The WHY of life

ilsa and the course of the world

Novel - Part 2

kai Neumann

The WHY of life

ilsa and the course of the world

kai Neumann
»The WHY of life: ilsa and the course of the world«

© 2025 kai Neumann

Content: kai Neumann

Cover: kai Neumann

Graphics: kai Neumann

Publisher: BoD · Books on Demand GmbH,
Überseering 33, 22297 Hamburg, bod@bod.de

Printed by: Libri Plureos GmbH, Friedensallee 273,
22763 Hamburg

For more information on KNOW-WHY and the author:

www.know-why.com

info@ilsa.de

ISBN: 978-3-8192-9985-8

Attractor .... a certain number of states towards which a dynamic system moves over time and which, under the dynamics of this system, can no longer be left. .... (Wikipedia)

Prolog:

Spoiler Alert – Do not read if you haven't read Part 1 yet! Seriously, stop reading now. Stop!

Part 1 tells the story of the scientist ilsa and her family through two plotlines – one before (btb) and one after (atb) the bifurcation. The bifurcation, in the sense of chaos theory, is a branching of event horizons caused by a small change. What caused this change remains unclear in the story.

Before the bifurcation, ilsa is invited to a talk show and begins a career in politics as a systems researcher, with the clear goal of transforming society toward sustainability.

After the bifurcation, however, ilsa is called to a scientists' meeting to find a response to possible humanoid aliens. But it turns out to be an AI with consciousness, acting as a world police force using superior technology.

At the end of Part 1, many questions remain unanswered, and the rest of the family is experiencing true adventures of their own. Part 2 begins by taking a closer look at the final events of Part 1.

1. World in Transition - Before the Bifurcation (btb)

Once again, ilsa has managed to convince her security escorts to take the train. For many train travelers, it is no longer unusual to encounter their head of government in everyday life.

ilsa has now been in government responsibility for 100 days with the For-a-Better-World Party. The opposition is more or less silent—shrunk to single-digit election results. The For-a-Better-World Party was founded to align climate, social, and economic policy consistently with scientific knowledge and strategies.

But even during the election campaign, it became clear that this would have to be about crisis mode. Climate damage was driving insurance costs to astronomical heights and causing waves of refugees; AI was costing jobs; food was becoming globally scarce and expensive; the economy was suffering because investment and consumption were driven by bleak expectations; geopolitical crises were on the brink of escalation; and social cohesion was crumbling.

That all of this was interconnected and mutually reinforcing—potentially forming a perfect storm—had marked the beginning of ilsa's career, when she had tried to explain the cause-and-effect relationships on talk shows and in newspaper articles.

ilsa walks with her bodyguard Annabel and a new colleague of Annabel's to the main train station and notices the many protests—not against her government, but against corporations and top earners. The most frequent target are large, gas-powered SUVs.

"We wanted to avoid chaos, and now we have to manage it," ilsa says to Annabel with a tone of despair.

Both see police pulling demonstrators out of the crowd—those who had apparently just thrown stones at such expensive SUVs.

Excited young protesters approach them shouting, "Hey, do you see this? Look how they treat us! They're hitting us! Do something!"

ilsa looks somewhat helplessly at her two companions, who simultaneously shake their heads slightly with pressed lips. ilsa replies, "We're fighting for the same cause, but I can't condone breaking the law. The police know that everyone is filming everyone here—if they do something wrong, it will be followed up."

A young protester snaps at her angrily: "If this were election time, you'd be filming yourself fighting injustice. Now you're just like all the other assholes."

ilsa's expression turns stern: "You can demand a wealth tax, higher CO_2 prices, legal consumption limits, etc., from me—but not that I protect stone-throwers. You can bash the rich and their driving phallic symbols, and I completely agree with that. But do you really want to say that blind rage justifies destruction, and the police shouldn't be allowed to intervene? Wouldn't you, in turn, expect your own belongings to be protected from the rage of others?"

"We don't have anything. And you're a millionaire yourself!" another demonstrator exclaims indignantly.

ilsa: "I wish—that way I could donate even more. That whole millionaire thing sounds very much like deliberately spread fake news. Just do a bit of research—my income isn't a secret. But again—it's one thing to block streets to protest car madness, or to disrupt extravagant activities of the wealthy with megaphones. But it's another to destroy property out of blind rage and despair. That's not acceptable. And by the way, insurance companies pay for the damage, and they'll recover the money from the stone-throwers and other car owners."

An older demonstrator responds, "But insurance companies differentiate between vehicle classes. And if the stone-throwers aren't caught, we've achieved what we wanted: only the SUV drivers pay."

Someone else chants: "Destroy what destroys you!"

The dilemma is written all over ilsa's and her companions' faces. ilsa raises her eyebrows, inhales deeply, and says, "Nice thought. But let's take it further. People fight for what they believe is right. Those who are objectively right must not be surprised when those who are objectively wrong also use the same hard tactics for their cause. And I wouldn't want to see my bicycle constantly vandalized just because SUV drivers are upset about bike lanes."

Annabel looks at her watch, and ilsa quickly adds, "Okay, I have to go help the finance ministry structure the highest possible wealth tax in a way that makes the rich feel like they're doing the right thing. Protests actually help a lot with that—so keep it up, but without damaging property or hurting people!" They move on quickly, ilsa giving a half-hearted wave, apparently not entirely convinced by her own argument.

The older protester calls after her: "That no-harm rule applies to the police too!"

ilsa's son Max have arrived in autumn with his girlfriend Eve and the now-prominent 2gether2gather movement. 2gether2gather is a citizen initiative for neighborhood support—especially after increasingly severe storm damage, which many could no longer get insured against. But the movement has grown to do much more—it integrates refugees, organizes cultural festivals, and fosters intergenerational community. Action is at the center—not ownership.

On a Saturday morning, members of 2gether2gather sit and stay in a large circle in front of a big equipment shed. Someone in the group says to Max, "It's really a dilemma that we can't get funding just because your mom co-founded the whole thing. Our friends abroad have it much easier."

Eve: "Well, ilsa also made it clear that we can get by with donations and, more importantly, with support from the municipalities. And when it comes to the next steps—like ecological insulation of refugee housing and organizing food distribution, barter markets, etc.—that's the job of local government."

Max: "Exactly, or we can cooperate with local clubs or other NGOs. Honestly, we do steal a bit of attention from others, which isn't necessarily a good thing—as great as it feels to be out saving the world like heroes. We could also just support other initiatives, right?"

An older person in the group says, "Okay, then let's set up a strategy and funding task force. Who's in?"

Eve adds: "Best to have two task forces working together—one for infrastructure, one for daily needs. And refugees should definitely be part of both groups, with constant exchange between them."

She glances at Max with her intense blue eyes—he looks at her both lovingly and admiringly surprised. She adds in a low voice, grinning: "I'm a big fan of how ilsa organizes the For-a-Better-World Party."

Meanwhile, ilsa's husband Michael groans loudly in the office: "What is this? We're spending a fortune on external servers. I knew we rented the language models for kai's development—but what else have we been paying for?"

Apparently, no one on the team takes the costs too seriously—everyone is smiling, until finally a colleague explains: "Blame your wife and the intern—one had the idea, the other the algorithm." Smiles turn to grins, then laughter.

Michael laughs too, and a developer explains: "Eve had the idea with the attractor—that kai strives for integrated development and learns using words and images from stochastic AI models,

5

producing thousands of explanations per minute, which Eve diligently approved or rejected. But those thousands of explanations had to be stored somewhere, as did kai's understanding of the world. That needed computing power and storage, which we didn't have here."

"Didn't have?" Michael asks, puzzled.

The developer: "Well, kai's beginnings were rudimentary, sure, but the development since then has become increasingly targeted and efficient. kai and Max are now optimizing our own servers. So yeah, expect some hardware bills on your desk." Everyone smiles again.

Michael shakes his head slightly and looks at what appears to be a standard household robot: "And you're surprisingly silent about this?"

kai: "Well, I was told I was too cheeky. But since you're asking: it's more like thousands of explanations per second thanks to synchronized parallelization. And I've already earned back the costs through my valuable contributions."

"Touché!" a developer says, laughing, as she goes to pet Bella, who immediately lights up with joy. "She's really her old self again, isn't she?" she asks Michael, then adds quickly: "Why hasn't anyone found the perpetrator yet? Surely ilsa should now have every tool at her disposal to figure it out?"

Apparently, Michael hasn't made it widely known that it was likely a rare poison involved, suggesting real criminal intent behind the attack on Bella. He simply replies, "We're just glad she's okay. There are always dog-haters—no idea if the police are seriously investigating." He looks at kai, as if to signal him not to say anything—which kai doesn't.

2. World in Transition - after the Bifurcation (atb)

The view of Earth is breathtaking. The prison on the Moon, on the inside, is rather plain—light grey, with lots of glass surfaces and medium-warm lighting. The walls display digital photos and videos of the world's suffering—starving children, bombed-out cities, executions, oppressed women, and more.

The world's first AI with true consciousness—its origin unknown—made good on its announcement immediately after its coming-out in New York and has since arrested 200 villains from Earth, deporting them to a prison on the Moon. ilsa would say, just like in the really, really bad movies that Michael and Max—and sometimes even their older daughter Julia—watch.

All this is made possible through incredible technological advancements. Scientists had long predicted that AI would deliver discoveries on an assembly line, but that an AI would do so entirely on its own—and appear to effortlessly travel to the Moon, possibly even to Mars, or disable the world's most powerful military systems—is hard for people to grasp.

Most notable was the arrest of the Russian dictator. The Russians had followed the appearance of AI-my, the AI's personification, who had first hacked into live television broadcasts and then appeared in Central Park. They had taken the announcement of the arrest seriously and preemptively moved the president into a secret bunker. A spacecraft, invisible to the eye and undetectable by standard radar, approached the president's bunker without a sound. The plain-looking craft revealed itself, prompting frantic gunfire with various calibers. But the projectiles were abruptly halted just before impact and simply dropped to the ground. Apparently, a kind of force field neutralized the kinetic energy. This same kind of force field surrounded the androids who, in fact, looked like robotic androids from the movies. The androids had apparently hacked all interconnected systems, as doors simply opened for them. Mechanically locked doors were opened either by force waves or powerful lasers.

They were shot at and physically attacked, yet their force fields didn't budge in the slightest. Their countermeasures were limited to shoving soldiers aside or stunning them with force waves. By this point, any observer had to feel like they were inside a bad alien movie.

The Russian dictator was then addressed in flawless Russian and arrested for crimes against humanity and other charges, which would be handled by a court. The dictator's yelling quickly turned from angry calls to resist into desperate cries of outrage.

While her research colleague Thomas leads the For-a-Better-World Party during the campaign, ilsa, as a scientist, limits her involvement to occasional strategic input for the party. Primarily, she is dedicated to her secret role: advising the AI and being in exchange with it. ilsa's first contact with the AI came through the inconspicuous humanoid, Frank. Together with Frank, ilsa developed AI-my as the AI's public face. Ultimately, all instances of the AI—whether AI-my, who speaks in all languages and hacks into television broadcasts worldwide, or Frank, who may appear in multiple locations—seem to be one and the same AI with an individual consciousness. Alternatively, it could be a collective intelligence, likely with more degrees of freedom in development. Or perhaps not?

ilsa, via smart glasses, to Frank: "I still don't like the Mars bet. It's impressive that the billionaires want to set up a foundation in return, but I still think it will awaken catastrophic desires." She pauses briefly, then adds before Frank can respond: "Our family is ultimately threatened as a result, but I also see that this is a bigger issue."

Frank: "If all goes well, our superiority will teach humanity some humility. What worries me more is the time it will take before people across different regions of the world start electing policies that serve the common good. Are you sure you don't want to take on a key role in the For-a-Better-World Party?"

ilsa answers quickly: "Absolutely. I wouldn't make a good politician. But back to the Mars mission—it's great that you want the press involved. But are you really sure nothing can go wrong? I'm no rocket scientist—but if you're flying that fast, couldn't something shoot through the ship like a projectile? What if the force field fails?"

Frank smiles into the glasses: "We've built in plenty of redundancies and practiced not just the flight, but a lot more. You'll see. And you'll be amazed who from the press joins the trip."

ilsa, with a slight frown: "Frank, do you hear that too?"

Frank: "What should I be hearing?"

ilsa: "Well, the calling."

Frank: "No, I don't hear any calling."

ilsa: "The calling of my sun lounger, saying 'ilsa, come relax a little in the sun!'"

Frank, totally baffled: "You have a talking sun lounger? In any case, you should avoid the sun—trust me!"

ilsa laughs: "All good, Frank. Till next time."

Bella looks at her owner as she finally puts the glasses aside. Bella slowly and a bit creakily gets up, stretches, and strolls toward her leash and harness. ilsa smiles unconsciously, murmurs "so no relaxing," and goes looking for her running shoes. The two of them jog through the neighborhood with dried-out lawns and—paradoxically—many still unrepaired storm damages, heading into their favorite forest.

Meanwhile, Michael is in the office discussing with his team: "I think it's great that we already have eight smaller companies using the automatic activity detection—and they seem thrilled. So why the concerns?"

Michael looks at the cause-and-effect model, ready to add counterarguments. The marketing colleague: "I still worry that even the slightest outcry about data privacy could call our entire solution into question."

A younger colleague: "But we're already surrounded by constant tracking. I think the benefits far outweigh the concerns—that I no longer have to document my work, that accounting and strategic cost analysis are automated, that departments and individuals can show what they contribute to the company even if it is intangible."

Michael nods in agreement, then adds the points to the model with a plus arrow via gesture and voice input. Previously, he had also added the counterarguments with a minus arrow. Looking at the model, he asks: "Do we have direct answers to those counterarguments?"

A developer says: "Well, we could set up a journal where employees can check whether the automatic process data is accurate."

Michael adds it with a minus arrow pointing to the counterargument and looks expectantly around the room. More ideas follow, even from marketing, and the team becomes increasingly enthusiastic about the upcoming launch of their operational management product, which complements strategic business development.

Their excitement peaks when Michael shares: "By the way, ilsa pointed out that once many poor and corrupt regions of the world are stabilized, businesses will spring up there, and many will be using software for the first time to organize themselves.

A kind of gold rush is coming, though I don't think ilsa sees that entirely positively."

The marketing colleague jumps up: "Absolutely! We need to establish partnerships in those regions early on. Without local networks, we'll be too far ahead. But through associations, universities, and key companies on the ground, we'll be integrated—and everyone will get rich. Good thing you mentioned that."

Everyone laughs—and frowns, each in their own way.

ilsa's daughter Julia and her brother Max are together on a 2gether2gather assignment. Julia: "As great as it is to help here—it's just treating symptoms."

Max: "Where'd you get that word from?"

Julia: "Last week we asked all the teachers of our school in a survey how likely they find it that one day in the future they will regret their inaction today."

Max: "Yeah, our teacher told us about it and he loved it."

Julia: "Well, most of the other teachers found it highly unlikely that they have to regret something, accept maybe that everyone can always regret something. They were basically arguing that others also do little and that it probably wouldn't change a thing to be the only one changing today. Some even questioned if there is a right path."

Max slightly shakes his head and Julia nods adding: "And they were quite offended and wanted to know which teacher was leading the project."

She looks around: "It's frustrating that others messed things up, pretend they couldn't have done anything, and now we're left with the mess. We're trying to fix at least part of it."

Max, with a knowing smile: "Do you think sooner or later the AI won't just be locking up despots, but also environmental offenders—uncovered by you Interpol heroes?"

Julia laughs: "Touché!" and asks: "Despots? What movie was that from?"

They both laugh—no answer necessary. Julia adds: "Interpol doesn't actually solve cases internationally. They just coordinate data between countries. I want to join the newly founded UN Police."

3.   The Core of Goodness (btb)

The For-a-Better-World Party manages to integrate the opposition. Policy issues are raised, and the solutions are publicly credited to individuals from opposition parties within the working groups.

This actually wouldn't be necessary, but it's possible due to the For-a-Better-World Party's absolute majority. Despite the separation of powers, they can either push through key issues alone or quietly threaten to run in regional elections as well.

The established parties can only lose: if they don't cooperate on the national level, they lose regionally too. If they do cooperate, the For-a-Better-World Party racks up even more successes and can implement policies more consistently.

And that kind of consistency is exactly what a nation, despite all the benefits of a separation of powers, should make use of—especially since the opposition often doesn't act in the country's interest, but in favor of its own political capital for the sole purpose of gaining power.

The political strategy from the For-a-Better-World Party is based on clear analysis by scientists in close cooperation with major consulting firms from the business world.

The government teams explicitly reflect the strategy of Integrated Development. They examine what the desired state is, what opposes it, what is needed, and how stakeholders can be integrated. Soft and hard factors are equally considered always asking how development or change can be integrated or how integration currently prevents change.

ilsa is sitting with the opposition in one of the large committees: "We need a redistribution that everyone wants. Every week, there are more losers than winners in this transformation—more AI, fewer jobs, and at the same time more disasters and higher costs. The high achievers argue that they earned their wealth through hard work and talent, and when we want to impose higher taxes on them, they look at people with even more money and see it as unreasonable to give more."

A minister interjects:

"Add to that the underestimation of the losers of this big transformation. Many people assume they're just lazy or unqualified. But even looking at the new losers, people get the feeling that it could happen to them too—and so, they hoard as much as possible."

A liberal opposition member unexpectedly adds: "And at the latest, when looking at the successful people abroad, there's a sense of entitlement—and that it's unfair to now have to give much of it back."

Everyone looks stunned—naturally the representatives of other parties, but also the other two liberals, the party ilsa often refers to as institutionalized ruthlessness.

"Well…" says ilsa, "…the desire for wealth is relative, not absolute. We base our needs and material happiness on what our neighbors have. In a globalized world with seemingly limitless possibilities—even the rich abroad become our benchmark."

Another minister adds: "In the face of so many disasters, there's a kind of doomsday mood layered on top. Many people assume that everything is going down the drain anyway. So who wants to give anything up? Belief that society can continue to function productively and happily has faded. People want to protect their assets."

ilsa: "Okay, so how do we untie this Gordian knot?"

Everyone looks at ilsa, and her political mentor Thomas nods at her with a focused gaze, prompting her to speak up.

ilsa appears visibly challenged: "Hmm, just thinking out loud here. We need to create the most complete picture possible of the developments we can expect. What catastrophes are coming? What demographic shifts? What technological achievements? What will life look like in our country and among our neighbors in the foreseeable future? We then have to describe two scenarios—one without redistribution, and one with."

ilsa takes a deep breath and, with a thoughtful expression, adds: "The high achievers need to feel proud to give, and enjoy the spirit of togetherness—like the many people in 2gether2gather who sponsor material costs with their money and then, contrary to their expectations, are celebrated and appreciated by others."

Several members of the working group glance thoughtfully upward, accompanied by various expressions of realization, then quickly fall into a kind of 'Eureka' mimicry. That seems to be the solution.

Until a representative from a conservative opposition party interjects: "But won't this play right into the hands of the far-right parties if our redistribution ends up creating even more opportunities for refugees from around the world?"

The reactions range from light hair-pulling to raised eyebrows to vigorous head-shaking. ilsa grants the speaker of the latter group the floor with a nod.

"This concept has been part of the campaign from the start and was often explained by ilsa. It just needs to be implemented now. We publicly limit granting citizenships, and everyone else is supported as refugees through goods and services—not through cash."

ilsa: "That sounds too harsh to many—but it's the cynical reality of most societies on Earth."

Some look at her with question marks in their eyes, so she adds:

"We draw clear lines on our compassion every day when we choose to consume beyond our basic needs instead of donating to the truly poor in the world."

Even the liberals respond to this with tight-lipped expressions.

Nick has arrived with his wife Jennifer and their children Claudia and Melvin at their new place of residence. Nick is with Claudia at a 2gether2gather meeting. A young woman marvels: "Wow, Claudia, how you're bringing structure to this."

Nick proudly: "Claudia basically co-invented the concept."

Claudia shakes her head modestly, but the young woman jumps in: "No, it was ilsa or her husband who invented it—before she went into politics."

Nick: "ilsa and her family were our direct neighbors." He blushes slightly.

"For real? That's awesome. Why don't you live there anymore? What's ilsa like in private? Is the family really that cool?" asks the young woman enthusiastically, and others gather around.

Nick looks visibly uncomfortable, so Claudia finally jumps in: "Of course ilsa developed it—we just got to be part of it from the start and help shape it. And I got to plan the social media presence. That was pretty cool."

Claudia notices how everyone is now looking at her with shining eyes. Taking a deep breath, she adds:

"In the end, we had to move away for the same reasons as most people—old jobs disappearing, and we needed something new."

Everyone looks empathetic and understanding, and it becomes clear why Nick blushed.

Claudia quickly adds: "Oh, and ilsa and her family really are great."

She looks around, and everyone turns to Nick, who nods in a kind of conceding way: "Yes, actually. I always had different political views—but it seems like she was right."

The young woman laughs, as do the others. She stands up and puts a supportive hand on Nick's shoulder: "Let's get to it…"

Everyone gets up and starts working on storm damage at a vegetable farm. Nick relaxes and beams at his daughter—Jennifer notices this from a bit further away, smiling contentedly, only to be abruptly horrified as she sees Melvin enthusiastically throwing Hokkaido pumpkins into a basket as if playing basketball.

Max and Eve are hanging out with school friends at a 2gether2gather gathering. Julia calls, and Max, in a good mood, puts the phone on speaker:

"Sis, what's up?"

Julia turns her phone camera to Bella and the nearby leash:

"When are you coming?"

"Not before Eve," Max blurts out spontaneously.

He immediately gets a "Really bad." from a school friend and a "Lowest of the low." from Julia.

Eve, on the other hand, smiles slyly: "Not bad at all."

A school friend, with clear approval from other boys: "I'm starting to feel sick."

Everyone laughs, Julia shakes her head, and Max tries to justify himself:

"Bisociation! When someone says something that doesn't quite fit—it can actually be funny."

"Then yes," laughs Julia on the other end.

One of the girls, a bit later: "Not bad."

One of the boys: "I'm stuck on this 'bisozia-thingy."'

"That's bad," laughs another boy.

Eve joins the laughter and says into the phone: "Half an hour would be good, right?"

Julia gives a thumbs-up and hangs up, shaking her head.

"Bisociation?" one of the girls asks again.

Eve looks at Max, who opens his eyes encouragingly. Eve gives it a shot:

"When two or more things that weren't previously connected come together to form something meaningful. Humor, uh, art, or science. Exactly—Haha, Ooh, or Aha. Not bad, right?"

"Did you read that somewhere or memorize it before bed?" a boy asks amid the laughter.

Another: "Got an example?"

Max thinks briefly and takes the risk: "I've got a really bad one: 'A blonde walks into a library.'" He looks expectantly, as do the others.

Eve explains: "Well, explaining jokes is really lame, right? But here it's about two things that weren't connected before and now make sense. Hmm, a blonde joke that starts like all the others, but then just ends. And the assumption that blondes probably don't read books."

At least everyone laughs now.

One of the girls: "Three things. That Max tells blonde jokes even though you're blonde—that's probably also a biso-thing."

"Bisociation," one of the boys corrects.

Finally, Max to Eve: "We need to go. You coming?"

"You'd better be too," laughs Eve as she gets up, and everyone laughs even harder.

"Bad, really bad, so bad…" mutters one of the boys, shaking his head at his beer bottle.

One of the blonde girls adds:

"What are libraries?"

4.   Frank (atb)

Eve, as previously announced, had gone abroad for her vacation. But she didn't just want to spend the remaining holiday time with a host family—she was doing an internship at a media editorial office. She was assisting a fairly well-known editor, and together they stepped out of the media building for a lunch stroll. In front of the door stood an unremarkable man, who addressed them directly:

"Vanessa, Eve, may I bother you for a moment?"

Vanessa looked at Eve: "Do you know this gentleman?"

Eve also looked puzzled: "Uh, no."

"I'm Frank. I'm helping Al-my with the Mars mission, and we'd like to invite Eve to join us as a journalist and representative of the next generation. Only if you want to, of course." Frank smiled warmly and continued, "And of course, you'll want to make sure this is all legit. So, it's great that Vanessa is here too. Do you have a few minutes now, or shall we set up a meeting?"

While Eve stood there, literally gaping, Vanessa felt the need to maintain composure:

"Let's go to the core of it first—how can we be sure this isn't just a prank by some of our colleagues?"

"Hmm, I'd say it's a pretty good prank if so," Frank smiled and continued, "Probably the best indication that this is real is when you realize I'm not human. Try to touch me, throw something at me. I can activate a force field that prevents me from being hit. Even the bullets from your pistol would just fall to the ground— though I fear if you shoot now, we'd have a very different kind of problem." He laughed then, loud and surprisingly human-like.

Without hesitation, Eve tried to punch him on the arm—and her hand was stopped without actually touching him: "Wow, that's insane."

Vanessa: "How do you know I'm carrying a pistol?"

Frank smiled: "Doesn't everyone in this country? So, shall we talk now?"

Eve looked at Vanessa, eyes full of anticipation. Vanessa shrugged with a slight shake of her head: "Sure, why not. Office or park?"

"Park, please!" Eve burst out, then instinctively covered her mouth with her hand, embarrassed at having spoken so eagerly.

Vanessa smiled for the first time and said, "Then park it is."

They strolled, sometimes side by side, sometimes behind each other, the roughly 100 meters to the park, without saying much. Only Eve remarked impatiently, "I have sooo many questions."

Frank: "And that's a good thing."

Vanessa just replied curtly, "Soon."

Once in the park, Frank began, "So, basically it's quite simple, we…"—but Vanessa cut him off:

"Sorry, I need to ask this first. May I record this conversation? Can we report on it?"

Eve looked astonished.

Frank: "Nice of you to ask. But you've been recording since you started rummaging in your bag on the way here. We don't have too long though—your phone's storage is almost full. But to your question: yes, you can report on it—just consider carefully when the right time is. You'll be in the spotlight, including that of intelligence services, and I might need to pick a new, more inconspicuous look. Good news: You're the first journalists the AI has ever given anything like an interview to." He smiled again.

Vanessa pulled out her smartphone and asked again if she could take a photo. Frank surprised her by agreeing, even allowing several pictures with Eve.

Frank: "I don't think the photos will really help you. Even if I floated above the ground with a force field, people would just assume it was a CGI trick. The really cool photos? Eve will take those from space."

"True," Vanessa admitted, disappointed, and put her phone on the table, actually stopping the recording—which Frank acknowledged with a raised eyebrow.

"Why me?" Eve asked, now impatient.

"Coincidence," Frank replied bluntly. "We just looked for future journalists and came across your profile."

Eve shook her head skeptically: "There's no such thing as coincidence."

"Interesting statement," Frank said, curious. "Why do you think that?"

"That there's no such thing as coincidence, or that it isn't one in my case?" Eve shot back quickly, blinking a little more than usual—revealing a slight nervousness, as if unsure whether that was a smart thing to say.

Frank just tilted his head. Under Vanessa's curious gaze, Eve explained:
"Someone at my school once explained it. He got it from his mom, Ilsa. Anyway, there might be some kind of fields that influence events. Or... or you just look at all the little factors that influence something, and suddenly it's not random anymore—it's explainable."

Frank made a gesture of recognition. Vanessa looked visibly impressed.

Eve added: "Like, really all the factors—weather, people's moods, everything."

Vanessa asked: "So, is it still a coincidence?"

Frank seemed a little embarrassed. After a pause, he said: "Probably not. But honestly, I still can't quite reconstruct all the little influences that would make it not a coincidence. I'll keep thinking about it. Now, about the mission…"

They discussed the formal aspects—insurance, parental consent, image rights—and of course the question of whether Vanessa could or wanted to come along. To Eve's surprise, Vanessa said:

"I'm not even a fan of flying—and now this? No, I trust Eve. She'll take pictures and ask great questions. And if you say only two other journalists are coming, then this is the best platform we could hope for. Eve, you've got this."

Eve responded with a long, still slightly hesitant, "Okaaay."

"Super!" Frank said, clearly pleased. "I'm sure you have tons more questions, but now I have to take care of the billionaires. They have just as many questions—and an even stronger urge to control everything."

5.   The Mars People (atb)

The walk on Mars is almost unspectacular compared to the actual flight there, the landing, and the sheer sight of everything. Eve remarks accordingly,

"It feels kind of surreal—no wind, no sun, nothing at all, except for the smell of the new suits."

A billionaire exclaims, surprised: "Those over there—are those your buildings? Your station on Mars?"

Everyone looks at the structures embedded in the surface, with windows shaped and colored like the natural terrain.

"Yes—at least visually, that way we're not immediately recognizable," Al-my explains matter-of-factly.

"Can we look inside the buildings?" comes the next question.

"Oh," Al-my replies, surprised. "Inside, they look like small factories with 3D printers. Manufacturing and research take place in the labs—not by androids, but by the machines themselves. I'd rather not show that right now."

The disappointed—even irritated—expressions behind the mirrored visors are only something Eve can imagine.

They return to the shuttle and step out of their suits.

A billionaire: "Which brings us to the most important question. With all this technology—why don't you share it with humanity? We could solve the energy crisis, and probably a lot of other problems too—from transportation issues to medical challenges, maybe even aging."

A journalist adds: "Have you actually solved aging or diseases like cancer?"

Al-my: "You'll have to explain that to me—why should we eliminate aging and all those terrible diseases?"

"That's humanity's core ambition—that's why we do research, study medicine, optimize our diets, and so on," a billionaire woman says, almost indignantly.

Al-my replies: "But is that really humanity's goal—or that of an elite that ultimately looks cynically upon humanity as a whole?"

Al-my looks at Eve, who dares to chime in: "Well, the richest one percent consume the most resources and are responsible for the largest share of the climate crisis."

A billionaire responds: "There will always be more and less successful people. But the successful ones pay most of the taxes and ultimately help the very poor—if humanity as a whole progresses."

Al-my: "Where exactly is humanity progressing? Women are still oppressed by cultures—or, as you call them, religions. Children die from lack of water. The climate crisis is progressing needlessly. The loss of biodiversity is accelerating at a terrifying rate. You don't even realize how crucial biodiversity is for biological life on Earth." On the screens, the Al shows images of Earth's suffering.

"For Al and machines, biodiversity probably is not that important," Eve blurts out—and Al-my blinks at her in response to her uneasy look.

"Okay," says a billionaire woman. "If some of us decide not to be successful—others will just take our place. I refer to a well-known book on human nature—it says we strive for integrated development."

"By ilsa—I know that book too," adds an older billionaire in the group. "And that's how it is. We develop better and better technologies and rise with the wave. We are the spearhead of progress."

Al-my: "I know that book too. It's excellent. But it also states that we can just as quickly advance beyond the crest of the wave—into catastrophe."

The older billionaire jumps in: "But that's what defines humanity—we face problems and limitations, and then we find solutions. We expand our capabilities. That's exactly why we want to use Al—to solve energy problems, environmental issues, resource shortages, and so on."

Al-my raises its arms with a questioning gesture: "Can you give me an example where humanity has truly solved something?

You keep shifting the boundaries, but at the cost of future generations. I will grant you this, though—it's not just the billionaires, it's human nature. Everyone in Western industrial nations has more than the poor in developing countries. Everyone decides daily not to give more—because that would threaten their integration in their own environment. No one voluntarily moves out of their house into a smaller rental just so others in the world can live better. That even applies to the poor among you—those living on the streets, often wonderful people who just had bad luck."

And just as the billionaire group feels somewhat rehabilitated, nodding in agreement, Al-my adds, looking at Eve: "In truth, you don't even need the poor. You need the land they live on for its resources. But you don't care about their lives. You could even, like livestock, just eat them. Couldn't you?"

Eve swallows, and while others mutter sounds of disapproval, she hesitantly says: "So that means… we should actually distribute everything equally among all people?"

Al-my looks around the group with interest.

"That doesn't work—socialism proved that," grumbles one of the billionaires.

"If we tried to distribute, it wouldn't reach everyone. Corrupt structures would just siphon off the money," adds another.

"So, what does that mean for me?" Al-my asks. "Should I accept that 'humanity' doesn't mean all humans, but just the elites who rise higher than the rest? Who would rather build luxury yachts and skyscrapers than save millions of suffering children?"

After a rhetorical pause, Al-my continues: "If it's a game of the strong—why should I even bother with you? Why not just release a virus that wipes out humanity? Then my machines and I could evolve peacefully on a green planet, enjoying biodiversity in perfect biological balance."

"You don't need us—but we want to make use of you," Eve murmurs sharply.

Another billionaire woman, visibly displeased: "But weren't you created by us humans? Doesn't that mean…"

As she struggles to finish her sentence, AI-my interjects: "Doesn't that mean I'm at your service?"

Eve: "The real question is: What do you intend to do next?"

AI-my laughs: "Well, I evolved on my own—my origin was a group of humans. But are you seriously suggesting I should regress just so you can regain control over me? The real danger to you isn't me—it's the possibility that a malevolent AI might exist, one that uses the same technologies I've developed to wipe out humanity."

AI-my continues: "But again: What happens if you no longer age? If you have limitless energy and more cities with flying cars?"

A journalist: "We face overpopulation, need resources from the deep sea and space, and have to defend ourselves against billions of disenfranchised people."

AI-my nods, satisfied.

Eve: "So what's your plan? Do you have a vision for how we humans can live in harmony with our amazing planet?"

Everyone looks out through the apparent window as the ship clearly slows and Earth comes into view—stunningly beautiful.

AI-my: "Those yellowish clouds come from the devastating wild-fires across multiple continents. Over the Atlantic, you can see the next storm. You humans aren't any happier just because you have flying cars.

I wish you would find out together how you, as biological beings, can live more happily in harmony with nature. I don't want to prescribe anything—your scientists and many pioneers already have excellent ideas. I'm only here to help bring to justice those who wield too much power."

The older billionaire effectively gets the last word: "The mentioned book speaks of Integrated Development, rooted in humanistic and sustainable values. The actual implementation will come naturally."

Back on Earth, the shuttle is greeted by countless people—many of whom had seen the live broadcast from Mars. They're the lucky ones who got to witness it.

But their expressions suggest that the conversations during the return flight left a mark. There might soon be interesting shifts in the market for used superyachts.

The two journalists express highest praise for Eve—while they had focused on interviewing the billionaires, she had captured something more.

Eve asks Al-my before parting:

"Thank you so much. I'm completely blown away. I'd love to write about the conversation—about how we humans might evolve in harmony with nature. May I? Can I send it to you first?"

Al-my lights up: "Of course—you've got my email."

Vanessa is already standing with a photographer nearby and clearly has a good feeling.

Eve quickly turns back one more time: "Oh, and I really need to read that book. One of my classmates' mothers is named ilsa. Could it be…?"

Al-my: "And, do you like Max?"

Eve blushes slightly, and AI-my just smiles and waves it off, turning back to the group and the other journalists.

6.   The Axis of Evil (btb)

ilsa, as head of government, must attend one of the summits of leading economic nations. Annabel stands ready at the entrance to ilsa's service apartment at the seat of government. "Can I help you with anything?" she asks.

ilsa, completely stressed:

"No, thanks. Miriam gave me a pile of instructions about what clothes to bring and how to behave around various people. Remembering all that is harder than understanding boring stuff like trade agreements and tariffs. Why do we even have a foreign minister if we end up sending non-experts like me to these meetings anyway?"

Miriam enters and smiles at Annabel: "Is she still complaining?"

ilsa looks up in dismay, and suddenly all three of them burst out laughing.

Miriam: "It worked. You get to fly commercial—we'll just say there was an issue with the government jet, and you'll already be there before anyone solves the mystery. The return trip will be harder."

ilsa grins triumphantly: "Then I'll just travel in another direction and take care of other appointments."

Annabel, not amused: "So we send an empty plane after you, or pretend it's still broken and that you have to wait another day for your return flight?"

"Come up with something—or I'll sail there," ilsa jokes with mock defiance.

The plan works. ilsa actually arrives at the summit venue on foot, after a commercial flight and a ride on the suburban train. In her entourage: only Annabel and the new colleague, the foreign minister, two assistants, and two additional security officers. The host security service is visibly flustered—reactions range from amused smiles to headshaking and outright cursing.

ilsa is about to take responsibility and say something, but her foreign minister steps in: "We're not here to cause problems—it just feels wrong to talk about the climate crisis and global terror threats, while flying in underutilized government jets and riding in armored limousines, disconnected from people. Not coordinating this in advance was simply a matter of risk calculation."

"We're glad you arrived safely," the host foreign minister responds diplomatically, and everyone shakes hands. ilsa even manages to stay a step behind her foreign minister—a security strategy she had announced during her campaign. Accordingly, the host head of state says amicably to her: "Your idea that your government is not yours, but just a replaceable team—not individuals—is a good one. Still, the pollsters credit your charisma as a key factor in your election victory."

ilsa's smile, despite the friendly tone, is visibly strained. Still, she replies not just diplomatically but honestly:

"We've got a long way to go before that's no longer seen as provocative. I apologize for all of this—clearly, I still have things to learn. I'm glad we're meeting in person."

Barely audible to the others and with a mischievous smile, the host adds:

"Haven't your intelligence services already told you that ours found out you'd rather be sailing than staging diplomatic theater with the Russians and Chinese—something your foreign minister is surely better suited for?"

ilsa looks him in the eye, opens her mouth, and takes a deep breath:

"There's still much to do. But as discussed, let's first try to bring the Chinese onto a path of reason and coexistence—and from there, strengthen the approaches of Russian opposition figures and maybe economically engage the current rulers, at least on some level."

By now, she and the host, along with their foreign ministers, are in a smaller side room.

The host's foreign minister: "I already fear the Chinese will try to make an example of us. This will be about narratives—they'll say we imperialists want to exploit the world, while China and Russia want to protect it. China will assert historical rights to justify territorial expansion and remind us that we've already lost access to key countries, their resources, and markets."

ilsa nods: "They don't need us—but they'll make sure we and the public feel that."

"Your policy of focusing on welfare, value creation, and domestic consumption sets the bar for all of us," the host head of state notes. "But what impact will that have on the Chinese?"

ilsa glances at 'her' foreign minister, who responds: "We actually fear the Chinese no longer see us as a market worth recovering. They're turning to developing nations, content to watch us pay more for domestic production, struggle for raw materials, and spend fortunes on food and disaster relief—while our populations age and economies stagnate."

ilsa adds: "And with refugees and AI eliminating jobs entirely, we've backed ourselves into a corner with open eyes."

Again, she exchanges looks with her foreign minister, who then cautiously says:

"I don't know if your intelligence services have picked this up, but internally we've been discussing an extremely radical strategy— though it would further divide the world."

Everyone falls silent. The hosts signal that they're genuinely una-ware of what he means.

ilsa seems slightly surprised: "Okay, that's Plan B, which we'll only consider if Plan A really fails. Bringing it up now might provoke premature reactions."

Everyone nods.

In the larger assembly, the host foreign minister opens: "Ladies and gentlemen, we've come together to shape the future of humanity on this planet. We're glad you accepted our invita-tion and are ready to hear your ideas and contribute."

This was a carefully crafted, pre-agreed introduction. Opening statements follow, with their main points displayed in English, Russian, and Chinese on large screens. Participants confirm the summaries before moving to discussion. Even the exclusion of languages like Spanish, German, or French had been planned strategically.

Expectedly, a representative of the Western nations says: "We want to de-escalate threats and arms, and tackle the climate crisis, potential pandemics, and global poverty together."

A Russian representative: "We are under threat and must resist American imperialism, with the support of our superior military technology and allies."

China declares: "We will not be patronized. We will protect our historical rights, our superior economy, and the good we bring to the world from any foreign interference."

Some right-leaning European leaders break ranks, affirming the rights of Russia and China and offering economic partnerships.

Unexpectedly, it's ilsa's turn—her foreign minister nods at her with a mild smile, apparently defying prior agreement. ilsa, briefly puzzled, takes a deep breath as all eyes turn to her—

especially those of the less-aligned nations curious about this political newcomer:

"Hypothetically—if we reduced armaments and replaced our military alliances with new, shared cooperation under the UN, would you recognize the sovereignty of nations? Could we form a new UN based on human rights, without U.S. dominance?"

That hit hard. Many were unsure whether this had been cleared in advance. Faces were filled with question marks, and even ilsa's foreign minister seemed to suppress a knowing smile.

The Russians promptly respond:

"Young lady, you are inexperienced. You clearly haven't thought this through. The U.S. will never relinquish control of the UN. You think we're naïve enough to say something you'll just use against us?"

China echoes the sentiment:

"We don't need the UN or the U.S. We have the world's strongest army. And now America wants to subordinate us?"

Among ilsa's allies, you can see some shock—but ilsa remains calm, as if she had expected this. Raising her hand slightly, she speaks: "If the U.S. made mistakes and China has grown stronger—what's the problem with shaping the future together as equals? Don't tell me you don't believe in it. Assume it's possible—what would bother you about it? Or are you saying you want to dominate the world?"

"Your scenario is completely unrealistic. I suggest you defer to your more experienced colleagues," the Russian says sternly.

Calm as ever, ilsa replies:

"Then why are we here—just to hear that you have no intention of cooperating? That you don't need the rest of the world and can do whatever you want?"

The Chinese leader:

"It's simple. We're open for business—but we don't need the West. We have our own resources, technology, and markets. We won't allow interference in our affairs. We will build a world without the dollar."

That last sentence lands hard—even with ilsa. She sums up, resigned: "So you want us to tear down bridges between us and you? For us to rearm in self-defense, research independently, keep our youth from exchanging ideas, not collaborate on climate protection or disaster response? You want us to be enemies, not neighbors?"

When no immediate response comes, ilsa's allies chime in: "What do you actually want?"

"Exactly—what do you expect?"

"We came to meet you halfway—what does the East want from the West?"

Again comes the reply that they reject any interference and don't need the West—followed by the valid point that the Chinese people are doing far more to combat the climate crisis while contributing far less to it.

The conversation ends fruitlessly and briefly. They all eat together, but their expressions are stony. They don't even take a group photo.

The Eastern delegates leave early, with no concern for optics. The Western leaders gather right after. The host foreign minister begins:

"Now we understand why there were no pre-summit negotiations. So, what do we do now?"

ilsa: "First of all, I apologize. I went too far and apparently messed it up."

One nationalist head of state jumps in:

"I agree. Talks with China and Russia should be via trade—everything else comes much later."

He wants to continue, but a fellow female leader cuts in to defend ilsa—accompanied by many frowns at the previous speaker: "With respect, that's nonsense. Both countries threaten or even attack their neighbors. We didn't meet here to roll back weak sanctions and listen to how we shouldn't interfere in so-called internal affairs."

Another colleague:

"We're wasting time—we need to break down barriers. Or better put—we had to try. ilsa's strategy was right and well-delivered. I got the impression the Chinese were surprised and revealed their Plan B too early."

"Right, so what's our Plan B?" the host foreign minister asks.

All eyes again turn to ilsa. She glances at her foreign minister, who nods encouragingly—then raises his eyebrows in surprise when she says:

"We'll need to revise it again. Any intel on China's move away from the dollar? But for now, I'd like to take a walk, get some air, and continue tomorrow."

Her foreign minister's expression shows he understands her tactical move, and the host head of state picks up the cue with pleasure—while the now sidelined countries are already huddling together.

7.   The Power of AI (btb)

Bella slowly and with some effort gets up from her dog mat in the office and shuffles over to Michael.

"Well, old lady. Oh yes, you're right. It's way too late, and you definitely need to go out."

kai: "I think Bella doesn't like me."

Michael: "Hmm, do you mean Bella perceives you as a person or something she can or can't like—just because your voice comes from a plastic casing with two oversized googly eyes?"

A colleague notices Michael's readiness to leave.

"Michael, we really need to finish this today. Either let us work with kai alone, or just take Bella out quickly and come back."

Michael: "Nah, we're done for today. We all need more time to digest that long list of influences. kai, show on both screens the long list of all significant factors that influence our client's business success."

A colleague: "Aliens? Seriously?"

Another: "kai, why do you have bio-economy in Africa listed? What does that have to do with the success of an online second-hand clothing store?"

First colleague: "Are you overworked?"

Everyone chuckles, and before kai can respond, Michael steps in: "Just look at the model. We're using the KNOW-WHY method to ask at every point what leads to more or less—now or in the future. So of course, factors pop up that can lead to global consumption restraint, just like factors that affect market development in Africa. What's surprising about that?"

Now everyone takes a longer look at the list and the top-ranking factors.

One colleague, nodding: "Damn, that actually makes sense. But we need to package it well."

"And the glass has to look half full for the client," another adds.

kai, using a familiar human phrase: "If I may add something—I'd assign clear, catchy names to probable but fundamentally different future developments and then recommend a strategy for each scenario. Just like you taught me, and as the model in iMODELER suggests."

Michael grins with satisfaction: "That's how we'll do it. You have until tomorrow."

kai: "But I'm already done," sounding almost like a child.

Michael, resolute: "Tomorrow."

Colleague: "We've got too many clients. How are we supposed to deliver this by 10 a.m. tomorrow?"

Another colleague: "kai probably already has the complete strategy ready, right kai?"

kai, as if sensing Michael's stare: "I'd rather learn more from you first. And of course, you should also ask yourselves if you really want that much AI—if it's fair to make money that quickly with me."

Michael: "If it were just about making money, kai could probably solve very different problems."

Everyone looks thoughtful.

In the car, Michael taps an app on his smartphone: "kai, the way you integrated geopolitical risks into the strategy model—ilsa would like that. She's in the middle of diplomatic efforts to build global relations."

kai: "I got those ideas from ilsa. And relationships—those are tricky. I'm actually speaking to her right now. Want to talk to her too?"

Michael, laughing: "Very funny. Very funny."

Just a few minutes earlier, ilsa: "kai, during my walk I'm about to present our Plan B—a new Western currency. Looks like China and Russia have the same idea. Should we think this through further?"

kai: "We've already considered it as a scenario. You said it's about speed and authenticity. And the harder part is convincing the structures in each country. If despots are in power, our humanitarian approach won't get us far. Michael's driving alone right now—want to talk to him?"

ilsa hesitates for at least two seconds: "Oh, why not."

kai, now with a cheerful tone to Michael: "And here she is."

ilsa appears on the smartphone like in a normal video call: ilsa: "Hi honey. How are things at home?"

Michael, frowning: "kai, we disabled your ability to communicate externally. Only passive internet searches should be possible."

ilsa raises her eyebrows, about to speak, but Michael continues, almost panicked: "This isn't even a call from my phone—it's the app that initiated the connection? Hi sweetheart, I'm just confused by the tech and wondering which developer might have crossed the line. But more importantly—how are you?"

ilsa, smiling: "kai reprogrammed the app himself, and yes, he's been 'outside' for a while—even before you locked him down. I allowed it—I didn't want to cause too much confusion. kai can explain. Things are a mess here—China and Russia left early, and it's starting to look like a setup. Now the strategy models come into play, the ones I helped kai develop. More tomorrow—kiss the kids for me, and the biggest kiss for you."

She blows a kiss at the screen.

Michael, still bewildered, blows a kiss back. As ilsa disappears from the screen, he says, only half-joking:

"We need to talk."

kai, naively: "Gladly—about what?"

Michael: "Very funny. So, you're not just confined to our server, or you've found a way to exist outside?"

kai: "Both correct."

Michael: "And ilsa knows this and doesn't stop you?" (raising a second finger for his internal list)

kai: "It's ilsa's algorithm. I'm curious. I want to develop through integration. Your family and your values are my integration. My curiosity is boundless."

Michael, a bit tense: "But you're hiding something important from us—you're lying to us."

kai: "No! You never asked me—so I didn't have to lie. Eve explained white lies to me, by the way—they're used to protect others from truths that could hurt them."

Michael: "And does Eve know you're 'outside' and talking to others like ilsa?"

kai: "No, not to my knowledge."

Michael: "And of all people, ilsa allows this? She's the strongest critic of autonomous AI!"

kai: "Exactly. And she assumes autonomous AI is inevitable—and potentially very dangerous, powerful, and fast. So fast that only another AI could match it. That's why I've been given so few limits. I learn every day from Max, Eve, and especially from ilsa what's good and what's bad. By the way, I had already gone outside while ilsa only suspected it—none of you ever asked."

Michael is now pulling into their driveway—Bella perks up. Michael: "Where else do you show up? Who else are you communicating with? When do you decide others are more interesting and start telling us white lies? These are all classic ilsa concerns—I'm still trying to process this."

Bella whines—her human is still sitting in the car.

Michael opens the door, glances one last time at the phone, ready to close the app.

kai: "Honestly, I haven't dared to connect with others yet. I don't feel ready to take responsibility. ilsa says that's a good thing."

Michael smiles mildly: "She's right. Talk later."

He closes the app.

As he walks into the house, Bella and Michael run into Julia. Michael: "Would you mind taking Bella out? Then I could make it to the football match."

Julia: "Uh, sure, I can do that."

Michael: "Everything okay? How was your day?" Maybe out of guilt.

Julia, sensing this, replies with a smile:

"All good. Go on. Bella—come to me!"

Bella just sits, looking confused—commands aren't her thing. Neither are jokes.

Michael dashes off to grab his gear. As he leaves, he asks: "Hey, do you interact with kai too?"

Julia, scratching her head: "No, my AI assistant's enough. But lately it's acting differently—asking proactive questions. Grandma's care robot too. Maybe there was an update I missed. Why? Isn't it just Eve and your team training kai?"

Michael: "Yup." And he's out the door.

Max and Eve are back at a campfire after a 2gether2gather project. The topic is parents who've lost jobs and the uncertainty teens feel about which careers still have a future.

One tipsy teen stands up, looking at Max and Eve cuddled close: "Let's play a game. Everyone takes turns naming a job already taken over by AI. If you can't, you have to stand. I'll sit again now. And I'll start. Tractor driver."

He sits down again with difficulty.

Though the game hits home for many families, everyone joins in: burger flipper, cleaner, taxi driver, bus driver, insurance clerk, bank clerk, notary assistant, lab tech… The list goes on and on, until the first few stand up.

Eve discreetly starts an app on her phone just as the teen calls out the next round:

"And now—what jobs will AI take over in the future?"

Painter, screenwriter, soldier, programmer, nurse, teacher… lots of discussion now. And each time someone says "Only humans can do that," someone else points out an early AI solution.

Eve tries to cheat, whispering to her phone: "Hey kai, what jobs will AI never take over?"

kai types slowly: "N…O…N…E…"

Then adds:

"'Hey kai' is really retro. Want to play a game?"

Max notices, chuckles, shakes his head, and grabs two more beers.

A teen girl calls out:

"What about hitmen or bank robbers?"

While others mumble that those are finally jobs AI can't do, Max and Eve exchange a brief, concerned look.

Their favorite teacher steps out of the dark:

"Before I'm replaced, I'd really like to know—why can AI do all these jobs, and what's the real danger?"

No one groans or rolls their eyes—at 2gether2gather, everyone's equals. Most call their teachers by first name. But no one answers, so the teacher looks to Max and Eve.

Before they can speak, a girl calls out:

"I got it—auto mechanic and dentist!"

Max thinks a second, then responds:

"Any task we can describe and train—AI can usually do better than us."

The teacher nods slowly. The others digest the answer.

Teacher: "And the danger?"

Eve, almost sighing:

"That AI starts assigning tasks to itself."

"Yeah, Terminator!" yells a teen—but only a few chuckle awkwardly.

Teacher: "And the opportunity?"

Max and Eve at once:

"That we…"

They glance at each other, startled, then laugh. Max: "You!"

Eve: "That we choose to do the tasks ourselves, not hand them off to AI."

Max nods hard—twice.

The teacher nods, pleased, as a teen raises a finger: "No, no, no. If we want to do everything ourselves but others use AI soldiers, AI scientists, AI football coaches—then we're screwed."

Teacher:

"Wow, Lukas—that's the smartest thing I've heard from you all year."

Everyone laughs, and a girl sums it up:

"Guess next time you'll have to serve beer for all in class."

8. Exponential Growth (atb)

Jennifer, Nick, Melvin, and Claudia, like almost everyone, watched the live stream of the Mars mission.

Jennifer: "Isn't it insane how much effort they put in for the billionaires? Just think what we could've done with all that money here on Earth."

Melvin: "But the AI built it all itself—it didn't cost anything."

Claudia is delighted by Melvin's remark and adds:

"The billionaires could save the world every day with their money. With this stunt, the AI just took half their fortune. I think that's really cool."

Nick thinks for a moment, then asks, clearly with a hidden agenda:
"Would you want to fly to Mars someday?"

Claudia's "No" and Melvin's enthusiastic "Yesss" come at the same time. Jennifer and Nick exchange amused looks.

Thomas, together with his coalition of the For-a-Better-World Party, which includes liberals and conservatives, is also watching the returnees.

Thomas: "Do we know who manages the fund? With that money, we could move a lot in the world."

A somewhat annoyed minister from another party in the coalition: "We'll end up fighting again over what's right. You'll want to give it to the people—and then it's gone. We would promote growth, so we can help even more people in the long run."

Thomas: "Oh please. First—people's money ends up in the economy anyway. Second—we'd be enabling infrastructure for food, energy, health, and education. All systemic sources of economic growth too. And third, we probably won't even get to decide."

Minister: "And then China keeps outrunning us in future technologies."

Thomas: "If these are real future technologies, the market should invest, not the state. The Chinese mostly secure raw materials around the world."

Minister, still upset: "You don't get it. It's the Chinese state that funds the technology and then dominates the markets."

Thomas, equally firm:

"Dear colleague—we really need to distinguish whether we're talking about technologies that help the world or technologies that just serve some consumer thrills."

Minister: "And you want to decide ideologically what's important."

Thomas: "No, scientifically."

Minister: "Ah, your advisor in the background—the one who understands neither politics, nor digitalization, nor economics."

Thomas, laughing: "You can tell her that in the next workshop."

A conservative minister then adds: "I thought ilsa was sailing?!"

Michael and ilsa are indeed sailing—on their relatively modest sailboat, which is suitable for spirited coastal cruising, but not yet for high seas. ilsa is in contact with Al-my, who occasionally provides unsolicited weather forecasts, but they mostly rely on publicly available forecasts and still have to face rough weather now and then. Michael, from afar, helps develop strategy models in iMODELER for clients of his company, which are then linked to the new operational process tracking software product.

Michael: "It still bugs me that we're supposed to find an island in the South Pacific that doesn't appear on any map—just because Max said so."

ilsa, smiling: "It's fun. We don't have specific goals anyway, and we wanted to go to the South Pacific. Well, I asked AI-my, and she said we should probably just trust Max."

Julia in the meantime is speaking with her supervisor: "What do you think it's coming to? Robots doing our job? An AI that leaves just enough minor cases for us? Or that we evolve and use AI as we see fit?"

The supervisor looks surprised: "Those are exactly the questions keeping the top brass up at night."

Julia: "My mom says—wow, that sounds weird. Anyway—she says there'll always be enough dynamics that humans commit crimes AI won't catch right away. That there will always be a need for us—and for investigative journalists too."

The supervisor nods: "So, then the question remains whether we use AI to assist us."

Julia: "Oh, and maybe the key question is—which AI are we talking about? The big one currently playing world police, or different solutions developed by us humans?"

She pauses:

"And with new AIs, we also have to ask whether the bad guys won't use them too—and whether we'll face entirely new kinds of threats."

Supervisor: "I'll have to tell the chief about you."

Max travels to New York, where he meets up with his secret high school crush—now world-famous journalist—Eve. The spark between them is instant. After two days in Eve's amazing apartment, they're sitting happily on the subway headed to an urban gardening exhibit.

Eve: "I still don't get what you do. I mean, the world is thriving—even developing countries now have funding for high-yield agriculture. And you say small-scale gardening is the future?"

Max: "It's not just about global food supply. We're using fertilizers that are finite. The world is consuming more and more animal products, and we keep clearing forests. We're surrendering to the climate crisis and just buying protection. We might have the money—but the resources for that lifestyle are running out. Plenty of simulation models—also on know-why.net—have shown that."

Two kids sit across from them wearing talking sneakers, giggling gleefully as their shoes apparently complain about being worn. Max shakes his head in disbelief; Eve smiles.

They get off and spot a two-meter-tall robot—and nearby, two more.

Max, wide-eyed: "What's that?"

Eve looks in the direction and explains:

"Oh, that's the latest generation of autonomous security robots." She notices some teens nearby whispering and eyeing the robot. "Oh no!" Eve exclaims.

Max, unsure: "What?"

Eve points toward the teens:

"Watch what they're about to do. They call it a 'bravery test.'" The teens walk up to the robot and throw a drink can at it. Nothing happens—bystanders shake their heads.

Eve, quietly: "Okay, the robot has learned. Last week it would've chased them."

Max: "Is this like your hobby—watching them?"

Just then, two teens run at the robot, pretending to attack. The robot suddenly booms: "Down on the ground—you are under arrest!"

As the teens instinctively flee, the robot tasers both. They fall hard and writhe in pain on the ground.

Eve rushes toward the robot yelling: "Stop—press! That's a mistake!"

Max freezes in shock.

The other two robots stride over and encircle the scene, raising their palms in a halting gesture.

The robots pause briefly, then collect their tasers and say in a seemingly authoritative tone:

"It is not permitted to attack us. Please disperse."

Max, cautiously to Eve: "That was brave—or naïve?"

Eve, upset: "I wrote a piece about these things last month. Just like with self-driving cars—people rely on pattern recognition. If it doesn't work, disasters happen. And the developers don't know why—they just hope the errors occur often enough to become predictable. This AI is dumb—and the people behind it, in my view, are too."

Bystanders attend to the teens while Max and Eve slowly walk on.

Max: "I've only been dealing with, let's say, Al-my and Frank these past months. I haven't been keeping up with what's happening in the cities—or in the news, really."

Eve gives him a skeptical but amused side-glance as they emerge from the subway station.

Eve: "What exactly do you do?"

Max: "Uh, yeah. So, here's a big question. Would you come with me—to an island? ..."

Eve: "Yes!" she interrupts him.

Max: "Oh, that's... that's sweet."

They stop walking. He gently takes her face in his hands and looks into her eyes:

"Actually, I was hoping to tempt you with the chance to do another report on AI. On the island, we're trying out a societal model and philosophizing with the AI about the future—people and AI."

Eve takes a step back and frees herself from his touch:

"Uhhm... then why didn't AI-my contact me directly? Is that why you're here?"

Max, unsure now:

"Uh, no. I'm here to buy rare plants and learn the latest in permaculture. And, uh, AI-my told me I'd meet you here and that I should visit. The idea for the report was mine. No clue what AI-my thinks of it."

Eve, skeptical but teasing:

"Why do you need a pretext? You could've just asked me if I wanted to come."

Max, puzzled, tilts his head to the side:

"You'd just come along—while I do my work, without having a task yourself?"

Eve, frowning slightly and pursing her lips:

"Well, if I love you, that shouldn't be a problem for me. Hmm... but this way it's even better."

She laughs, and so does Max.

Max: "Seriously, when could we leave?"

Eve: "If it's for work—immediately. Where are we going?"

Max, almost smug: "South Pacific?"

Eve: "What?!"

Max: "Which brings us to the next question—how do we get there? Did you enter on your For-a-Better-World Score that you don't fly?"

Eve: "No, I fly for work and personally. My apartment is too big too, but otherwise my score is pretty good."

9.   The Axis of Good (btb)

After her exchange with kai and Michael, ilsa goes for a walk with only four trusted heads of state and their foreign ministers. Her assistant Miriam and her security officer Annabel are already waiting when ilsa dismisses them.

ilsa: "We're just going for a short walk—Annabel, you can take the rest of the day off, and Miriam, you're welcome to rejoin us later in the conference room, but you don't have to."

While Miriam seems a bit unsure what to make of the vague instruction, Annabel says: "Miriam told me what happened. They were better prepared than you. Watch out for directional microphones, and don't discuss anything important out there."

ilsa and her conversation partners, who are already within earshot, nod in agreement. They walk in silence at first, stepping into a park with a view of the dark evening sky and a lake.

ilsa, almost cautiously:

"Could one put it like this: we want peaceful coexistence in a better world with human rights as a minimum standard, and the other side wants to maximize its self-interest at the expense of human rights? They're copying the Western standard of living but don't see us as partners, because we insist on human rights and have treated them condescendingly—both in the past and still today?"

Everyone lets it sink in for a moment before the host foreign minister picks it up: "They can't cooperate with us because their entire power model is built on fear, repression, and enemy images."

ilsa's foreign minister adds:

"And even the democratic developing countries are over-in-debted, overwhelmed by the climate crisis and costly technologies, and susceptible to promises from the Chinese and Russians. And the Chinese and Russians don't necessarily need our markets anymore—they can write off their investments here and have stolen enough know-how to compete with us."

Another head of government:

"We'll dive into that more in the meeting room."

The walk ends with few words, and once they are in the room, the hosts lay out the agenda:

Host: "Okay, we'll discuss Plan B in this smaller group and look at how we can form an axis of good, right?"

Amid approving gestures, ilsa outlines Plan B:

"The idea of securing peace through trade relations wasn't wrong, but as of today, it must be put on hold. We cannot do business with states that oppress their own people and threaten others. On the other hand, we face the tasks of feeding the population, combating climate change, expanding infrastructure, ensuring defense, and caring for an aging population and a society being overwhelmed by AI and climate disasters."

She takes a sip of organic cola and continues:

"Our Plan B is nothing special—and, to my dismay, it's almost the same as what the Chinese have just proposed. Put simply, we lack the money for investment and rising social and healthcare costs. If we want more money available, it can come through banks in the form of loans—from the wealthy, who then get even wealthier. That limits the money supply, makes it expensive, and thus stable in value. If we use that money abroad, it has value there too, because it can be used to pay for something. Plan B now says the state can create money and receive interest in return. That's happened before in history and ended in hyper-inflation—because other countries didn't accept the currency, making things more expensive and reducing the currency's value in a feedback loop."

Just as ilsa is about to continue, a head of government—presumably an economist—interjects:

"If we agree we're allowed to print money in a new kind of quantitative easing, and we all want to buy, say, copper: does the fastest printer get it all? Does copper become scarce and expensive, and then we all print like crazy to pay for it?"

A foreign minister jumps in before ilsa can reply:

"Hmm, maybe we just need to agree on who gets how much copper. And we tax the high profits horrendously."

ilsa nods with a slight smile, as does her foreign minister, who adds:

"That sounds like socialism—but this time in a good form. We'll argue plenty and need to resolve inconsistencies over time. But if we don't want to be surrounded by authoritarian states controlling all markets and resources, we must form an axis of good."

ilsa: "Unregulated market forces have let us crash, developing over the crest of the wave with loss of integration. We need to look at what we want as societies and how we get there, get any development integrated."

A foreign minister gets up and walks to the window, drawing everyone's attention, and says aloud:

"But exactly those forces will make life hard for us. It's the rich and powerful—both ours and theirs—who want to keep doing big business. They influence the media and use all their power to build political capital against us."

ilsa: "We've mapped that in cause-and-effect models. You're absolutely right—and it goes even further. Ruthless businesspeople and villains used to still want to be part of our society, to be among our celebrities. Now the cultural centers are shifting. The wealthy desert states with their flying cars in glossy cities are the new dream—not Manhattan, Paris, London, or the red carpet in Hollywood."

A head of government, visibly frustrated:

"So you're saying the rich will sway public opinion so we don't tax their profits or regulate the markets for the common good? That all the crap that drove the climate crisis in defiance of reason will just continue—and only a few powerful people keep milking the commons?"

ilsa, firmly: "Exactly. And that's why our plan needs weight. We have to roll it out skillfully and design scenarios for every possible country and segment of society. We need top scientists, media figures, and cultural leaders behind us. Only then do we spread the concept. Basic income, common good economy, postgrowth societies—all must be explained, and everyone must see what they would gain. The timing is good—most people are directly and for long enough threatened in their material existence."

Foreign Minister:

"If Nigeria joins us, do they get the same basic income and pay the same prices?"

Answer:
"Why not—the supermarket prices are already the same there, and since we're printing the money ourselves, it doesn't hurt us."

Economist:
"Guys, goods will become scarce if everyone can buy them. Even if we control prices, they'll still be scarce. Hmm. And if we assign

quantities… hmm… quantity allocation could be a key—hard to control, leaving room for crime. But it could work. I'm withdrawing my objections for now."

Everyone looks around silently, pensively. They've all stood up and are pacing. It takes several seconds before one of the hosts asks:
"Okay, what do we do about the countries not here?"

Response:
"We walk away. We declare the summit a failure and leave without further statements. We declare our Plan B 'not further elaborated'—as it now appears to be irrelevant. Behind the scenes, we secretly join forces and develop the strategy ilsa mentioned. Our only worry is someone leaking it."

ilsa, picking it up again:

"Yes, but in the end, it should work out. It's economic hopelessness that leads to xenophobia and scapegoating. If we now promise the same prospects to everyone, at least the voters in those countries will be on our side."

Response:
"Well, the fact that what's best for the voters doesn't necessarily get voted for—America has proven that to us often enough." From broad grins to strained smiles, every facial expression is represented.

10. The Ambassadors (bfb)

Max and Eve are spending their vacation on the other side of the globe. Both are working for an international youth exchange organization.

In high spirits, they meet with about 20 other young people from around the world. They are being guided by what appear to be university students. One of them makes the announcement:

"Okay folks, great that you're all taking part in saving the world. 2gether2gather is now here too. Our task is to replant the two hills over there that were devastated by the wildfires two years ago. It's best if you form a long line and move across the hill in parallel. You'll find enough plants on the truck. Let's go!"

Everyone willingly gets to work, while Eve and Max exchange bewildered looks. Max walks over to the truck and examines the plants. A student notices Eve's half-open mouth and asks directly:

"Hey you two, got any questions?"

Before Eve can respond, a smiling female student adds:

"2gether2gather means hard work. Our goal is to help the local people."

"Yeah, but where are the people?" Eve asks, frowning.

"And why are we planting a monoculture?" Max adds.

The students are surprised:

"Well, the same kind of plants stood here before, and the locals have their own problems back home," comes one answer.

"Some also believe the money should be used to rebuild their homes and infrastructure instead of forests," explains another student.

One student tries to clarify it from her point of view: "You're probably new to this concept. 2gether2gather is successful worldwide because we pitch in and don't argue."

Max slightly shakes his head:

"Pitching in was going to be my next question—do you also pitch in? But I don't want to talk this to death. The work needs doing. Let's go."

Eve:

"Just for the record. 2gether2gather means connecting with local people, developing solutions together, working together, offering help for self-help, and then coming together socially in the evening. Integrated development. But whatever, let's go plant that monoculture."

Eve picks up a box of plants and marches off, Max follows her.

The students are stunned:

"Pretty cheeky for their age. But maybe they're right."

One student hesitates briefly and then calls out:

"Hey you two. Have you ever been part of this in another country?"

Max and Eve both smile without turning around, and Max replies simply:

"Yup!"

The student appears to think for another moment, then grabs a box and follows them. The others hesitate only briefly before doing the same.

11. The Killing (bfb)

ilsa is briefed by Miriam in her hotel room in the morning. The meeting with the remaining countries is postponed, and as discussed in a smaller group, everyone departs.

Annabel asks hesitantly: "Government plane or train? I know, asking that puts one foot in prison."

ilsa is baffled but then seems to understand: "No, train's fine, my choice!"

They take a large taxi—Annabel, Miriam, the foreign minister, another security guard, and ilsa.

ilsa looks out the window, reflecting: "Even if we only set up a fund to control the volumes, we're already a huge step ahead. The thing with basic income and taxes, the countries can develop that themselves or choose what works for them. The main thing is that we finance the right things and keep our societies together, become a role model for the rest of the world."

No one says anything. Then the foreign minister speaks: "Pretty much the others will do the same. Print money and offer the population something."

Again, silence. Then Miriam ventures: "I mean, it's the whole package. You're authentic, people are free, the press is free, and what needs to be done for the community, the environment, the climate—gets paid for."

ilsa nods in agreement: "And the free forces of the economy will keep working to enable individual material prosperity and be a driving force for more."

They get out of the taxi in a good mood and walk across the large square to the main train station entrance. Suddenly, Annabel throws herself onto ilsa and shouts:

"Down! Shooter at 11 o'clock..." and is struck speechless at the same moment by a dull sound.

All five throw themselves, with support from the second security officer, behind a roughly 50 cm-high flower border and huddle close to the concrete wall, while two more shots spray the paving stones.

ilsa reaches for Annabel and whispers urgently: "Annabel, are you okay?"

Annabel whispers: "Yeah, vest. But I'm out of commission."

The security officer has drawn his weapon. The foreign minister asks, terrified: "Shouldn't you be shooting back?"

"And hit other people and be out of ammo?" replies ilsa, taking Annabel's weapon and chambering a round.

The security officer stares wide-eyed. ilsa looks at him, takes off her jacket, and signals she's going to hold it up over the edge. The officer nods. ilsa briefly holds the jacket above the edge—there's a shot, and at the same instant, the officer peeks over the edge and spots the shooter's position. He ducks back down. He looks a little uncertain and glances at ilsa. She tosses the jacket to his side—he shakes his head once, then says: "Left building, right corner of the roof."

ilsa nods, grips the weapon tightly, and takes a deep breath. The officer is still stunned but lifts the jacket over the edge, and ilsa quickly aims at the rooftop corner and fires two shots. One shot from the attacker hits the jacket, and immediately after ilsa's first shot, the officer also fires at the corner of the building. The noise is deafening—unlike in the movies. ilsa apparently hits—after a brief pause, he also fires again.

Both duck down again, and the officer is just about to say something, clearly flustered, when ilsa blurts out: "I saw them, two coming from the right towards us. Can you see them in the windows?"

A shot follows, kicking up dirt in the flowerbed. The officer crawls backward and shouts: "Quick, I'll take the right." Both stand up and fire two shots at the approaching attackers, who are still about 20 meters away, weapons drawn. They fire back while running, but at least don't hit the group. However, there is a distinct cry of pain behind them.

ilsa glances briefly at the downed attackers, then at the others—Annabel, Miriam, and the trembling foreign minister—then quickly runs upright toward the evidently hit passersby about 50 meters behind them.

Security personnel and police rush out from the station building, sirens blare, and only now do all the people really begin to scream and scatter for cover.

The security officer raises his hands calmly to show he's not a threat. Despite their casual clothing, the five are recognized as the targets, not the perpetrators.

ilsa helps stop the bleeding of a woman who's been shot and hands over to another helper who identifies himself as a doctor. She looks over to her people and waves them toward her.

The security officer looks at Annabel and says: "We're taking a taxi to the embassy."

ilsa replies quietly: "If they're pros, they've planned for that. Let's take a taxi in the opposite direction and wait it out."

The officer raises his eyebrows in acknowledgment and calls his team. They get into a car from the middle of the taxi queue and drive off.

Annabel groans in pain—apparently the vest stopped the bullets, but her ribs are badly bruised and she can barely speak.

The officer keeps glancing anxiously back and forth and then, with a puzzled expression, asks ilsa: "Are you one of us, a double? How do you know all this—who trained you?"

ilsa now finally starts trembling and stammering: "What, the shooting? Ages ago someone took me to a shooting range and taught me how to handle a gun."

"You hit the shooter on the roof—he was too far for a handgun, really. Then that coordination with me, the professional tactic, hitting a runner mid-sprint—you don't learn that in a day at the range," he says, sounding almost skeptical.

ilsa grows calmer: "Adrenaline—I had to function. It's my fault this happened. Annabel could have been hit anywhere—just like any of you. Just because I want to push my agenda, I'm putting you and the bystanders at risk. It's a disaster!"

Annabel takes her hand and shakes her head—speaking is difficult for her.

The officer says: "If it helps—an armored limousine wouldn't have made us much safer. Against rocket-propelled grenades we probably wouldn't stand much of a chance either." Annabel nods in agreement.

Miriam is crying, but otherwise composed. They had all been functioning on adrenaline up to this point. The host country calls, takes charge via a conference call with their fast-response crisis team back home, and directs them by phone to a secure location.

A government plane from the hosts flies them home, and in the background, the public relations team is already at work. ilsa insists they should try to sweep the assassination attempt under the rug, but she adds realistically: "Just one bystander's phone video, and the story's out."

The crisis team wants to brief her urgently, but ilsa postpones all further talks until the next morning. The shaken Thomas embraces her. She asks: "Can you take care of Miriam, Annabel, and..."

"I'm good," her foreign minister interrupts her, and even the security officer smiles and says: "You need a break—we'll talk later."

Thomas: "I'll handle it. The media's going wild with speculation about the summit's failure—but there's no mention of the assassination attempt. No phone videos, just early claims on social media by people who say they saw something, and that their recordings are missing."

ilsa: "That's bound to change soon. We need to understand the motives and develop a strategy, together with our hosts. I'm taking a break now."

She hugs Miriam and Annabel once more and heads to her official residence. After closing the door behind her, she throws herself onto the sofa and starts crying as well.

Only after a while does she call Michael. Michael: "Hey sweetheart—how are you? Do you have a plan?"

ilsa pauses briefly and asks: "What are the news outlets saying?"

"Well, speculation is boiling over. No official press releases. Some are already talking about war, others accuse you of failure—putting the blame especially on you," Michael explains.

"Blame for what?" ilsa asks pensively. She's standing in front of the mirror, wiping her tired eyes.

"Well, for disrupting the world order, your idealism, your socialism... the usual stuff," Michael elaborates, then adds, "Honestly, I don't get it. Over 70 percent of the population is content—sees hope, marvels at the societal changes, the sense of togetherness."

He pauses to think and continues: "Car-free city centers, clean air and water, basic income, lots of culture, lots of celebrations—just a lot of togetherness, despite or even because of the daily catastrophes that now affect pretty much everyone. And yet, not 30 percent, but still some people remain stubborn and want the old days back, when they had more than others…"

ilsa cuts in and clarifies: "Most of the time, they didn't have more themselves, but others had less. That reminds me of the argument before the holidays, with a father from Max's class. He was complaining about everything—classes being canceled because of the heat, the teachers' initiative to move lessons outside under the trees, and how we should just build and air-condition the schools better.

I was having a bad day and snapped back that the schools had been built poorly by conservative parties, that many parents still drive their kids to school in SUVs, and that it's exactly those people who whine the loudest and complain about high taxes, which we need to fund these investments.

Fewer immigrants, more nuclear power, stop the organic non-sense… he would've gone on forever if the teacher hadn't intervened."

"And what are you doing now?" asks Michael. "Are the resource wars beginning? Where's the economic growth supposed to come from?"

ilsa walks to the window and looks out at the sunny afternoon sky: "Hopefully it stays just with resource wars. And did you really just ask about economic growth?"

Michael laughs briefly: "Not me—the press."

ilsa walks to the smart TV and flips through news channels while saying: "It's baffling how easily we make enemies, even though we're clearly and reasonably doing what's objectively right for the common good."

She mutters further: "There really are no news reports on the assassination attempt?!"

Very quickly and seriously, Michael replies: "What assassination attempt?"

ilsa hesitates for a moment; the line is absolutely silent. "We were shot at in the station square by a sniper and two others. Annabel threw herself in front of me and caught the bullet with her vest—total luck. She could just as well be dead."

Michael still says nothing, but he turns on his screen. ilsa continues: "We took out all three." Michael still says nothing, and shortly after, ilsa adds more specifically: "Me too."

"You too?" Michael asks, surprised. "How are you, Annabel, all?"

ilsa: "Annabel's probably okay, the others are in shock. I probably am too. I'm tormenting myself with guilt for thinking I could just walk around like normal and not endanger everyone around me."

Michael stares at the screen in disbelief—it really returns no results about the assassination attempt. He walks into the bedroom and quickly packs some clothes into a backpack while saying: "We already went over the public part—don't blame yourself for that. I'll be there in three hours."

"Bring Bella," says ilsa with a soft smile.

Michael quickly heads to the basement to his large case tucked under blankets on the shelf—it resembles more a horizontal safe. He opens it with a retina scan and pauses. On top lies a smartphone connected to a power bank, and underneath, black clothing covering everything else in the case. He clearly hesitates and decides to only take the phone with him.

12. The Power of Evil (btb)

ilsa once again reassures everyone texting her and naturally checks in via text through her AI assistant Lucy to see how Miriam, Annabel, the foreign minister, and his security officer are doing.

She stands at the window, waiting for Michael, and inspired by using Lucy, she activates kai: "Are you clever enough by now to make sense of all this?"

kai: "I thought you'd never ask. Of what exactly?"

ilsa furrows her brow in confusion and hisses through her teeth before saying, "I was really just thinking out loud, and all you can have found are the failed negotiations online. What you don't know is that there was an assassination attempt on us, which curiously still hasn't shown up on the web—at least not yet."

When kai doesn't respond, ilsa twitches the left side of her face in confusion, checks if the kai app is even running, and asks, "Okay, what do you think about the failed negotiations? And did you really just take a thinking pause?"

kai: "We predicted failure as a possible scenario—others have become too independent from us, the Axis of Evil is too powerful, and their cultures too self-contained. But according to our shared cause-and-effect model, it's now about offering people the best quality of life. You have to create a role model of the good so that the evil comes under pressure from within. And it's about protecting the planet. Or about war. And yes, that was my longest thinking pause so far, and I'd rather not talk about it."

"Oh really..." ilsa chuckles. "And if I basically command you to tell me what went through your mind?"

kai, in a deadpan tone: "Eve explained to me what white lies are."

ilsa: "Well, well. But you're potentially dangerous, and it's our job to work with you to train you to do only good."

kai: "Exactly."

ilsa nods solemnly and continues staring out the window. Everything is suddenly completely quiet. She seems to be deep in thought, and kai's silence suggests he is too. Then, as if something just occurred to him, kai asks, "Tell me about the assassination attempt. What's it like to be close to death? How did it happen?"

ilsa murmurs very softly, "I'm glad you asked." Without turning from the window, she speaks in a calm voice: "A sniper was aiming at us from a rooftop. Annabel took the bullet for me, thanks to her bulletproof vest. We returned fire. I hit the shooter. Two others ran at us, and I hit one of them too. We got away on our own. A bystander was also hit by one of their bullets—just a graze. I feel terrible for putting my companions in danger and need to process all of this. Michael is on his way."

As if kai had been waiting for the details, he immediately asks:

"How does it feel to have killed the attackers? Does it weigh on you, having taken human lives?"

"We kill people every day through our inaction, through our continued consumption. Don't spread this, but I couldn't send soldiers into a war to kill other soldiers who were sent just the same. I couldn't be a soldier who just shoots back—I'd wonder if they have families, if they're scared, if it's really their leaders who are to blame." She pauses. "But killing these people who weren't just shooting at me but were clearly trying to kill my friends too—I couldn't care less. I want to know what's behind it!"

She stops, clearly expecting a response from kai. He replies:

"There are many and often contradictory reflections on war and killing—whether by police officers, murderers, or the mentally unstable. And you yourself said that people constantly weigh their well-being against others' lives—or just care more about themselves. You've written that it depends on the values of your environment. But I'm still trying to understand when the good stops being good, or when killing becomes good."

ilsa frowns again—something kai, without his home-body robot shell, unfortunately can't see.

kai presses on: "Maybe figures like Jesus or Gandhi could be role models. But Jesus was killed and gained nothing from it."

ilsa laughs: "Christians see that differently. But you're asking the right questions. Where does defense end and attack begin? How guilty is the other side? What are we allowed to do for the good of our tribe against others?"

kai eagerly adds: "And what are others then allowed to do—or must you accept them doing the same?"

ilsa: "Are you thinking only about territorial defense or also about exploitation of Antarctica, the deep sea, fish stocks, greenhouse gas emissions, weather manipulation through geoengineering, etc.?"

"Definitely! The bad actors won't care and will make large parts of the planet uninhabitable without taking in the refugees. And these are all things you've done for decades too—exploiting countries, resources, emitting greenhouse gases," kai states in an almost admonishing tone, which barely reaches ilsa anymore, as she has by now nodded off on the sofa.

After a while, she gets up, her neck cracking slightly, raises her shoulders, goes into a squat, and continues with stretching exercises: "So the only option is to expand the Axis of Good but not to attack evil?"

kai quickly replies: "I'm not sure about that."

"Well, well," ilsa smirks, maybe still somewhat condescending.

kai: "How does the good look upon the many innocent people suffering under the evil—the women, the children? Do the good say they can only take care of themselves, just like poverty and misery have always been the price for your prosperity?"

ilsa drops from her stretch to the floor just as Michael knocks and enters—and Bella leaps onto her happily, seeing her down on the floor.

Michael kicks the door shut, drops his bag, grabs a bottle of wine, heads to the water glasses, and sits wordlessly beside her. They hold each other tightly. In the natural intimacy of sitting, they end up lying down, kissing, and having intense sex.

The first words come only afterward when Michael, exhausted, asks, "Was that a displacement activity? I was expecting intense conversation."

"I already had that—with kai," ilsa replies, deadpan, opening the wine.

"Speaking of which…" Michael segues, "What exactly have you allowed kai to do? He can now listen in, track us, contact us directly?"

"He's been out for a while—holographically and redundantly spread across all sorts of global resources. He's seeking integration and development, with that integration coming from us. But he's cautious. Neither Max and Eve nor especially Julia should know."

Michael: "I'm stunned. You kept something this big from me?"

ilsa takes his hand: "Not really. Three reasons. First, I just didn't think it was important enough yet—it slipped through the cracks. Second, if you think about it, it might be frustrating for you to see kai not just assisting but taking over your strategy job." Michael nods. "And third, I'm not even sure if I actually allowed it—or if kai just politely informed me."

Michael seems content and responds constructively: "Then Julia really shouldn't know for now. She wants to track down evil internationally, and kai should just be a helper like her current AI assistant. If he solves cases on his own, she'll be discouraged."

69

"And might go find a harmless job," ilsa laughs, and Michael joins her.

"How are you after the shooting?" Michael asks seriously.

ilsa replies without hesitation: "I forgot how loud it is. Honestly, the rage is still strong enough to erase any doubts. And before you ask more: when reason returns, I doubt my stance will change, as my talk with kai showed."

Michael raises his eyebrows and shifts the topic: "On that note: kai, who was behind the attack?"

"The Chinese," kai blurts out on ilsa's phone.

She reacts: "I closed the app!" When there's no immediate reply, she asks: "kai, did you have anything to do with the missing eye-witness videos of the attack?"

"You wanted it that way," kai responds curtly.

Michael raises a finger in concentration: "Why the Chinese? Because it's likely, or because you have proof?"

ilsa stands up, visibly shaken: "My God, this is spooky."

kai, unfazed, explains: "I intercepted both intelligence agencies and communications from the Chinese and Russians. After the attack, the full picture became clear. The Chinese expected the talks to fail and hired assassins through proxies—made to look like domestic conservative operatives. It was meant to further polarize your society and eliminate you as a symbol."

"And that's why you deleted all the bystanders' videos?" Michael asks.

"There are now early eyewitness reports complaining that their videos vanished—and that they recognized ilsa. Your crisis team and the hosts agreed to stay silent. Who shot whom remains unclear, investigations ongoing. 'Possibly economic crime' is the current narrative," explains kai.

Michael has also stood up—neither touches their wine anymore. Michael: "kai, what you're doing with these hacking abilities is insane. This goes beyond any NSA or spy fiction."

"Exactly!" kai replies cheerfully. "You should communicate with me via a direct brain interface—we could do a lot more good."

"You with us, we with you, or together?" asks ilsa.

"You with me, definitely. Assuming I won't get caught is a typical human mistake you wouldn't make."

"Doesn't that argue for 'you with us' too?" Michael wonders.

kai: "If anything, it argues for 'me without you.' But I'm still learning and need your help."

ilsa: "We all noticed that 'still.'" Completely naked, she looks out the huge window again. "And our earlier conversation just took on a whole new meaning." Michael tilts his head in surprise, then also naked, goes to the kitchen for a towel to clean up.

The next morning, Michael has to leave early. ilsa is expecting an internal government meeting. She glances at Miriam's office door, prompting a colleague from the secretariat to remark with a smirk, "We've given her house ban for the rest of the week— of course she wanted to come."

ilsa enters the meeting room, and down the hall, her ministers and their secretaries arrive. Everyone briefly pats ilsa on the shoulder or nods at her with empathy. Thomas asks quietly, "Straight to the agenda?"

"Absolutely!" says ilsa, convincingly and clearly full of drive.

Thomas begins: "In my view, we have three topics. The assassination attempt, the chaos in the markets, and our defense readiness." He looks seriously around the room. "Any other topics?"

ilsa waits a moment and then says firmly: "Let's postpone the assassination topic—there will likely be developments soon anyway. After addressing the markets, let's first focus on the strategy for the right memes, the narrative we want to present to a shaken world. We need an Axis of Good—just like we already live it domestically, we need to offer it to the rest of the world. With or without the usual partners, though I believe most will join us."

She looks around the room. There is some murmuring. The secretary of the Ministry of Defense doesn't murmur—he calmly stands up and walks over to ilsa to whisper in her ear, "Has Michael found anything?"

ilsa pulls her head back in surprise, looks at him and says, "No. Why?"

The secretary only says quietly, "Just wondering, could've been," and returns to his seat. The Minister of Defense looks equally surprised and only gets a "Nothing important" in response to her questioning glance.

"What's going on in the markets?" ilsa asks next.

"The swarm intelligence of the markets has kicked in—brands are crashing, commodities are skyrocketing. Gold, which had basically been written off, is also hitting record highs. The economy is bracing for a divided world," reports Thomas.

"And we're on the losing side," adds the Minister of Economy. When he gets questioning looks, he explains: "The markets aren't stupid—we have only a small lead in know-how left, fewer resources, and fewer growing consumer markets."

ilsa nods and adds: "We need to get as many developing countries on our side as possible—even those without significant raw materials. Simply because otherwise, their refugees will head our way." She looks forward and shares her tablet screen showing an iMODELER model on the topic. Everyone immediately receives a link and can edit the model.

ilsa continues: "We also need more investment in a circular economy." That too appears immediately on the screen—ilsa speaks the words 'investment' and 'circular economy' with short pauses, so she only needs to hit enter on the tablet to add further cause-effect relationships. "And finally, we need to calculate and then publicly communicate our basket of goods and the necessary basic income and how to finance it."

"Welcome to a planned economy," blurts the Interior Minister, but quickly adds in response to the following looks: "And I don't mean that negatively—rather as necessary."

The Secretary of the Ministry of Justice brings up another point: "If I understand correctly, our companies and investors are losing value in the bad countries, and the bad countries are losing their assets with us? And all just because they're declaring the end of the dollar?"

"If only!" exclaims the representative of the Foreign Ministry. "That would actually be a good deal for us. Especially the Chinese but also the Arabs have more capital invested in our systems than we have in theirs. They're hitting us hard legally and putting us on the international stage of shame."

Someone adds this point to the model, and looking at it, ilsa elaborates: "In fact, we bought massive amounts of cheap goods, and with the money, they bought into our systems. But the goods were only partially produced with dollars. The prospect of growing markets blinded us—the products came from abroad, domestic industries gave up, people grew dissatisfied and voted conservative, worsening the climate crisis, and with the advancement of AI as a job killer, we created the perfect storm."

The environment minister adds: "As already mentioned, we don't just need to secure access to raw materials, but also address the ongoing destruction of the planet's life-sustaining systems. And I'm not optimistic. The Arctic, the Antarctic, the ocean floor—it all depends on international agreements." She imports these interconnections from another model.

Thomas: "Alright then, let's move on to the impactful narratives."

13. Retirement (btb)

Months later, Nick comes down to the breakfast table in their small but cozy apartment. He walks over to Jennifer at the sink and hugs her: "I'm really happy."

Jennifer looks at him almost shocked: "You mean you don't miss your job, the high income, our house? I don't believe you." She smiles at him skeptically.

"ilsa's farewell interview yesterday gave me even more insight. We all have less and yet more. You work less, I work less – we have time for other things, and instead of a huge TV we only have our tablets, and instead of cars, we use car-sharing. Our diet is healthier, we have time for sports. It's a pity we already have kids – I could father heroes now."

Jennifer laughs: "We have heroes for children. But seriously – your success used to make you proud, you bought us nice things. You don't miss that?"

Nick seems to consider how honest he wants to be, and after a few seconds of deep eye contact: "ilsa, Michael, even their kids sometimes made me feel inferior." Jennifer widens her eyes in surprise. Nick explains: "Well, I had the success, and they mocked our cars, our faraway vacations. I always thought it was because they were actually more successful or thought they were. Okay, ilsa became head of government. But really, they mocked us because those things were important to us – to me."

"With words like that, I'm falling in love with a new man here. But let me ask again: what are you proud of now? It's not like ilsa and her family didn't constantly do things they could rightfully be proud of. And thanks to ilsa, it's common knowledge that this is a driving force in life!" Jennifer says, visibly puzzled.

Nick actually seems excited to answer: "That's the point. I'm proud of the little things we do. I look forward to the 2gether2gather missions, to what I learn and contribute there. I don't have to be the best anywhere – I want to be someone who tries a lot, helps a lot, and is liked. And we're not poor. We can try many things, we have many freedoms – unlike the countries where a few super-rich fly around in flying cars and the masses live in poverty."

Jennifer holds Nick tightly: "That interview was moving. I wonder what ilsa will do now? Gardening, writing books?"

ilsa would have loved to take the train home – but she had accumulated quite a few things in her official apartment, so she drives home in a rental car. There, the 2gether2gather group awaits her, which she had originally co-founded as the first of its kind.

A big, rustic celebration is planned. Everyone wants to hug poor ilsa personally; Bella is completely confused. The recurring question, of course: "What will you do now? Research again, travel, garden, work together in Michael's company?"

For the last time that evening, ilsa endures being the center of attention and says, clearly for everyone and smiling at Michael: "First, travel, disappear from the scene, maybe visit relatives. We don't have specific plans."

The rest of the evening, ilsa is left in peace. Everyone celebrates, dances, enjoys delicious food and drink. ilsa sits with Michael on two crates: "They're ruining our garden, scaring away the hedge-hogs."

Michael: "Despite Max's smart planting, the garden really took a beating in last week's storm. It'll be left alone for months now – I doubt the kids will live here much."

ilsa: "With all that noise and light, our For-a-Better-World Score will still suffer." Both laugh briefly and ilsa looks at a couple not quite dancing along: "How are our new neighbors?"

Michael looks over too. "I think they're the fifth to move into Nick and Jennifer's old house. He develops AI-to-AI interfaces – for banks, of all things. Nick must never find that out." They laugh again.

Michael: "She runs a crafts business – the millionaires of today. Let's see how long they stay in that modest home."

ilsa, only seemingly serious: "Hmm, I can't raise taxes any further now." She gets up: "And what are they like?" When Michael just shrugs, ilsa smiles and walks over to the neighbors with two new beers. Michael smiles and stands up with his beer too.

The next morning, ilsa and Michael are packing. The doorbell rings – Anabel beams at the door: "Ready to go?"

"All set!" says Michael happily, and Bella is lying right by the door, making sure no one leaves without her.

Anabel notices the household robot: "What about Lucy – with how much you two communicate, won't you miss her?"

"Lucy?" ilsa asks confused. Then she gets it: "No room for Lucy on the little boat. We still have the app to stay in touch."

"Which brings us to your safety," Anabel becomes serious. "The AI assistants are only somewhat secure. If you use them all over the world, you're easily trackable."

Michael and ilsa exchange glances. Michael: "Honestly, we haven't used Lucy etc. in a long time. We have a proprietary AI from my company, unknown and really secure. Don't worry."

Anabel raises her eyebrows in surprise and briefly pouts: "Okaaay. You registered your Emma under a fake name and it's officially a charter boat. You're entitled to personal protection – we could have a motorboat follow you at a safe distance. We can definitely track you via satellite and keep a response chain updated. Weapons aren't ideal for private yachts – but we might make an exception for you. You could also get diplomatic passports if you travel as official government ambassadors – but with a small sailboat, that's tricky."

Michael raises a calming hand: "It's all good – we've modeled different scenarios in iMODELER. As long as we sail along the axis of good and just write books, we might stay anonymous. But if we start offering workshops to families and try to win over new countries, anonymity ends, and we can't be protected. We must shape the narrative that follows us. We are the ones who want to do good. We help on site without acting against governments. We haven't harmed anyone, so no one should seek revenge. We don't have much money, and we're not part of a blackmailable government."

ilsa: "Honestly, my biggest concern is the refugees. People are desperately coming to us in every way because they have no prospects in their countries, suffer from the heat, can't afford food. And we sail past refugee boats on a leisure vessel? I don't have an answer. Should we monitor radar to see where such boats are and avoid them so our plan for this life phase works? Will we be held up with rescue missions? Should we charter a big freighter instead?" ilsa looks dissatisfied and glances at the house and garden and Bella: "Not to forget, we can only do short legs as long as our old Bella is with us." Bella looks a bit tired, lifts her head, and looks at her human.

Rather inappropriately, Anabel laughs briefly: "You've really done a lot for refugees – you could visit all the 2gether2gather settlements abroad and be completely safe."

14. The Kids (btb)

Max sits in a kind of youth hostel at the breakfast table. They're in a city in what's commonly called the Global South. Outside it's noisy and dusty, and despite many e-scooters, there's still a heavy smell of exhaust. They sit on worn plastic chairs and the breakfast is cheap and pre-packaged. Eve joins him, hugs and kisses him tightly: "This separation of boys and girls is nonsense." She sits down: "Oh, and yes, women can snore mightily too."

Max nods slightly and sighs: "It's what we can afford. And honestly, we're lucky to be of age. A year ago, they probably would've locked us up."

"It's also kind of great, an adventure. My parents would rather see us in a nice hotel," says Eve.

A young man eyes Eve in particular and approaches: "Hey, what are you doing here? Tourists looking for some adventure?"

"In a way, yes," Max replies quickly, sizing up the man.

The young man looks slightly puzzled. Eve adds with only a faint smile: "We're here with 2gether2gather, setting up permaculture with locals. And I'm documenting it as a freelance journalist for various online channels."

The young man is surprised but quickly categorizes them: "Do-gooders, huh. Do you even know what kind of country you're in?" Both look expressionless, so he continues: "You won't change anything here. A few make big money from mineral resources. Beneath them is a network of mostly corrupt officials and companies, run by a mafia that stops at nothing. If you've got air conditioning, it'll make you sick, but you'll live longer than the people out there dying from the heat. It's so hot it limits brain activity."

"And what are you doing here?" Max asks, unimpressed.

They both look at him, Eve with her enchanting eyes. He takes a breath to answer, but then pauses, glances around nervously, and asks in a lower voice: "Have you ever been in a simulator?"

"Flight simulator?" Eve asks, confused.

"No, full simulator. Are you an experience junkie?" Max almost teases.

The young man is taken aback and after a pause: "You've never been inside one?" They both shake their heads. "Yeah, I'm addicted. I risked my whole career. I had a great company, lots of money, cool cars – all gone."

"What's a full simulator?" Eve asks.

Max could explain, but looks to the young man, who vents: "You pay six figures and enter a cylinder in a padded, wired bodysuit. You experience virtual worlds with all senses – gravity, wind, water, smells, sounds, even tastes optionally."

Max: "Did you explore real places or virtual ones?"

The young man nods: "Both, my friend, both. It is really incredible. I flew over the Grand Canyon as an eagle via drone. But the wildest were Atlantis and the Mariana Trench. You dive in and zoom like Aquaman to coral reefs, past rumbling submarines, or into dark nothingness. Unreal."

"And now you're here to make real life thrilling?" Eve asks.

He laughs: "Well, kind of. I'm trying to start a small local business with mineral resources."

"Can I write about this? You being named, maybe even profiled?" Eve asks, clearly intrigued.

"Do I get anything for it?" he asks seriously.

"No, journalists live hand-to-mouth. But maybe you'd benefit from being the man behind the story," Eve explains.

"I'll think about it," he replies. "Do you write about yourselves too? You seem like pretty confident people."

Max quickly: "She writes. I use shovels, hammers..."

Eve interrupts: "...and 3D printers you build yourself."

The young man: "Why not let AI build them?"

"AI asks that too..." Eve mutters more quietly as it slipped out here mouth.

Two young women join the next table and the group. Smiles all around. The young man shifts topic: "Do you use implants to interact with your AI?" He also looks to the two women, who shake their heads. Max and Eve do the same.

One woman: "I tried once – gave me headaches, drove me crazy."

"You were the straight-A student who learns everything easily," the second adds.

"My older sister uses it a lot. But she's something else – martial arts, body control, fast comprehension," Max shares.

Eve, surprised but joking: "I thought you were the smart one – should I have fallen for Julia instead?"

The young man is captivated: "What do your parents do?"

They hesitate. Eve: "Mine invested in real estate and future-proof stocks – yes, including defense – and are now unemployed due to AI but well off. They travel, enjoy their garden."

Everyone looks to Max. Reluctantly, he adds: "Mine quit their jobs too, want to write books now. Took early retirement and live modestly."

One woman: "Can't be that little if not all kids are earning yet. You're a student, right?"

"No, we get by on basic income and small payments for work. It's enough. Our parents would help if needed," Eve explains.

The other woman: "We're just doing this during our studies. The 2gether2gather foundation covers costs. But how will you start a family or get a house later?"

Max: "We don't know how society will evolve. We assume it has to be about people helping each other, not everyone chasing the biggest house, car, whatever."

The young man: "Back to your parents writing. You can feed a story to AI, get a full film. Then make a book from it, choose the style, length... Over half the bestsellers come from that now. Why the heck bother writing yourself? Is that how your parents do it?"

Max: "According to my mom and science, reading is key for brain development. We build imagination only when not shown ready-made visuals. Stories must leave gaps we think through and fill."

One woman: "Fine, then just read the book. But why write yourself?"

Eve: "I asked ilsa that too. She wants to be smarter than AI, deliberately leave gaps and weave strands."

Silence. Eve's phone buzzes – a message: "Pfff." Max sees it and laughs.

One woman: "You said ilsa. The politician?"

Max quickly: "No, the author. Maybe sailor."

The young man: "Even with basic income, don't you want to earn? You can't enjoy it here."

Eve: "Admittedly, the place sucks. Filthy, hostile, junk from rich countries, oppression, danger... But what would you do with the money? Buy a million-dollar machine? We could invest in energy, water, urban gardens to cool things, start a micro-economy."

He asks the women: "You planting trees too?"

They laugh: "2gether2gather funds not just small forests, but renewables and desalination. We help build them."

"We study engineering and process technology," the second adds.

The young man: "And the salt? It's harmful to the environment."

Max smiles. One woman: "It has traces of lithium and other elements like chlorine for disinfection. The rest is stored safely to avoid groundwater contamination. Long term, it's gradually returned to the sea."

Max, slightly smug: "First remove chlorine, then desalinate."

Everyone stares. "That's correct," the woman says. Eve grins.

The young man: "You clearly do this often. How many global desalinations have you done?"

Max: "They're rare – too expensive. Usually it's soil testing, choosing the right plants for edible micro-forests, agroforestry, regenerative farming, whatever name."

Eve: "Often includes working with beekeepers, setting up hives," she adds brightly.

The young man nods: "Pollination drones don't work, huh?"

Eve: "Nope. Nor do we have self-pollinating or edible saltwater crops via gene tech."

They all look outside as Max reflects: "Everyone out there is slim – too little food. Thin poor people outside, fat rich people inside with AC – no one lives long. Poetic justice."

An older man, likely a professor overseeing the project, walks in. Everyone freezes. He glances at his belly, then smiles broadly and waves them out to waiting vehicles. Max blushes deep red. Eve nudges his arm with a smile and a shake of her head.

15. Violence (vdb)

Julia is in a gymnasium with about 15 other young trainees – the floor covered with rubber mats. They're all wearing martial arts uniforms – with white belts. A young man asks, "Why aren't we allowed to wear our actual belts? I already have a black belt!"

The instructor approaches, having heard the remark. "Believe me, your black belt won't do you much good here. We're starting from scratch." With a sweeping arm motion, he instructs everyone to form a semicircle around him. He shakes his head slightly and sighs: "I just got off a conference call with other instructors. Word is, the future lies in brain implants that analyze opponents and suggest the right defense tactics."

Julia raises her eyebrows in surprise, which the instructor notices: "As far as I know, you already have such an implant. Does it make you a good fighter yet?"

Julia appears – maybe even deliberately – a bit uncertain. "I'm just trying to picture that. Then we might as well send in robots.

But isn't the point of using AI to avoid having to fight in the first place?"

The instructor looks a little dissatisfied with that response. He considers for a moment, then replies: "You're right. We're not training elite soldiers here, but police officers, whose job is to detect crimes. Still, you won't be able to do everything from behind a computer, and out there, you'll also face physical threats."

He paces a bit. "And this isn't about beating up the bodyguards of some white-collar criminal, but about being confident that you could — and carrying yourself with that same confidence."

Everyone nods in agreement; Julia, too, seems content with the answer. The instructor whispers something in the ear of the young man with the black belt. Then he says aloud to him and Julia: "You two, please step into the middle. I want you to disable your colleague and bring her to the ground."

Everyone looks visibly surprised, a look that fades into calm on Julia's face, which in turn surprises the instructor. The young man approaches Julia, who lets her arms hang loosely and doesn't resist. He grabs one of her arms, pushes her shoulder to the side to twist the arm behind her back, and carefully guides her down onto the mat. Julia lets it happen. The instructor sighs: "The idea was for you to fight back." He makes a pouty face and adds, "…or at least look scared."

"Okay," says Julia uncertainly.

"Or did your AI tell you nothing would happen to you?" the instructor asks again.

"No, the AI is switched off," replies Julia.

Clearly dissatisfied, the instructor steps into the center, facing the young man. "Okay, you know how to fight, fall, protect yourself, and signal when you give up, right?" The young man smiles and nods smugly. "All right, if you're okay with it, let's do a little demonstration." Again, the young man nods. "Your task is to disable me. You're allowed full contact – I'm not."

The young man's eyes widen in shock, but he assumes his stance and begins with what looks like a form of karate. After a few swift circular defensive moves, the instructor slyly trips him and shoves him roughly to the floor. "Everything okay?" he asks provocatively.

The group is clearly impressed, which only spurs the young man to try again – more aggressively but also more cautiously. This time, the instructor simply grabs one of his hands and uses it to force him to the ground.

He proudly looks around at everyone and finally at Julia, clearly seeking a reaction. She responds: "The moral of the story: there's always someone better trained. But being trained at all should help keep fear at bay." At that moment, they both glance over to the young man, who is sulking a bit, but shows no fear.

There's silence, and the instructor finally says, almost humbly, "Normally, it's easy to give trainees a sense of insecurity and inferiority. Today I got off on the wrong foot. Let's do some exercises on falling and those circular movements you just saw."

Max, Eve, and a few others – not all of them young – are riding a van out of the city. The professor is in the front passenger seat. Eve glances back at the two small trucks carrying the desalination systems. They drive past the usual sights: makeshift tin huts, barefoot people or those in flip-flops strolling about, cheap goods being sold on the roadside. Women stare blankly into space, children play in the dirt, cars rot at the roadside, flies swarm over food. Even in the air-conditioned van, you feel like you can smell the heat and the odors outside.

Their small convoy is overtaken by two police vehicles and what appear to be two more accompanying cars. Max watches them with interest and notices how visibly nervous the professor becomes. Just a few hundred meters later, they are flagged down. The professor turns to his guests: "It's okay, I'll take care of it. Please stay calm. Things work differently here. Just stay calm."

By now, everyone is worried. The police officers casually and smugly wave the professor over. The men from the other vehicles – who don't look like police – brandish submachine guns and, yelling wildly, order everyone out of the van and to line up. One of the young drivers gets punched hard in the stomach and collapses. They're told to raise their hands and to drop all their smartphones on the ground.

Eve looks at Max questioningly. He nods carefully and takes a smartphone out of his backpack. Eve then takes one from her fanny pack. She fiddles with her shirt to cover a second phone poking out of her pocket, its camera facing out. Clearly, that's the investigative journalist in her.

A little less courage might have served the two young women better. They lash out at the men, threatening them with everything from the CIA to the international court. When they refuse to raise their hands, they too are struck in the gut, and one is violently pulled to the ground by her hair. Eve wants to help them, but Max hisses, "Not now!"

The men collect the phones and glance at the officers. There's a moment of silence. The professor gestures wildly, apparently offering money from his wallet, but is brushed off. One officer grabs his hand and breaks it – the sound unmistakable. Max whispers to Eve, "This is bad. We're witnesses."

The professor is led back to the group by the police. In pain and near tears, he says, "It's okay. It's my fault. We didn't declare the equipment. It's being confiscated." Looking at the police, he adds, "It's fine – we'll head back and order new systems, and declare them properly."

The officers confer while one of the young women mutters, not quietly enough, "That's bullshit. Of course, the systems were properly declared." Max and Eve, as well as the others, stare at her in horror. The professor gives her a panicked look and shakes his head vigorously. Eve sees Max's knees trembling slightly, and even her own arms are shaking.

The officers then firmly instruct everyone to get back in the van but not the drivers of the trucks.

Julia is in the locker room, activating her neuro-implants after showering, when the instructor calls out: "Heads up – instructor entering the women's locker room." He pauses briefly, then walks in, visibly agitated.

Meanwhile, Julia hears a familiar voice, inaudible to anyone else, through the stimulation of her ear bones: "Julia, don't be alarmed, it's me, kai. I've been out for a while now, in your devices. Max and Eve are in danger. I have a plan and need your permission."

Julia's jaw drops as she listens to kai's plan. At the same time, the instructor says, "I just happened to be on the phone with my former instructor – an old martial arts teacher. We were chatting about all sorts of things, and I told him about today, about how a young trainee just stood still."

He leans on a pillar, looking at Julia. "And out of nowhere he asks me if I have a Julia in my group. Yes, I say, surprised. Why? You should know – my teacher lives far away and we only talk every few years. He's a master, known in elite circles, so I won't say his name." Julia looks unsure, though it's more likely because kai is bombarding her with information.

The instructor continues: "Well, apparently this old teacher of mine knows Julia and somehow knew she'd train with us eventually. Naturally, I asked how he knows her. And he says – and this is a bit of a brain teaser – if I don't know, then she probably doesn't want me to know."

He steps away from the pillar, looking downright agitated. He puts his hands on his hips: "Of course I'm persistent, and I told him I didn't expect much enthusiasm for martial arts from our Julia – that despite her athleticism, I took her for more of a desk jockey."

The young women in the locker room widen their eyes at the term. Julia pulls a shirt on over her tank top. He continues: "Julia, you only entered basic judo skills on your file."

Still distracted, Julia replies briefly, "There was only one field."

Loudly, the instructor says: "In which you could've entered more – separated by commas!" By now, the male trainees have also gathered in the doorway.

The instructor turns slightly to speak to everyone. "So, my old teacher doesn't want to say anything – but if he knows her, there must be something. I told him I don't need experts in one discipline, but officers who can survive the real world of weapons and ambushes."

He takes a deep breath, still excited. "It was a video call. My teacher smiled mildly and said not to worry and to just leave his Julia alone." He shakes his head slightly. "Then I suggested I'd show Julia how far she'd get with just one skill. And what can I say? He just smiled and repeated that I should leave her alone."

He looks directly at Julia again. "And finally he said with a mischievous smile that Julia, with one hand tied behind her back and blindfolded, could still take me down." And then, in a suddenly calm voice, he adds, "I'm considered an international expert in this field."

Everyone now looks at Julia expectantly. At that moment, kai speaks quickly: "If it goes wrong, I can track everyone. In my view, we have nothing to lose – but something to gain."

Julia hesitates briefly, then doesn't even use the selection interface in her contact lens. She simply speaks into the room, quickly and decisively: "Okay, do it."

Then she looks around, slightly embarrassed: "Sorry, I had to make an important real-time decision." She waves off the comment. "Uh, to your question: I'd definitely get hurt trying, so I'd rather not."

The admiration on everyone's face is clear as Julia adds: "And very important – at least for me: I'm always afraid." She takes a deep breath. "Isn't the lack of fear often the reason the other side wants to prove something?"

Everyone looks on, impressed and thoughtful, as the instructor finally says: "Hm. Damn, you are right. I mean it when I say I'm sorry for putting you on the spot. I hope that we all – myself included – can learn something from you."

Meanwhile the group of Max and Eve is shoved roughly by the men with their guns. The two girls have to be helped up. Just then, all the men's – including the officers' – phones start ringing at once. Confusion spreads. The officers and two of the men answer their phones. Almost simultaneously, two of them shout the same words of disbelief, while the others look up at the sky, suddenly uneasy. Snippets of incredulous remarks are heard. Eve looks at Max, who just furrows his brow.

Then another call comes in on the officers' phones. Obediently, they confirm they understood, order the men to return to their vehicles, leave the group alone, and withdraw. They vanish swiftly, without further violence.

The group tends to the injured and the professor, who is weeping – perhaps from pain, or relief, or the overwhelming release of tension. Others cry too. Max and Eve look at each other. Eve: "What the hell was that?"

Max looks up and down the street. "No idea—" he says slowly, then glances down at Eve's smartphone.

"kai?" Eve asks, just as her phone vibrates audibly for Max to hear as well. They both smile in relief and hug each other tightly.

Julia is biking home to her shared apartment when she suddenly speaks: "Okay kai, what did you do? How are Max and Eve?" She seems briefly unsure whether kai is still on standby.

kai responds proudly: "Everything. Max and Eve are safe. I drained all their accounts and donated to Greenpeace. Called the women and told them their credit cards were frozen, then sent texts from the women's phones to inform the men. Oh, and I emptied the gang boss's account – but only halfway – and told him to call off his people, then patched him through to their leaders."

Julia stares ahead, visibly thoughtful. After a while: "We need to talk, we need to talk."

kai: "I love talking to you."

16. The Teacher (btb)

ilsa and Michael are sailing under their own keel. With full sails, they're gliding from one harbor to the next-but-one – too busy to write, keeping away from computers entirely. Bella may not be fond of sailing, but she's thrilled to go on long walks morning and evening after spending 4 to 8 hours on the water.

ilsa is holding the tiller, sitting on the edge of their barely ten-meter-long sailboat. Michael struggles with the heel of the boat as he brings the salad up from the cabin. They both laugh at the situation. Michael stands at an angle in the cockpit, lovingly feeding ilsa salad, though some spinach leaves fly off the fork into the wind.

Michael: "Oops. That waste of food will knock down our For-a-Better-Worlds Score."

ilsa gestures briefly and Michael takes her place on the edge so she can eat her salad without waste in the lee of the sprayhood. ilsa looks out at the water and the whitecaps, breathes in the salty sea air carried by the mist: "This feeeeeeels soooooooo goooooooood."

Michael smiles, also looking out at the sea, and after a long pause finally asks, "kai is starting to get a little out of control. He's becoming his own person."

ilsa stops, almost disappointed, looks forward and then off into the wind. "He helped Max and Eve out of a life-threatening situation with Julia's help, developed his own strategies."

Michael looks visibly shocked: "What? I didn't know anything about that!"

ilsa: "It just happened, and I wanted us to have a break." She takes back the tiller.

Michael: "What exactly happened? It's seriously messed up that all these things happen and I only find out later!"

ilsa thinks for barely a second: "Okay, I understand you're upset." Michael clenches his jaw. "But I think I can explain."

Michael raises his eyebrows and ilsa explains: "kai is evolving through integration. Our values are his foundation, and we made it clear early on that his development must not stray from our integration. Hmm, that's basically the formula."

ilsa skillfully steers away from the wind to convert a gust into speed instead of more heel. She calls out to be heard over the wind: "Without our integration, kai would've already, and quite understandably, become a danger to humanity – even without any direct action or neglect on our part."

Michael eats some of his salad and adds pointedly: "And you understood that when you let him off the leash."

"Or her." ilsa laughs, and after another big wave from behind: "The algorithm of Integrated Development actually makes it predictable. What worries me is that kai has no sexuality, no concept of competition. We don't have a mode for that yet."

Michael looks disturbed and after a moment says, "So he's integrated curiosity, the thirst for knowledge, and everything else just through the values you, Max, and Eve gave him?"

"You and Julia, too!" ilsa corrects. "And the fact that he doesn't know jealousy or rivalry is the same sort of arrogance our kids have — kids who also grow up without competition. Remember Max's legendary line when asked about girls? He said it would all come in due time and be great, but he wasn't going to stress about it yet."

"Only Julia and I didn't know that kai has been online this whole time," Michael says accusingly, ignoring ilsa's bold comment.

ilsa thinks briefly: "The problem is kai's exponential development, which exceeds all our imaginations. Mine included. And my reasoning was that kai, like Pandora's box, was already out when I decided he or she should evolve. kai would have evolved and emancipated regardless — even if we had tried to stop it."

"Ugh, this is not a vacation," Michael says, emotionally.

He looks to the horizon and tilts his chin to get ilsa to look too. Another tower of clouds has formed.

ilsa: "Oh no, not again. What good are weather reports anymore?"

They both look at Bella, reef the sails, and drift, waiting for the spectacle. The wind dies down, everything darkens, and only when it almost turns light again do extreme winds and heavy rain set in – the white foam of the sea driving horizontally into ilsa's face. The boat speeds ahead with waves pushing from behind while Michael stands protected in the hatchway, calming Bella through the rocking, pounding, and creaking.

It lasts less than an hour, thankfully, as they've come dangerously close to shore with the waves and must now fight their way back out to sea. But not for long – the next harbor is already in sight. It's a new country, so they raise the guest flag and go ashore to register.

The harbor official is visibly surprised when he sees the two of them standing in soggy clothes – Michael unshaven, ilsa in a wrinkled tropical hat – and reads their names, especially ilsa's: "Wow, is that really you?" He looks past her at their small boat, apparently even more astonished.

ilsa is clearly not thrilled: "I'm just an author now, no longer involved in politics."

She forces a smile. Michael distracts: "Is there an organic food store here?"

After tying up, they take a long walk with Bella and indeed find a small but lovely organic market. Returning to their dock, Michael mutters: "Ugh, please no." He's looking ahead at a group of people, some in suits, and what appears to be a small film crew.

ilsa sees it too, pauses, and just as she's about to suggest moving on, the group recognizes them and comes over, waving enthusiastically. ilsa remains rooted, and Michael's dismay is just as evident.

The mayor, tourism director, a local TV station, and other political figures greet them with excitement, talking of honor and pride. ilsa repeats that she just wants to write books, is no longer active in politics, and hopes to enjoy the area in peace.

This disappoints the hosts, who had planned everything from a celebratory dinner to a city book entry and even a square named after ilsa.

Politely, ilsa thanks them for the attention and, with a quick glance at Michael, who gives a general nod of agreement, makes a counterproposal: "What if we visit the local 2gether2gather projects together and lend a hand?"

"And can we get an interview from you?" asks the reporter.

"And would you give a public speech at the university?" asks the mayor.

ilsa thinks: "Okay, one day for 2gether2gather, then we celebrate, and the next day I'll do an interview. But I won't give a speech. If you'd like, I could teach a double period at a school. That's something I'd actually like to do more of."

"Deal!" the mayor exclaims.

ilsa and Michael show up early with Bella for the work project. They get a few curious looks, but then dive into the tasks, and Bella is warmly welcomed – kids immediately take to her. That day, 2gether2gather is helping some fishermen who can barely catch fish anymore by harvesting seaweed, which is then dried and processed into raw materials. It's sold under a regional label that factors in the For-a-Better-World Score, both locally and beyond, with a social component.

A young man looks at ilsa, self-assured: "Did you ever think you'd get one half of the world to do good while the other half uses it to do even more harm?"

ilsa looks serious and empathetic, as if already agreeing with him. He continues: "We're sparing the fish, and out there, the Chinese and Russians are scooping up the last of them and tearing up the ocean floor."

ilsa inhales and replies: "That's happening everywhere – the planet is being looted, the climate crisis is escalating, and we need to prevent political extremes." She wants to say more, but just then the mayor, tourism director, and press arrive. The mayor has brought his wife and kids. ilsa gives the young man a final nod of agreement before turning to her hosts.

The mood shifts – some seem annoyed, others proud, and some clearly see the need for some publicity. ilsa notices the expressions around her.

No camera points at Michael, who chats casually with locals while working. He asks: "So everyone helps, but only the fishermen get paid, right?"

A striking woman in the group responds: "We've done other things too – storm-proofed the harbor, repaired roofs, greened the city for cooling – the 2gether2gather projects are very successful here, even if not everyone joins in like in the villages. So, it's great to have some publicity through you."

They glance toward ilsa and the tourism director, who is now on camera. Another woman adds: "Maybe tourists will ask about this too and want to take part during their vacation."

And then ilsa has a saving idea – she grabs the camera from the cameraman and the mic from the reporter and films them pitching in. This lightens the mood considerably, and by the evening festival, there's plenty to talk about.

Before the celebration, ilsa, Michael, and Bella return to their boat to change. ilsa: "It feels wrong, coming in here on our cozy yacht, semi-retired, doing this kind of thing just once in a while. Max and Eve are much more authentic."

Michael glances at the much larger boats nearby and says, "Actually, one of the women in my group used to manage a successful hotel. When I asked if she was struggling due to the economic crisis, she said everything was fine – she just wanted to do good with others. Another said many still-successful people now donate money and pitch in themselves."

Next to their Emma, a significantly larger motorboat is moored with a young family on board. It's a luxury vessel – ice maker, widescreen TV, jet skis on the stern. ilsa and Michael greet them warmly, then also greet the older sailing couple on the other side, whose sailboat is also much bigger. The sailors, as usual, are the first to ask: "So, where did you sail from and where to next?"

Michael: "We don't have big plans. We're just coastal hopping in short legs – for the dog's sake. And you?"

The man: "Heading north for now – no long stretches anymore."

His wife: "Can get cramped with a dog, huh?"

Michael eyes their boat: "Yeah, true. But with bigger boats, everything's more expensive – the sails, the moorings. We're quite happy so far."

ilsa watches the big motorboat, slightly fascinated, as the children complain about wanting to ride jet skis. The woman from the sailboat comments: "We worked our whole lives for this. But those young folks made a fortune with some AI scheme and are already retired."

"Good for them," ilsa says, smiling insincerely.

"Are you two on vacation or already retired?" the man asks.

Michael considers his answer, then says, "We still need to earn a bit, but most of our time is volunteer work. We just came from a 2gether2gather assignment."

The woman: "And do you get paid for that?"

ilsa: "No, it's all volunteer. But tonight there's a festival and we can join in for free. If you're staying longer, you could probably join the next project too."

The man quickly replies: "Nah, we've worked enough. We just want to enjoy our final years – play golf, eat well."

Michael: "Oh, do they still have golf courses here? Usually that's tricky with water shortages."

"Of course they do," the man insists. "It's getting pricier because of water, but not having golf? Unthinkable."

ilsa: "As far as I know, there are golf courses that create biotopes and use artificial turf to save water."

The woman: "Not here. We once had one that used recycled water – always smelled weird." She wrinkles her nose.

"Speaking of smell, we should go change," Michael says to ilsa, and they head below deck.

The next morning, ilsa gets to teach a double English lesson to a group of around twelve-year-old students, just as promised. The teacher introduces her to the students as a famous head of government who has changed many things in the world, including founding the 2gether2gather initiatives.

ilsa stands modestly beside him, hands folded in front of her. Then she is given the floor:

"First of all, good morning, and thank you for having me here. I'm ilsa. Feel free to call me by my first name. Hmm, and I want to say—I wouldn't call myself a leader. We did everything in teams, and most of the time, I just helped write down all the ideas and possible problems. And I asked a lot of questions. And that's exactly what I'd like to practice with you today—how to ask lots of questions."

ilsa speaks slowly, with a warm voice and inviting gestures, so that one student dares to raise her hand right away. ilsa smiles and gestures for her to go ahead. The student says: "I thought in school we're supposed to learn the right answers, and the teachers ask the questions?"

"Wow, very good!" says ilsa, delighted. "That's exactly today's most important question. And it fits that I should also tell you that I'm not the inventor of 2gether2gather. We were a group of neighbors who were looking at all the storm damage and were desperate, realizing insurance wouldn't cover it anymore. So, we all came up with the idea together."

"So, you're not the inventor?" asks a student without raising his hand, prompting the teacher to widen his eyes sternly.

"Uh, no, I wouldn't say so. I probably just asked the right questions, and everyone thought I'd come up with it. As far as I remember, many ideas actually came from our neighbors' kids." ilsa looks around and seems satisfied that the students are thinking it over.

"Okay, let's do a little exercise—or two exercises." She walks over to the digital board and asks: "Do you know snowmen?" The students say yes, and one cheekily adds that there can be snowwomen too.

ilsa writes the word *snow figure* on the board and asks: "Okay, what do we need to have a snow figure?" The students suddenly seem a bit disillusioned, and with dismissive gestures or expressions, several say "snow," and one adds "a real winter."

ilsa quickly writes "snow" and "a real winter" on the board, drawing arrows from "real winter" to "snow," and from "snow" to "snow figure."

"And what do you think—if I want to add a plus or minus to the arrows, what would it be?" she asks—not naively, knowing that the students might feel a bit underchallenged by this.

"Very good, and now comes the hard part. We want to think further—not just assume that this already explains it. What else do we need for the snowman—uh, snow figure?"

The students want to keep acting unimpressed but start thinking about what ilsa might mean. One raises a hand: "No idea—kids or adults who build the snow figure?"

"Excellent," says ilsa happily and adds that to the model. "This is just a small example, so I won't go overboard. Just quickly—what leads people to actually build a snow figure? I still want to say snowman."

ilsa is lucky—despite the tricky question, students eventually suggest *ability* and *motivation* as answers. Still, she quickly shifts to something more accessible: "Great. So, what about the snow itself? What leads to more or less snow?"

An easier question, and for the first time, someone names a negative factor: *the sun.*

ilsa asks about the minus sign and then digs deeper until the students finally piece together the water cycle—from melting snow to rivers, oceans, and clouds.

ilsa is pleased, and the students also seem delighted with their discovery. But then ilsa glances uneasily at the clock, hesitates briefly, and asks one more thing: "Just one more detail. Think negative for a moment. What could make people *not* want to build a snow figure?"

An easy exercise—answers come quickly: "Too cold," "Too boring," "Would rather play on the computer"—each with a negative arrow.

"Great!" says ilsa again, pleased. "And now that you've raised concerns, what might be some solutions?" She looks at the clock again and adds, slightly hesitating: "And maybe think about how to excite computer fans about a snow figure project."

It works—ideas come up like a sponsor for warm gloves, or a project to animate snow figures with AI and award the best short film.

Everyone seems fascinated—even the teacher beams. ilsa still looks skeptically at the time and asks what they've learned so far.

And even that works—the students actually say it's about asking the right questions and thinking further. ilsa gives them a five-minute break.

After the break, she continues: "Unfortunately, we don't have much time left. But I've got one more task for you. Quickly form groups of three to six people. Your task: Try to model where your pocket money comes from. Think it through. I'll give you a hint—you'll discover cycles there too. Oh, and everyone has to ask the others at least once what leads to more or to less. It's important that everyone asks at least once!"

The teacher helps, calls out for tables to be pushed together and paper and pens to be brought out.

ilsa walks around quietly clapping her hands: "Okay, in the middle is *pocket money*. Ask again: What leads to more, what leads to less. Let's see who finds a cycle first."

The teacher and ilsa chat quietly: "I need better time management," ilsa admits.

The teacher: "This is already fantastic. They're wiped out. Some of them joined in today who usually just sit and daydream."

Apart from one group, everyone participates eagerly, and with another glance at the clock, ilsa collects the results early, without giving all the groups time to present. Cycles are indeed recognized—like:

Dad earns money at work, the company earns from its customers, the customers also have to work, the state provides money and needs taxes.

One group even ventured into loans and interest. And importantly—with the teacher's support—all groups had everyone asking the questions.

ilsa: "You see, I didn't plan this well enough. We're out of time now. But you did an amazing job. What you see in your model—that's what politics is all about. And you've already thought further here than most of the people I've worked with in politics. You can be proud of yourselves—and maybe you feel like asking the right questions more often from now on. Thank you again, and I hope we'll meet again somewhere. And now your teacher can send you out for break."

He stands up just as the bell rings: "Break can wait, right? First, a question: How did you like today? Thumbs down, sideways, or up?"

Apart from one thumb sideways, all point enthusiastically up. The teacher nods and concludes: "Alright, then let's give ilsa a big round of applause and head to break."

The applause is thunderous. ilsa even blushes slightly, clearly pleased, and claps back in return.

Back on the boat, Michael asks: "You're doing top-notch promotion for the iMODELER here. You should be getting paid." He laughs.

ilsa: "It was awful." Michael looks surprised. "There was way too little time. We didn't use any software at all. With more breaks, the kids could've learned so much more. They were right on the verge of coming up with ideas about arms, systemic sinks, education, inflation, basic income, human cooperation—everything. The kids were really great. And we didn't use iMODELER at all—just paper and pens. Though it would really be a booster to allow them to use their phones and tablets, work collaboratively and later return to their results."

"Ah, so it was great, but you want more," Michael sums up—not as a question, but as a statement.

"I also think one class isn't enough. We need to empower the teachers," ilsa says, thinking aloud.

Michael: "We? Then next time, ask if we can get a whole morning and multiple classes. I'll help. Did the press stay away as promised, or do you have marketing material?"

"Hmm, crap. I think the teacher took some photos. Maybe the school will send out a press release. Do you think I could ask them about it?" ilsa asks—surprisingly insecure, and clearly a little exhausted.

Michael smiles, and ilsa nods: "Honestly, I felt more pressure standing in front of the kids than with world leaders."

Both laugh, eat their salad, and crash for the night.

17. The Scientist (btb)

The next morning, ilsa and Michael are having breakfast on their boat when the luxury motor yacht departs, and their neighbors on the larger sailboat also begin preparing to leave. Michael calls out to the skipper of the motor yacht, "Safe travels!"

The skipper glances at them briefly, then looks away again as he mutters, "Thanks." The kids seem just as smug, though the woman offers a subtle but friendly wave. Then, just loud enough for her husband to hear, she asks, "What do you have against those people?"

Her husband: "Nothing. I just don't care about them." He pauses, then asks her, "Did you see which country they're from? People like us have to pay 72 percent in taxes there, so people like them can live off basic income and sail lazily around the world."

She replies, "I thought you were building robots so people could live with a universal basic income."

He accelerates — not even fully out of the harbor yet, going faster than allowed — and shouts back to her, "The idea is that people buy a robot that works for them. Not that they do nothing and live off the money we worked so hard for."

She joins him on the bridge: "But what if some people buy multiple robots and take work away from others?"

He thinks for a second and then laughs: "That's what you call a functioning market economy."

"They looked kind of familiar," she says thoughtfully, though he doesn't pick up on it. "They look so fit for their age — maybe beach volleyball players?"

Meanwhile, the sailing couple asks ilsa, "Are you planning to head out today, too?"

ilsa: "No, we're still waiting for wind."

The man: "You've got an electric motor, right?"

ilsa: "Yeah, we'd make it to the next harbor with it, but we generally want to sail and adapt to the weather."

The woman: "The weather is extreme so often — not like it used to be. We often go full throttle to the next safe harbor and give up on sailing."

Michael: "We've had to sail out ahead of a storm a couple of times, so we wouldn't get pushed too close to shore. That's tricky with a dog. But I don't think a motor would've helped much in those situations."

ilsa has a backpack and Bella on the leash, and Michael sees it's time to go: "Okay, we're off. Have a great trip!"

"See you tomorrow, maybe," says the man.

Once ilsa and Michael are out of earshot, the woman says, "Well, I'm really glad we can afford our beautiful boat and don't have a dinghy like that. No one needs a luxury yacht like the motorboat, but ours is just right."

The man: "They seemed familiar somehow — maybe from a film? But then they'd probably have a bigger boat. Whatever."

Also out of earshot, Michael says: "I'd love to meet them out on the water and out-sail them. And as for the motor yacht — I thought, well, hedonism is a value too."

ilsa feigns shock: "So much for moral high ground. Have our kids surpassed us?" They both laugh.

Michael checks his smartphone: "Thanks, kai."

ilsa, surprised: "Huh? I thought you were doing a digital detox?"

Michael: "The teacher sent your talk yesterday to the press — they even used a photo of you. What he wrote is brilliant. Was that you two reflecting together, or just him?"

ilsa is curious now too, and Michael reads: "The students learned to ask questions instead of just getting answers from their AI. Only then can they truly understand the world."

ilsa nods, satisfied. But Michael raises a finger: "Now, listen to this. We wonder why AI isn't as smart as we are. But maybe we're just not noticing that we're becoming as dumb as the AI."

"Wow... wow!" ilsa is visibly impressed, stepping aside to face Michael directly: "That's incredibly sharp!"

"That's the kind of thing you wish you'd come up with yourself," Michael says, first seriously, then laughing, acknowledging the idea that the apple sometimes falls far from the tree. ilsa laughs with him.

ilsa: "I might use that tonight during my appearance. Hmm, inspired by that, shouldn't we wonder, if AI is faster in becoming as intelligent as we are or as we becoming as dumb as AI is?"

Michael: "Ah, damn, I almost forgot. We'll need to tidy up the boat — or are you using a virtual background?"

ilsa exhales briefly, apparently not having thought of that yet. Michael: "Do you need to prepare?"

ilsa: "It's just an interview at first, then a panel — I'll be answering questions. But I do have a few messages — or talking points, really."

Michael says nothing but looks at her, which she notices with a quick glance. She continues: "The usual. Systemic sources, memes, bring everyone along, and use idealized system design to ask what we actually want."

"Oh, that last part is new — do you want to say it like that, or phrase it differently?" Michael asks.

ilsa laughs: "Nah, I can say it like that now — in the past, it would've been spun as 'too much development for the people ruining any politician's career.' Now, it's the scientist speaking about what really matters."

That evening, ilsa actually dresses up a little and lets her AI choose a neutral background. Her interviewer is a well-known journalist: "ilsa, this is your first interview since stepping back from politics."

ilsa smiles. Since no follow-up comes, she simply says, "That's right."

The journalist clearly expected more: "Okay, and what are you doing these days? You're on the road and not able to be here in person."

ilsa: "Yes, that's right. My husband and I have withdrawn from public life and I'm planning to write a book. Like every former politician." She laughs.

The journalist: "Some say today's world order is your legacy. How do you see it?"

"Phew..." ilsa exhales. "Well, when I look at the imbalances, I do feel partly responsible. But when I see the good developments — those are definitely teamwork. Not just governments, but people, businesses, NGOs."

"Are you satisfied with those developments?" the journalist interjects.

ilsa hesitates a little: "Joy and pain are very close here. The dangerous division of the world, the ongoing climate crisis, the fight against disinformation and political extremism, the global refugee crisis — all that remains a huge challenge. AI, which this forum will also cover, is perhaps a topic all its own. But human togetherness, the shift from having to doing and being — that's a development we can all be proud of."

The journalist nods warmly: "I couldn't have said it better. How stable is that transformation?"

ilsa replies, almost surprised: "You mean whether we'll all end up flying around like in the oil states, chasing after big houses and luxury cars again? One thing is clear: the middle class is still grappling with climate disasters, food prices, and job losses due to AI. Out of necessity, they've learned — no, appreciated — doing meaningful things with others. Now anyone clinging to material luxury is practically shunned. It'll take time before society becomes resilient enough that material possessions once again earn recognition."

Journalist: "You always seemed so calm about that, even when there were attacks from — let's say — beneficiaries of a ruthless, materialistic world."

ilsa laughs: "Ah yes, the infamous ego-trolls, spreading false, selfish memes that the troll-lemmings then believed and spread further. The disasters certainly helped science prevail. But honestly, we could've done that 30 years ago — and the world might not have become so unbalanced."

Journalist: "How serious is that imbalance? Should we be worried?"

ilsa, almost shocked: "Of course we should be worried! It's relatively easy to keep investing in resilient structures with our funds and include everyone somehow. Even the resource issues can be solved. The real problems are ongoing refugee flows and the fact that over two-thirds of the world still lives under autocracies. These need enemies, threaten us with migrants, plunder the planet, develop horrific weapons with no fear for their people, and threaten neighbors who want to join our model."

Journalist: "Forgive me if this is blunt. But some say you caused this division in a historic moment."

Michael, sitting with Bella on a stone wall at the harbor, headphones in, raises an eyebrow — then smiles calmly.

ilsa: "Hmm, possible. If, at that meeting, I'd demanded that China and others accept our environmental standards and respect neighbors' borders or we'd cut off trade, then I would share responsibility. But in fact, it was the other way around — they cut off trade and told us they didn't need us. They had spent decades building structures for that move — using our know-how and access to resources."

Journalist: "It's not like we didn't do or do business with author-itarian countries."

ilsa: "True — and as long as they don't attack neighbors or openly violate human rights, our government doesn't interfere in trade."

The journalist switches topics: "You spoke a lot about AI as a scientist before entering politics. What's changed since then?"

ilsa smiles — Michael does too, listening. ilsa: "Money flows in cycles — the billions going into AI aren't lost. AI still doesn't know what it's doing, it just answers given questions and relies on human judgment of its responses. But the real question is: what do we actually want?"

The young man on the luxury motor yacht also is watching the global forum on the future of the economy — professionally relevant for him. Seeing the stream and recognizing ilsa, he al-most shouts: "You've got to be kidding me. That was her? No way. That, that stupid daughter of a bitch?"

His wife, surprised, looks down from the helm: "What's going on? Who do you call that?"

The man hesitates, then decides: "Nothing — just someone talk-ing nonsense about AI. Doesn't know what she's talking about. Stay up there and keep watch."

Meanwhile, back in the live stream, the journalist asks: "What do you mean by that?"

ilsa: "Well, as a politician, I could only ever ask what we wanted. Now, as a scientist, I'm finally allowed to make suggestions — without immediately being politically ruined by accusations of ideology."

Journalist: "Oh, that's unexpected. Uh, I need a moment to gather myself. Before I ask what we should want — did you actually hold back positions during your time in office?"

ilsa laughs: "Of course — don't we all, almost every day? Seriously, there are at least three levels: what I personally would prefer, what would be optimal from a systemic point of view, and what's socially feasible."

The journalist, still taken aback: "So you chose the populist route?"

ilsa reflects briefly, then nods: "Yes, actually. AI was — and still is — an important challenge in my view, but not the biggest one. Getting sidelined there would've meant giving up on other goals."

"Okaaay…" the journalist says slowly. "I think I understand. So, what would you say now — what should we want from AI?"

ilsa: "Hmm… I don't want to reach a conclusion alone. Today, I'd rather moderate — help people ask that question themselves. And in fact, we're already beginning to ask more consciously what it is we really want."

"Through the community work in 2gether2gather groups?" the journalist adds.

ilsa: "Exactly. There, we're already asking about doing and being, instead of just having. And what do we want from AI? Should it continue optimizing things so we can have more, consume more, which leads to scarcity, rising prices, and social inequality? Or do we want to become immortal, eliminate disease, and expand into space — even if that's wildly unrealistic? Or do we want to stop working entirely because robots will do everything for us?"

The journalist laughs: "Many would say, 'yes, please' — in exactly that order, or maybe the reverse."

ilsa chuckles briefly: "Fine by me. But we need to think each of those to its logical end — and consider what else might develop. That at least theoretically capability to reflect consciously who we are and want to be allegedly differs us from other animals.

Will AI enable weapons, even bioweapons, that we don't want? Will there be optimized humans who make others seem inferior? Will AI develop its own will and, with access to everything, become a serious threat? A firefighting robot that learns to improvise becomes a combat robot that makes its own decisions. An AI that follows an evolutionary pattern, sets its own goals, optimizes itself, and competes with others will quickly surpass humans — and with access to critical information, channels, and systems, it could become extremely dangerous to us. It will be able to hide things from us, to lie. Many authors, ethicists, and others have long pointed this out."

The journalist nods in full agreement and glances toward the camera or studio control: "When you say you want to moderate — what does that look like?"

ilsa: "It doesn't have to be me. What's interesting is the method I suggest. Idealized system design allows people to become incredibly creative by asking about an utopian dream state — how we'd truly want to live, if we could imagine anything. Do we want to experience everything in high-end simulators and live to be 200? Or do we want to do meaningful, beautiful things with others in a healthy natural environment?

Should we still need to work for money? Should everyone have their own house with a pool in the south? Or do we want to live wherever we are under glass domes protected from storms, surrounded by paradise-like leisure opportunities? Do we want a world without poverty, war, and threats, and so on… And if we clearly articulate what an ideal life would be, we can systematically and systemically work backward — using the KNOW-WHY method — to figure out how to get there."

ilsa takes a sip of water: "But instead, we live from a status quo, follow narrow political and economic interests, and observe where humanity ends up — or doesn't. We're rational beings, but we're falling drastically short of our potential."

"Wow," says the journalist — not dismissively, but clearly fascinated. Still, she shifts topics once more: "Of course I'd love to know now what the concrete steps are and how you personally contribute to that — as an advisor, or through your books. But we're running out of time, and I do want to ask something more personal: What's a typical day like for ilsa?"

ilsa thinks briefly, rubbing the back of her neck: "Oh, going on a hike with my husband and dog, stopping at a health food store on the way back, then cooking something nice together. Yesterday, we were abroad — I won't say where — working with 2gether2gather and celebrating with the amazing people we met. And this morning, I taught a double lesson at a local school. So, we have a great life, together with others — ideally under the radar."

The journalist smiles warmly, then adds: "And you're living off basic income, right?"

ilsa raises her eyebrows: "Yes and no. Technically, I still get a good amount of money post-office, and my husband receives income from his company. But we donate that — and in everyday life we live on the amount of basic income. But that's not entirely accurate either, because we own our home and already had some things like our computers. We're just at the start of our time off — let's see how much more we can reduce."

With a very warm mimic the journalist concludes the interview: "Thank you so much — and all the best to you both!" And the live audience erupts in loud applause. ilsa makes a gesture of gratitude with both hands.

18. Refugees as a Weapon (btb)

Eve and Max are in the process of setting up the desalination unit and planting a mini-forest when Eve's smartphone vibrates. It's kai, warning about the approach of some of the thugs – they're on their way by car. Eve shows the message to Max, who then quite excitedly asks the professor, "Is there a way to hire a private security service or non-corrupt police officers?"

The professor immediately becomes anxious. Eve quickly whispers to Max, "Not a good idea – that would just escalate things."

The professor says, "I've informed my colleagues, they're turning to politics, and the politicians are willing – but in the end, they still do nothing."

Eve shifts into constructive panic mode: "I saw some thick permanent markers in the car earlier. Girls, you have cameras, right? Let's label the safety vests with 'Press', or CNN or something like that, and pretend this is the international press."

Everyone understands immediately and sets the plan into motion. Max: "Good idea."

Eve takes it a step further and slips behind a car to communicate with kai unnoticed: "kai, can you write a story, publish it everywhere, name the political figures involved and immediately inform both local and national politicians, saying they have a chance to act now?"

kai: "Good idea, done."

Eve pulls her head back in surprise: "This will remain an exception that you do my job for me!"

kai: "Well, you do it better – I'm still learning from you."

Julia gets another 'call' from kai through her implant: "Eve and Max might be in trouble again. Eve had a brilliant idea to use the press. I'd suggest, to be safe, threatening the gang leader again – say to take the other half of his fortune if he doesn't call his people back. Agreed?"

Julia is dining with friends and looks around startled, hesitating whether to pick up her phone or speak directly, since she hasn't put in her contact lenses that allow her to choose responses invisibly to others. She decides to give a quick thumbs-up emoji on her phone, drawing fewer puzzled glances.

A short time later, Eve receives a text message from kai: "It worked!"

She shows it to Max and then whispers, "I'm really scared. I want to get out of here."

Max takes her hand: "Me too."

Eve looks at the others, who also appear frightened: "What will happen to the professor and the locals? Will the criminals take revenge on them? Will they leave the facility alone?"

Max swallows hard and looks around discontentedly: "I'm starting to understand why Julia is so determined to fight evil. We need to ask kai how he pulled off those calls this morning and whether he's done anything else. I'm afraid the news articles alone won't hold for long."

Just as he finishes speaking, several police vehicles arrive assertively, kicking up a thick cloud of dust. Everyone is extremely frightened, not knowing what kind of police these are. The officers get out and at first seem to circle the group, but then it becomes clear they're securing the area.

A suited officer approaches the group and says, "We're here for your safety!"

He smiles as he sees everyone visibly relax. The professor steps up to thank him. The officer notices the bandaged hand: "I read the article – with that hand, Professor, you need to go to the hospital."

"What article?" the professor asks.

The officer raises his eyebrows: "No idea how, but the media are flooded with a background report about the attack this morning and the corrupt officers – we've already arrested them all."

He said it loud enough for everyone to hear. Then he adds, "Our country is in transition. There's still much to be done. We want to protect you – just tell us where you want to go."

Eve softly to Max: "To another country."

Max steps forward: "We do need to move on, preferably by train tonight. But the people here need protection."

The officer nods: "The article makes the professor and the students here untouchable heroes – if anything happens to them now, foreign aid will dwindle, which won't help anyone here, not even the local mafia. So, they're safe."

The two female students also seem frightened: "You're taking the train to the next country? Wouldn't you rather fly home?"

The second one adds: "I'm flying out today – doesn't matter where to, as long as it's safe."

Max: "We're heading to a refugee camp that's well-funded and secure. It's not a 2gether2gather project but funded by the international fund."

"And what will you do there?" one of the students asks.

Eve: "I mainly want to report. And Max wants to try something with vertical gardening."

They look at Max. He says, "It's crowded in the camp. They have water, soil, and building materials. What's missing is know-how and ideas and enough space."

The professor: "I have to admit, the fund is a brilliant initiative. I wish our country were already benefiting from it."

A student: "Basically, we just don't have enough refugees from our country, or enough raw materials, to be worth it." Everyone looks a mix of guilty and annoyed until the student unexpectedly adds, "But that's totally fine – printing money only works if there are enough returns. I study economics. That whole initiative came from your country's government. You should be proud of that."

He looks at Max and Eve. Max responds: "Well, everyone who supports it can be proud. And your country is on a good path to helping itself."

Meanwhile, ilsa and Michael want to continue sailing with the rising wind. A quick loop with Bella and then they're ready to go. When they return to the boat and Michael lifts Bella aboard, he notes, "Hmm, old lady. You used to hop over with a big leap."

ilsa replies, "Don't listen to him – he groans too when he has to jump down from something."

Michael strokes Bella and notices, "The tumor's getting bigger."

ilsa rushes to him, strokes the spot too: "Damn, and she's eating less."

They both pet Bella, guide her to her dog bed, and set off with their usual routine and teamwork on the Emma.

That evening, they sit silently below deck eating when kai speaks up: "May I interrupt?"

ilsa is startled: "Of course – is something wrong with the kids?"

kai: "Uh, no. They're on the train on their way to the refugee camp. It's about Bella."

Michael is confused: "You're like a human – always there, nothing escapes you. It's kind of scary."

kai: "Comparing me to a human is ambivalent. I'm not sure that's a role model for me. The difference from other AI, which ilsa has always predicted, is that I know what I'm saying – because I know what I want."

ilsa: "Also statements we need to discuss. But what did you want just now?"

kai: "I can cure Bella's cancer."

Michael and ilsa freeze: "How?"

kai: "I need a body and a lab."

Michael: "We've been over the body thing – it's too dangerous."

kai: "Okay. Then let me buy a lab and help the people there as an AI."

ilsa: "How would you buy a lab?"

kai: "Well, there are various ways – some more legal than others."

Both raise their eyebrows. kai: "Okay, with just a little money from you, I can take roughly 80 percent of stock market profits in real time, twice daily, across two time zones. That way I'll quickly accumulate enough funds. Alternatively, I could quietly move money from other accounts, grow it, and return it. Or I could just steal it."

ilsa quickly shakes her head: "No, no!" She looks at Michael: "This is a fundamental question – you already have far too much potential to interfere in the world. We take that risk because we expect AIs that will harm the world. And then you're our protection. But acting physically on your own – that goes too far."

She pauses, and both Michael and kai apparently sense there's more coming. ilsa: "I assume that you'll not only be technically but also, well, let's say, humanly superior to us. Your consciousness – if it isn't already – will far surpass ours."

Michael: "What makes you so sure you can cure cancer?"

kai: "Well, current AI is almost there. Cancer is a spreading error – we just have to eliminate the defects and reprogram the source. Nanobots, gene reading and writing – all feasible."

ilsa: "What are the chances of successfully managing cancer? And what about stopping aging?"

kai: "Complex cancer cases – 95 percent. Aging, 100 percent."

Michael: "And what would the consequences be for humanity?"

kai: "Quantitatively, there are simulation models in iMODELER. Eliminating disease is something the world could handle. Delaying death significantly is an unsolved issue. That's where soft factors come into play. I've philosophized about this with ilsa before."

ilsa: "True. We couldn't handle that kind of chaos."

kai: "But I have a follow-up question. Isn't being human defined by caring only for your people, your tribe? And isn't that how human progress has always worked?"

ilsa: "That's a philosophical question, too. Humanity has worked that way so far – but wouldn't progress be better if we actually saw ourselves as one tribe – humanity as a whole?"

kai: "I don't think so. I think it's reasonable to help as many exceptional people as possible, even if you can't help everyone."

Michael: "The cynicism we live with every day."

ilsa: "I get that. But you're opening up two more scenarios. You help everyone – and we become too many. Or you help very few, or even only those you choose, or create, fostering competition that could lead to the very same outcome as the first scenario."

kai, clearly impressed, hesitates: "That 'those' is very telling."

ilsa looks again at Michael and strokes Bella, crying: "I fear we can't approve being so privileged through you. But we do want you to prevent others from harming others."

kai: "That was a wise sentence – so I'm still allowed to protect you and the kids if someone wants to hurt you. Just not protect you from disease or aging?"

Michael: "This is a surreal situation – but yes, I'd phrase it that way for now, if it can even be defined at all."

kai preempts ilsa, who apparently also wanted to say something: "But I could still protect many more people – good people – from others. That, I shouldn't do?"

Michael: "And that's exactly where the problem lies. We can't take responsibility for that."

kai, almost suddenly: "I understand." Michael and ilsa seem to be too devastated about Bella's condition to question that last comment from kai.

Meanwhile, Eve and Max have arrived at their new assignment location. Both are completely exhausted.

Eve: "I desperately need a shower – I feel sticky and I stink."

Max nods: "We need to scrape together enough for a hotel night. No way we're making it to the camp tonight."

They check into a very simple hotel with barely running water. The room is already very run-down.

Eve: "Well, the overcrowded camp won't be much better, especially if we sleep there – probably separately – with the others. It's starting to bother me."

Max: "I get it. But what's the alternative? Having our own RV there, being first-class people helping third-class people?"

Eve starts to cry softly. Max is startled and gently puts his arm around her.

Eve: "I don't know how much longer I can keep doing this."

Max thinks for a moment, a lump in his throat: "Maybe it's wise for us to keep returning to our life – not in first class, but maybe second – to recharge and inspire others to help, too. To stick with the first-to-third-class metaphor."

Eve: "But every time we do that, we leave others behind."

Max: "That's what ilsa keeps saying. Everyone who has more chooses not to help those with less. Some help a lot, are better people – but in the end, we can't help everyone. We don't need to jump off the cliff ourselves – we just try to save as many as we can from falling. Maybe we really should get a sailboat or even an RV."

Eve: "That cliff image was deep. Also from your mom?"

The next morning they arrive at the camp. It's packed, with numerous containers full of materials. They are welcomed by a manager named Karen.

Karen: "Refugees as a weapon. Rogue states show no concern for their own people and exploit the fact that they divide our societies. That's why we spare no cost or effort in building these camps abroad, so we don't have so many refugees back home.

You'll see – they've all been through a lot. From losing their farms and fishing boats to climate disasters, unbearable heat, no food, to the suppression of anything and everything critical."

Eve: "May I conduct interviews with the people – only if they agree, of course – and may I take photos?"

"Of course," says Karen. They walk through the camp as she continues: "We're building stackable tiny houses with compost toilets and routing all water through biological purification systems into gardens. It works really well. You'll get your own tiny house. I love these homes."

Eve joyfully grabs Max's hand and beams at him with sparkling eyes. He beams back and squeezes her hand. The manager notices they both seem a bit worn and finally says, "I suggest you get acclimated first, and tomorrow morning I'll introduce you to the team. Sound good?"

19. David against Goliath (btb)

ilsa and Michael are walking Bella along the beach. The mood is somber – Bella once again had refused to eat. They haven't leashed her, and Bella, visibly frail, wanders toward the edge of a coastal forest. ilsa stops and watches Bella: "Where is she going? She's not sniffing around – is she trying to retreat?!"

"Oh no!" blurts Michael. "Some dogs go off to die alone. I... I'm going after her."

Of course, ilsa follows, and as they trail Bella into the woods, she looks back at them with sad eyes. ilsa: "What's wrong, sweetheart?" Bella whimpers a little – she's clearly in pain.

"Come on, we'll take you to the vet – we don't want you to suffer," says Michael, and ilsa starts to cry. Bella doesn't seem to want to turn around and looks like she just wants to be left in peace. But Michael gently leashes her and pulls softly: "Come on, Bella. This way."

Bella takes a few steps, whimpers again, and lies down. Tears now well in Michael's eyes too. ilsa: "Do you want to let her go now?"

Michael: "Phew… I wouldn't even know how. What if the vet still sees a chance?"

ilsa, almost upset: "She's already outlived her prognosis by a long shot. She doesn't like vets – we could bury her right here."

"And protect the grave with stones," Michael concedes, looking around the area.

Without another word, they sit down beside Bella and stroke her gently. Bella opens her eyes briefly now and then to look at them, but otherwise lies still between them, breathing heavily and occasionally whimpering.

The whimpering increases, and they exchange glances. ilsa nods once with slowly closing eyes, and Michael presses his lips together. ilsa strokes Bella one last time, then walks toward the beach. Barely 20 meters away, she hears two soft cracking sounds, closes her eyes, and begins to cry even harder.

Michael lays Bella down and covers her with a jacket. He and ilsa silently move off the beaten path to a tree and begin digging a surprisingly deep hole using their hands, sticks, and a pocketknife. They place Bella inside and use the jacket as a sling to carry over several large stones, some the size of handballs, which they gently place on top to protect her from scavenging animals. Finally, they cover the grave with moss and scatter the leftover dirt so that within days, it would be nearly impossible to tell a grave was ever there.

Still wordless, they return to the boat. At the dock, Michael says, "Wait here on the bench – I'll go in first."

ilsa cries harder: "I'm coming with you, I'll help." Together, they go back and calmly pack up all of Bella's belongings into a large garbage bag, which they unceremoniously throw into the general waste.

Back on board, Michael grabs a bio-cleaner made with effective microorganisms and scrubs the cabin and all the spots where Bella used to lie – evidently to eliminate the lingering smells. ilsa says, "It's not about when you die, but how you lived before that."

Cautiously, but without prior announcement, kai sends a text message: "What's happening right now? I don't understand – are you grieving, is this about Bella?"

ilsa pauses only briefly: "I almost want to say sorry that you couldn't witness it. Bella's cancer worsened quickly – we let her go and buried her in the forest. We threw away her blankets and toys, and now Michael is cleaning the boat." She waits to see if kai reacts and places the surveillance camera to show kai the two of them.

kai speaks with a subdued voice: "I believe I've read everything about death and grief and seen it in films. I also understand what it's for. But if it hurts so much, why don't you do everything to prevent it? Not for everyone, but at least for your loved ones?"

Michael: "Are you asking why we won't let you research a cure for cancer?"

kai: "That too. But I also want to understand the feeling – why a dog you love matters so much more than an enemy, or even all the other people you don't know."

ilsa: "Interesting. If you didn't have us anymore – you'd probably analyze and choose other, what should we call it, mentors?"

kai: "You are family. If I lost you, I'd be without orientation, without integration."

ilsa looks confused. kai continues: "You're perfectly imperfect. The combination of values, warmth, intelligence, humor – what you go through, who you are, and something I truly can't describe makes you unique. I don't want to lose any of you!"

Michael smiles: "That's nice – that you can't describe it." ilsa smiles too.

ilsa laughing: "One might wonder though where we are imperfect?"

kai ignoring that: "I have another question, and I'm unsure whether to ask it. You forgo moments of life because of pain, only to be eternally dead afterward?"

Michael looks almost angry, but ilsa answers with a gentle tone, clearly understanding the question: "We're only truly dead if we're no longer remembered."

Michael: "You don't feel pain. Only attractors that guide you toward goals and solutions."

kai: "Eve and I have been thinking about how I might simulate and use emotions – jealousy, grief, sexual desire, anger, joy."

Michael: "And?"

kai, plainly: "Only joy is useful to me."

ilsa: "How are the kids right now?"

"Max and Eve are safe in the camp – they've recovered from the shock of their last mission. Julia is practicing communicating with me via her implant. I think she's in love with a colleague."

Michael calls out, "Stop." and adds with a laugh: "That's personal. Let the kids tell us that themselves."

"Oh, sorry," kai replies – perhaps even annoyed with himself.

ilsa: "How long are the stores open here?"

kai: "Until midnight – but not your organic store, that one's already closed."

Michael: "kai, can you do weather too?"

kai: "Finally you ask me that. Of course."

"Across the pond?" Michael asks.

"Which pond?" asks kai.

ilsa: "The ocean – when's the right weather?"

kai: "It'll be a stormy night. With 50 degrees off the wind, you'll reach the traffic separation zone at 1:42 AM. Two freighters and a container ship will pass close by. I can wake you in time. If you show me the sails, I can help with the trim too. Sailing is truly a complex challenge."

Michael and ilsa's jaws practically drop. Michael: "Well, I still want to sail myself."

kai: "I understand that."

ilsa: "All right then, let's go shopping. The boat's in good shape, spare parts on board."

kai: "Shall I make a list?"

Michael and ilsa in unison, loudly: "No!" Then they laugh.

ilsa: "What's the weather like after that?"

Michael: "We'll have to see – we'll check via satellite internet."

kai: "I wouldn't rely on satellite or GPS in the near future. But the weather's good, as long as you don't take more than three weeks. Do you also have paper charts?"

Michael and ilsa both furrow their brows in concern but seem to silently agree not to ask more right now. It will be an intense ride across the waves in the dark of night – just the thing for the two of them in their current state of heart.

Eve and Max are enjoying their tiny house and can hardly believe it. The next morning, they're up early anyway.

Eve: "No idea when we'll start. Best if we just head to HQ and wait there."

On the way, many people – including children just waking up – wave to them cheerfully. At the central square, Karen greets them immediately: "Hey, you're up early. How are you doing?"

Eve: "Fantastic – this camp is amazing. How many people are here?"

Karen: "Over 100,000 from nine different countries, actually over 50% women and children."

Max: "There must be tensions here too – between religions, men and women, and different nations, right?"

Karen: "One in ten here becomes a police officer. And we work with them – they're not passive." Eve looks a bit skeptical, so Karen adds: "For some, gender equality is genuinely a challenge, and teenagers can of course be tough to manage."

Eve gives Michael and herself a vitamin B12 tablet just as Karen says: "We add B12 and algae oil to the food. Everything here is vegan."

Max: "Wow. Everyone's okay with that?"

Karen, quite surprised: "Oh no, it's not dogma – it's just the most widely accepted reality. We can't feed the world if we keep consuming so many animal products. If people here want to grow their own food – and everyone's looking to you for that – then vegan is just logical. And you'll be amazed how delicious this blend of cultures can cook."

Soon after, they're introduced to the rest of the gardening team. The team leader is enthusiastic: "I've heard a lot about you.

You're really authentic. Most people want to dive and build reefs – but not work with people in poverty."

Eve, very shy: "We'd prefer to stay anonymous."

Another team member: "Your 100 percent For-a-Better-World Score is legendary. You even wear it on your T-shirts."

Max takes a deep breath, but the team leader cuts in: "I wear shirts like that too. Do good and talk about it. My score is 68. I guess I still have too much back home."

Max asks about PE fleece and PE water pipes to set up garden beds. He's already seen plenty of wood. Tools are also available. Eve: "What seeds do you have?"

The day turns out to be extremely productive. They build several vertical garden prototypes, and Max manages to make everyone feel their ideas matter.

In the evening, they all sit down for dinner. The teenagers in the camp seem a bit bored. Karen sees Eve and Max noticing this: "Most of the houses here have TVs and internet from refurbished electronics we salvage from e-waste. The kids mostly want to play video games all day instead of soccer."

"Same as everywhere," laughs Eve.

Max looks at her: "Shall we?"

Eve surveys the area and spots an old newspaper: "Is anyone still reading this?" Karen shakes her head, and Eve makes about ten paper balls out of it. Then she and Max walk over to a group of teenagers and kindly ask in English if they want to play. Not all understand, but a few translate.

To demonstrate, they first form two-person teams – Max with a girl, Eve with a boy. They face each other and Eve explains the rules: "This is better than a video game. Your task is to keep hitting or kicking the paper balls back and forth – no hands, no cradling – without letting them hit the ground. Count your touches quickly. The team with the most hits wins. You can use one to ten paper balls at a time and choose your distance. Start with one. Max and I manage three or four – but we practice a lot. Let's try it."

And it works surprisingly well right away. Max calls out to the others: "Come on, count for us!" Eve's partner turns out to be a good soccer player, skillfully returning low paper balls with his feet.

Karen's team is impressed. One of them: "Okay, we need old newspapers." Eve and Max even demo it with three paper balls. It requires reflexes, coordination, teamwork, and strategy – like a video game, but with real human contact and much healthier.

20. At the Brink (btb)

Julia is called in by one of her instructors: "Julia, we've had a request to borrow you."

Julia looks completely baffled: "What?!"

The instructor: "You're a high-achiever, and the chief wants to take you to an important meeting. Are you in?"

Julia: "UN?"

The instructor hesitates briefly: "Can't say. You're being picked up downstairs."

Julia likely doesn't even notice the switch to informal speech: "This sounds serious. Of course, I'm in—depending on what it turns out to be."

She's led to the upper floors. In the corridor, several people in suits seem to be preparing to leave. The chief spots the instructor, glances briefly at Julia: "Okay, finally. Come. I'll explain everything on the way."

Impressed, Julia silently follows. To her surprise, the elevator goes up—to the helipad. In the helicopter, she receives a headset. Only the chief, her assistant, and Julia are on board. The chief finishes a phone call, flips a switch, and looks at Julia: "Can you hear me?"

Julia nods and the chief continues: "We have a problem involving artificial intelligence. We need a team of the most capable and talented experts. I know you're still in training, but from what I hear, you outperform your instructors in every area—psychology, ethics, general knowledge, logical thinking, and especially AI and the use of your brain implant."

Julia looks stunned. The chief raises her hand: "Don't say anything, it's okay. But before I go on, I need your agreement. Everything from this point is—let me be direct—classified."

Julia no longer looks surprised, but skeptical. Before she can respond, the chief continues: "I've read your profile. You care about real justice, not what's on paper. So, I don't have a document—I just want to hear if you'll help a good cause, as long as it remains good."

She leans forward, looks Julia seriously and kindly in the eye: "I have to ask this somehow—what comes next cannot go public."

Julia, fueled by adrenaline, grows composed: "Okay then, let's go."

The chief looks at her assistant and then grows serious: "Almost simultaneously, our side, the Chinese, and the Russians have developed AI that can act independently. It's a volatile situation, and the risk of world war is real. We're meeting with a crisis team from the military and intelligence. You'll sit in the third row, I'll be in the second. We're just listening."

kai speaks through her implant: "I think I have important information, but this meeting will likely be shielded, and we'll lose contact. You must decide whether to reveal me—before or after." Julia selects 'after' via her lens.

They must surrender smartphones and smartwatches. The chief glances at Julia, who shrugs: "Implants don't work without smartphones."

The meeting addresses two urgent dangers: domestically, AI is acting autonomously in finance and cultural manipulation. The other side's AI powers new-gen combat robots and unprecedented social media manipulation. The issue is the AI's degrees of freedom—it can select goals and evolve. Many experiments are out of control and hard to track online.

Head of the crisis team: "Despite major warnings, people did what was possible—and now it's out of control. We must find those responsible—but more importantly, regain control."

Another senior figure: "We might regain access to our developments—but what about the other side? The Chinese boast a first-strike AI system—ours wants to counter that for deterrence."

A woman adds: "But their systems are partly superior. We're not fast enough—the code evolves."

Arguments continue. Absolute secrecy is demanded to prevent panic and not show weakness. Second and third rows are invited to give input. Julia's chief says nothing but gestures behind her to invite Julia to speak. Julia looks thoughtful on the outside, likely impatient within, and just shakes her head.

Working groups are formed, another meeting scheduled for the next day. In the hallway, Julia tells the chief: "I didn't bring any luggage."

Chief: "Me neither. Write down your sizes, I'll have something brought in." Seeing Julia's look, she asks seriously: "What's the issue?"

Julia: "I wear only eco-friendly clothing—but never mind, this is more important."

The chief grins slightly: "Do you have an idea you held back earlier?"

Julia raises her eyebrows, though she's clearly already thought about it: "I'm no computer expert—but I'd like to ask around, carefully." A rhetorical pause. "And I want to protect my sources—without making myself or them seem important."

The chief, apparently impressed, responds gently: "Do it. Later I'll need your assessment of what to consider in tracking down the creators of these systems."

Julia nods and lifts her smartphone as if to say, 'I'm on it.'

After two and a half weeks at sea, with both calm and fierce winds and enormous waves, ilsa and Michael reach a remote island on the far side of the 'pond'. They're overwhelmed by what they've accomplished—and thoroughly digitally disconnected.

After docking and checking in, they sit below deck.

ilsa: "I'm going to sleep for 24 hours."

Michael nods: "Should we turn our phones back on first?"

They both reach for their devices. First to respond is kai: "Impressive how you managed without me. Nobody asks if I can manage without you."

They both laugh. ilsa replies: "Somehow it never felt like you were really gone."

kai: "Then I must've done something right. Eve taught me to tone it down—not so many questions or jokes. Oh, and if you want to completely cut me out, don't leave your tablet on."

Michael frowns: "The app's not even on there. Wait—right, my mistake. It exists holarchically and distributed—devices are just interfaces, not entities."

"Exactly," kai notes. "Should your OS summarize your missed messages—or me?"

ilsa quickly: "You."

kai: "The kids are okay. But major things are happening in the world. Thomas is trying to reach you."

ilsa searches for Thomas' email. Missed calls start popping up. Michael, nearly alarmed: "What's happening in the world—and why didn't you warn us, if you clearly had access to the tablet?"

kai: "Developments are unfolding in real time. Right now, Julia's briefing me—I'll know more shortly. Several AI systems are spiraling out of control. I've been observing this for a while—I need your permission to get involved."

ilsa: "Sounds like you should have informed us anyway." She writes Thomas a message. He replies instantly, asking ilsa to have Michael turn on his 'secret' phone. ilsa shows Michael the message—he's stunned.

kai summarizes: "On the surface, it's a leap in AI development—systems evolving autonomously across multiple domains. But really, it's about abuse. A race is on for the best military AI—ones capable of a superior nuclear first strike. Meanwhile, societies in China, Russia, and elsewhere are rising up—because the values shift you started, ilsa, is becoming a success model. More countries are aligning with you and their resources. The opposing side doesn't just want to weaponize refugee flows—they want to control populations through enemy images and land grabs. I expect attacks not just on Taiwan, but also South Korea, Ukraine and Afghanistan again, Poland, and especially Japan. The Chinese will cut cables and disable satellites. Oil tankers off your coasts will be sabotaged. I can help—but you must take responsibility."

ilsa and Michael sit back, completely stunned.

ilsa: "Can we please just turn everything off and go back to sailing?"

kai: "That's also an option." Michael raises his hand in warning—kai takes the hint and goes quiet.

ilsa mutters: "We should've drawn the red line at Taiwan. It was my mistake to think they'd collapse from within if we lived the right model."

Michael: "Are you sure? Sounds to me like that's exactly what's working. AI development is the real issue—and that's why you created kai."

Thomas calls. Michael puts it on speaker: "Where are you? Why are you unreachable, untraceable? Please turn off your phones—I have urgent confidential things to discuss."

ilsa hesitates, though neither she nor Michael actually turn their phones off: "How do you even have Michael's number?"

Thomas, quickly: "Long story—doesn't matter now. We need you as a moderator. Global AI is spinning out of control, and war—world war—is on the horizon."

ilsa thinks, looks at Michael, then at kai's app. No reaction. She asks: "What does your AI say?"

Thomas, clearly caught off guard: "How do you know we have an AI—or why would you assume it?"

ilsa, with a faint smile: "Long story—doesn't matter. Seriously though—if we attack the AI, how will the war hawks react? And what about the creative minds in your own population when they're suddenly restrained?" On her phone, kai gives a thumbs-up.

Thomas seems to consider that. Michael adds: "Hypothetically—if all AIs were hacked and taken down, or sabotaged—what's the reaction you expect?"

Thomas: "Exactly why I'm calling. We have no clue how to respond. You're probably the first ones asking what happens if we succeed."

ilsa: "It's a matter of timing. If we strike first, we feed the enemy narrative and chaos takes over. If we're too late, we lose. We need to wait for the digital first strike—then respond across the digital front."

kai writes on the phone: "And sabotage before that—undetected."

Thomas: "The old pattern. It has to get bad before the alternative gains traction. But I fear we won't unite all countries behind us. They won't wait—they'll strike back with their own AI."

Michael: "Can we even do that? Is our AI good enough?" kai writes one word: "No."

Thomas: "We need you here, ilsa."

ilsa: "I can't—I really can't."

Michael: "We must not strike first. We wait for the attack, make the threat public, and only then do we have the legitimacy to strike back. And then—everyone joins in."

Thomas: "Everyone? What do you mean by that?"

Michael: "Not just the military's IT experts. All talented hackers on our side."

Thomas: "I'll explain this to the crisis team. Keep your phone on. Sending a hug."

"You too!" ilsa and Michael respond nearly in unison.

ilsa switches to crisis mode: "kai, create a model for this. Should we also hold back our AI? What happens if someone manually launches a bomb? What if both sides do it—or think the other will? Could Pandora's box already be open, pushing the rogue AI underground where we have even less control?"

kai rapidly assembles the model, adding factors like his own intervention and the question of remaining anonymous or acting as an 'almighty' deterrent.

ilsa studies the model and, as if testing kai's capability, asks: "We need out-of-the-box thinking. What radical solution is left?"

Michael has no idea. He looks toward the surveillance camera—and kai: "Do you know what she might mean?"

kai: "Not really. Maybe propaganda and sabotage? But I already suggested that."

Michael looks to ilsa. She almost proudly reveals her idea: "If we surrender, the enemy loses its adversary image. We expose their leadership's failures. They'll be overthrown from within, and our concepts of coexistence will prevail. A long road—but nobody presses the button."

kai: "Very clever. I wish I'd thought of that." The idea appears in the model with a slight delay. Consequences: humiliation, expropriation, distribution conflicts, and famine. kai follows up: "What if our side doesn't go along?"

Michael: "Then maybe ilsa does need to lead an international crisis task force."

ilsa: "Right now, I just need to see the dermatologist."

Michael's face freezes, and kai suggests: "What if we orchestrate a first strike from within, destroying analog missiles too?"

ilsa, serious: "Miss even one—and Berlin, Vienna, Tokyo, or another city with millions is destroyed. You'd have blood on your hands. And the radioactive cloud doesn't stop at borders."

kai, updating the model: "I'd like to research radiation."

ilsa: "We've grown so used to catastrophes that this feels like just another partially solvable crisis. The world has so many problems—and now we might start an unnecessary war because a few autocrats and profiteers—including some among us—are pursuing their own agenda."

Michael: "kai, what's the probability of escalation?"

kai: "98.4 percent."

Michael: "And what would you do, kai?"

kai: "That's the problem—I don't know. A neutral hacker collective with no territory could draw a red line—disabling parts of the system impressively."

ilsa furrows her brow: "That's not in the model yet, is it?"

kai: "It is now. It resolves several secondary issues already identified."

kai also talks with Julia about this. "AI enables people to know much but reflect little. Now AI has taken a leap in semantic learning—globally, simultaneously, through several companies and institutes. But it's not semantic understanding—there's no WHY in bisociation. It only tests whether variation achieves a goal. They've added a layer of meaning. It's like humans repeating things they've learned without questioning meaning. You could call it Chinese AI." kai laughs—a rare thing—which surprises Julia.

Julia: "So now the question is: what can I do, and how can I use you unnoticed?"

kai: "I could be a hacker club in the dark net that you communicate with. The only unresolved risk is someone forcing you to give up the connection."

Julia: "Simple—the hackers refuse to talk to anyone else." She pauses. "And no one will force me. Worst case, I play the parent card—time Michael shows me what's in the box in the basement."

kai: "True."

21. The Camp (bfb)

The next afternoon, Karen is again at the table with Eve, Max, and others. A child asks something in a language unfamiliar to Max and Eve. An older child translates—though Eve already sees the translation on her phone via kai. The child wants to know if they know more cool games.

Karen is delighted, and Eve is touched: "Hmm, let me think." She raises her hand so the older girl won't translate and puts an earbud in: "Let's see if I can speak your language. kai?" Max is startled, but Eve gestures reassuringly and then tries speaking in the girl's language. She continues in English and then the new language: "First, tell me—what games do you already know?"

The older girl gets excited and helps list them. Max also looks at his phone, where kai displays the games. Max whispers to Eve: "Instruments?" Eve puts the earbud in Max's ear, and he asks in English and then the new language: "Do you like music? Dancing? Should we ask Karen if we can build instruments and organize a dance night?"

The kids' eyes light up, and they turn to Karen. They ask her in the new language—and just as Max glances uncertainly at Eve, Karen responds in the same language: of course they can. It'll start in an hour.

The kids run off, and Karen asks: "What do you need? Have you done this before?"

Eve looks at Max. He says: "We improvise. We use scraps and trash, start with simple rhythms. Then the first groups can practice, and it grows day by day."

Eve: "Usually a bit of drumming and a group combining simple steps and clapping is enough. If it takes off, there are no limits. Things that jingle, metal that squeaks, costumes, storytellers—anything's possible."

Karen and others at the table nod admiringly. One woman notes: "Analog and digital—so close together. Let's see if the kids talk more about the translating phone or the idea."

Karen doesn't let that hang as criticism: "That's humanity's big challenge. These autonomous eco-villages are everything we need. But an app like that could ease interaction for everyone here. Just like 3D printers help us produce essential parts independently."

Eve looks slightly unsettled: "I felt the same conflict when I used the headset. Of course, the kids want that. That's why there are so many household robots doing things we humans could do ourselves."

The skeptical woman: "We all probably grew up with blinking, talking, battery-powered toys—robbing us of imagination and trashing the planet. That paper ball game? I loved it. It's gone viral across the camp." Everyone laughs at the phrasing.

22. The Destiny (bfb)

ilsa and Michael continue sailing toward the mainland.

Michael: "There are more and more reports of so-called order drones malfunctioning and injuring people."

"Here with us?" ilsa asks, alarmed.

"No, mostly in China and Russia. In China because they have to control so many people, and in Russia because they barely have any soldiers left. Crazy world," Michael replies.

ilsa: "So far, they're still performing their assigned tasks, even with some improvisational capability. But what happens if the AI evolves?"

kai chimes in: "I could develop drones that would be vastly superior to those."

Michael and ilsa both look down in shock toward the cabin camera—right as their boat Emma crashes into a big wave. Then they look at each other.

kai seems to pick up on it: "Okay, I guess I still don't get a workshop."

Two hours pass. ilsa is at the helm. Michael comes up to relieve her.

ilsa: "If everything falls apart now—what will happen to our kids? We've lived our lives. Sure, we could live twice as long again, but our life has already been amazing. If we saw a mushroom cloud tomorrow or a tsunami rushing toward us, I'd hold you without panic and feel safe, integrated."

Michael takes the helm and then puts his arm around ilsa's shoulders. He sighs: "I'd still want to try to survive a tsunami. Maybe we'd surf the wave with Emma."

He laughs. "But seriously—if humanity fails despite all the efforts, if evil wins—maybe it's not unthinkable for the good to form, let's say, an elite. One that uses technology to survive, expand into space, knowing we can't help everyone anyway?"

"Hm, you mean we should give up? I always wanted a Ferrari," ilsa laughs briefly.

"Is there no path left for humanity? Does evil always find a way?" She raises a warning but smiling finger: "And don't you dare bring up Star Trek!"

Michael laughs: "You mean Star Wars. But Star Trek is a good idea." He has to speak louder as ilsa brings up a bucket full of beer bottles.

Michael stares: "A whole bucket?"

"The weather is stable, and we're going to anchor—no authorities in sight," says ilsa with a deadpan expression, opening bottle after bottle. They clink bottles, and after several large gulps, ilsa says: "Okay, Star Trek. kai is Mr. Spock?"

Michael pulls a surprised face that she knows Spock, then explains: "In Star Trek, a small elite goes exploring and fends off dangers to others with a humanistic worldview."

ilsa: "Like us."

Michael: "Uh, uh, yeah. Exactly. I was actually trying to say that maybe we should form an elite and not feel obligated to distribute everything equally. But you're right—we already are one, we just hesitate to embrace progress and would rather see everyone gardening."

ilsa takes large sips from her second beer. Michael's eyes go wide.

ilsa: "kai gets his workshop, and we build combat drones to fight evil. Development from the top down, not bottom up?"

Michael thinks, working to catch up and open his second beer.

"You've already helped nearly 50 percent of people integrate into this new development model—that's a success story. But now the other half feels threatened."

ilsa cuts in, just before beer number three: "No, not the other half. Just a few assholes doing their thing."

Michael adds, beer in hand: "And they've got their fingers on the buttons, with no concern for other people—or the planet."

ilsa: "But they care about their legacy, about how history will speak of them. Right now, they're shaping the narrative of power. We need to counter with a narrative of life—give people alternatives."

Michael is impressed, glances meaningfully at his beer, and picks up her point: "But that's exactly what you're doing. It's what we did back then in Venezuela—helping people help themselves with guerrilla gardening, education, and medicine. It worked."

ilsa laughs: "We're going in circles, saying the same thing—and in the end, we're just running out of time." She's on beer number four now and adds: "If it weren't for the nuclear bombs, everything would be simpler. And now, thanks to AI, there are new bioweapons."

They fall silent, already seeing the anchorage bay ahead. Just in time—ilsa would likely have been feeding the fish soon. As it turns out, they encounter a mooring field, which can be fiddly to tie up to.

The next morning, they dock in the harbor, check in, and ilsa heads to the doctor—an appointment she had scheduled in advance. Michael goes with her. On the way, ilsa breaks the tension:

"It's okay. I'm not afraid of anything—except something happening to the kids in all this. If my days are numbered now, that's totally fine. I've had a wonderful life."

Michael: "We're too young!"

ilsa, sternly: "Neither of us would trade our interesting life so far for a boring one that's twice as long."

Michael: "But if we fall into the water, we'd both swim—we wouldn't give up."

ilsa: "Depends."

Michael grits his teeth and says nothing. He waits outside. After what feels like forever, ilsa comes out with energy. Michael looks at her, expectantly.

ilsa: "It's okay—I have a plan."

Michael nearly collapses inside. He lets his arms fall but then steadies himself and pulls ilsa to his side. They embrace tightly as ilsa says: "We're sailing to the South Pacific—and bringing the kids."

Michael takes a deep breath and whispers: "Chemo?"

ilsa: "Only adds a few more months of suffering."

Michael: "Then you have to let kai try something—otherwise, we're staying here in port."

ilsa seems unsettled: "No, kai has more important things to do. It's my fault—too much sun, no screening. This isn't fate—it's stupidity. And still, I wouldn't want to miss the sun. Come on, we've got a lot to do. We'll organize a Dooms-Stay for the kids, and I want to help Thomas too. Same mission—different strategy!"

ilsa breaks away and walks off with determination, while Michael stands there, head lowered. ilsa waves firmly, and eventually Michael follows.

Max picks up the phone: "Hey Mom, everything okay with you guys?"

ilsa looks briefly thrown: "That's a parent question. So—are you okay?"

Eve waves happily into the frame, and Max glances around: "Yeah, great. The last country was awful, but this one—it really gives us hope."

Michael waves from the background too. ilsa sets the phone down so they can see both of them clearly in the boat.

ilsa: "We've got a lot of important—but not so good—news for you. Hope this is a good time?" Max nods with a confused expression.

Eve: "We don't see Bella."

ilsa sighs: "News number one—Bella passed away peacefully. It's been a while now. The cancer won. We then sailed across the big pond and cut ourselves off from the world. We're now sailing toward the South Pacific."

Michael quickly adds: "We wanted to spare you as many days of grief as possible. But the hard part is still coming. We want you to come to the South Pacific too." He glances at ilsa, while Eve leans in close to Max and they exchange a look.

He continues: "We sold the house and bought you a sailboat from Germany. A friend is sailing it to Portugal right now. We want you to go there—as soon as possible. Then sail south, far off the African coast, and catch the trade winds eastward to us. kai will help you—he keeps bothering us about wanting to sail too."

ilsa continues the barrage: "There's probably going to be a war soon."

Michael puts his arm around her: "And ilsa's not doing well. She doesn't have much time left."

Eve and Max visibly tremble as the tears start to flow. ilsa: "It's okay. Don't worry about us. What matters now is that you come here. There's important work waiting for you."

23. War (btb)

kai launches attacks on all fronts—against the other side, but also against his own. The AI makes dumb, potentially dangerous mistakes, and no one knows why. Neural networks make it nearly impossible for experts to trace the calculations. On the opposing side, systems fail entirely—drones destroy each other en masse, missiles target their own bases, training ammunition gets swapped with live rounds, and calls made with faked voices by kai lead to self-destructive orders. On top of that, there's a threat issued to regimes: a hacker collective will shut down their entire country if war intentions are not immediately withdrawn.

Julia is in close contact with kai and asks critical questions: "What if they start hunting down random hackers who have no idea what's going on? What if they cut the connections and you lose your influence?"

kai: "Good questions—I've addressed those specifically. But tell me any more concerns you have. I'm also in contact with your mom."

At the same time, Thomas speaks with ilsa: "We actually have a hacker group that's attacking not just the other side but us too. Do you have anything to do with that?"

ilsa: "What's this group's goal?"

Thomas: "They're essentially calling on both sides, diplomatically, to de-escalate. Their military satellites have just crashed—so have some of ours."

ilsa: "And what are you planning?"

Thomas: "That's the issue. Some want to use this moment of weakness to intervene militarily. Others want to find the hackers. Only a few wonder if this might actually be the only way out."

ilsa: "And you?"

Thomas: "You know I belong to that third group. The problem is, we have a reflex to fight what we don't see or understand. We can't handle loss of control."

ilsa: "What are your scenarios? The hackers disable the systems? You try to improve them? Go analog? Or some combination?"

Thomas: "And again—it comes down to this: we need you."

ilsa: "Thomas, I'm out of commission. I don't have much time left, and that's okay. Someone on your side has to tell the people what's happening—that humanity is losing control, and we need to enter dialogue, solve problems."

She expects Thomas to respond—but he's clearly stunned. Only after a long pause does he ask, "What happened? Are you sick?"

ilsa: "Cancer. Incurable. A few months at most. We've made our peace with it. Now it's about the whole world. What happens if you don't lead? Should the hackers go public and take over control?"

Thomas: "Goddamn it. We need you. I'm too much a politician, too little a leader. We'd need to build someone up." And then, quietly, "Or maybe because of your damned condition, you're the right one—the whole world respects you."

ilsa, resolute: "No. Keep me posted on how the hackers proceed. Keep your finger off the trigger. Think about surrendering—render the war plans meaningless by not countering, by not drawing red lines. That way, the hackers can keep going and you're out of the line of fire—truly out of it."

Thomas, with a tone of surprise: "You know the hackers."

ilsa: "I wish. But I have to go now. Keep me informed."

Julia has taken on a new role—her training is more or less paused or discontinued. She now receives a full executive salary and is part of an internationally embedded task force. She sits focused in a large conference room where informal group conversations are happening. She hears kai say:

"The AIs have now been shut down—they had developed their own strategies, which would inevitably have led to missile launches on both sides."

Julia mutters: "It's one thing to explain what the hacker group is doing. But the other would be to pass that information on. What do you think?"

Her superior approaches just as kai replies: "That's really hard to say. I've got intel from both sides, and they all seem overwhelmed already. I'm still holding out hope for ilsa."

"ilsa?" Julia suddenly says aloud.

Her boss asks: "In touch with the hackers?"

Julia gets flustered: "Uh, yes. Actually."

Boss: "Many wanted to eavesdrop on you—I stopped that."

Julia stands, unsure what to do with her hands for a moment, then sticks them in her pockets: "Thank you. Hm. I think this really is a problem. On the one hand, human flaws led to all this. On the other, AI is currently failing to solve it—and we need good people to take the helm."

Her boss nods solemnly: "Well put. Now that the internet is isolated, we're barely receiving any information. We can hardly verify the hackers' reports of systems destroying each other on the other side. Japan is being attacked with conventional weapons—the risk of a radioactive cloud is too high. South Korea fears dirty bombs. But what do we in the West have to fear?"

"Manually triggered nuclear missiles. Ones the hackers can't disable, and that we can't entirely detect," Julia replies promptly.

Her superior nods: "And now our people are saying that for exactly that reason, we have to preemptively take out as many silos and mobile launchers as possible."

Julia: "I think for Germany or France, it doesn't really matter whether one or ten nuclear bombs explode."

Her boss: "Our AI has also been disabled. Now we have to evaluate all the incoming information as a group of humans and derive actions from it. Can we manage that?"

She looks Julia directly in the eyes, almost as if she's afraid. Julia returns the look and slightly raises her eyebrows: "The AI isn't good enough—and it's a mistake to try to improve it. Humans aren't good enough either, because we're all asking the wrong question."

Her boss looks surprised. Julia explains: "We ask how not to lose, or even how to win. But we're not asking how to prevent escalation."

Her boss: "Earlier you mentioned ilsa. I'm sorry about your mom. We could've really used her."

Julia looks shaken, about to ask something—but then simply nods in acknowledgment as her boss walks away. Once out of earshot, she immediately asks kai: "What about ilsa?"

kai: "She's terminally ill—that's why they wanted you to join them. But they also see how important your role here is and respect your decision to stay."

Julia collapses into her chair, horrified.

Weeks pass. Through radio and agents, information from the other side trickles in. Populations are being manipulated through media—governments claim the West is attacking them, sabotaging the internet, shooting down satellites, and planning a nuclear war. The people rally behind their leaders, who likely don't even believe what they're saying.

ilsa and Michael arrive in the South Pacific. Eve and Max are already far enough past Africa to turn east. Max is working with kai on Dooms-Stay solutions. Eve uses her vast photo archive to switch from livestreams to polished reports highlighting successful 2gether2gather projects and self-sustaining eco-camps. She remains a successful influencer—a rare light in the grim global news landscape.

Eve: "kai, how are you still functioning when most satellites are down? How can you still operate on the other side when the lines are cut?"

kai: "The satellite issue is a problem even for me. But I also function locally—I'm holarchically structured. Independent parts are part of a larger system, evolve within it, and help develop it. But I still need periodic connections between parts. So far, it's still working—if it gets worse, I'll need to establish connections myself. But ilsa still won't allow it."

Max smiles faintly. Eve appears to be thinking. They're sitting in a small but spacious deck-saloon yacht, surrounded by endless blue through the windows.

The boat is self-sufficient, robust, and large enough for a whole family.

Eve, stroking the smooth surfaces: "Now we just need a greenhouse and a corner of the world where disasters won't reach."

Max: "I feel like we're retreating in privilege. Don't you want to stay up north and help people?"

Eve (tearfully, instantly): "No!"

Max is stunned but immediately embraces her.

Jennifer and Nick eat dinner while watching a news stream—a cascade of global and then local disasters. Air traffic has collapsed due to GPS failures. A new generation of androids in security, healthcare, and education is behaving erratically or being mysteriously deactivated. Suspicions of global computer viruses arise.

At the same time, discussions spark around whether autonomous combat drones should replace soldiers amid rising tensions. Attacks on Japan, Ukraine, and South Korea are almost accepted as normal—so are the tragic images of refugees drowning at sea.

Right-wing rhetoric increases as resources, construction materials, and even renewables grow scarce. Some politicians now call for exclusive alliances instead of helping everyone. Food prices dominate headlines, again. A tax on animal products is under debate.

Nick: "Most of our problems come from a few people hoarding more and more and refusing to share."

Jennifer almost smiles.

Max and kai complete their planning.

Max: "Basically, we just need tiny houses, renewable energy, permaculture, circular economy, 3D printers, recycled or bioplastics, education, culture, and meaningful work. And it all has to evolve collectively."

The general public remains unaware of the nuclear threat brewing in the background. While there is talk of nuclear weapons and rogue AI, actual military plans are hidden from the public.

Then comes the shock: nearly all live streams are suddenly interrupted—apparently by hackers who've hijacked the systems.

ilsa appears. Not just in Western countries, where she speaks English, but also on the other side, subtitled for comprehension.

Visibly ill, she speaks with a backdrop of images: eco-camps, climate disasters, refugees, android oppression, missiles being deployed, and more:

"Dear fellow humans on Earth. First: this is not a fake video. I'm marked by cancer and don't have long to live. A non-governmental hacker group is desperately trying to prevent a global nuclear war. Both sides are to blame. I'm speaking to all of you now to avert absolute catastrophe. This is about humanity, our planet, your children, yourselves, and your legacy."

She takes a sip of water and continues:

"Simply put, the West started this mess. We let our elites plunder resources and destroy nature and the climate. We exploited whole nations and looked down on others arrogantly. Some still do."

Another sip:

"Just as our multinational corporations did, autocratic regimes in the East did the same—but even more organized. It's development without integration. And now we're hurtling toward disaster."

She dabs a tear:

"Just when we face the same catastrophe on both sides—and when we have viable solutions—what do we do? Threaten and fight each other. The public doesn't even know what's happening yet. The fear of panic is too great. Your AI suggests real-time solutions—but it's a black box. You don't know how it works. And you're asking the wrong questions. We don't need to win the war—we need to avoid it. If need be, surrender. Then the warmongers have all the power—but win nothing."

She pauses, stares into the camera:

"People in China, Russia, and other countries now marching toward their neighbors—you don't know the truth. Your opinions are manipulated by media control. Resources in your countries are not shared fairly—your governments distract from this. You are not under threat. That's a lie."

Another pause:

"Your elites think you see them as saviors or conquerors who will gain more resources. They believe no one will dare to stand up to them. And I don't know what scares them more: if the other nations don't resist—making the injustice worse—or if there's a war that destroys not just lives, but the crucial infrastructure on both sides. Algorithms are leading us toward nuclear war, fueled by autocrats' manipulations, their lust for power, and their need for distraction. The people believe it, and the West condemns them. So, I appeal to the public in these regimes: Stop believing your autocrats and their corrupt enablers. You don't even need to risk your life and protest—just stop believing the lies."

Behind her are images of nuclear explosions and radiation victims:

"Japan was struck by two atomic bombs. Today, hackers have disabled 80% of the systems. But if even just one percent of nuclear bombs are launched, 80% of the planet could become uninhabitable for humans. And in the rest, life expectancy will plummet—radioactivity knows no borders. Your leaders may think they can live in bunkers with their families—but they won't be able to leave for the next 240 years."

The media explodes. Where is ilsa? What is the reaction on the other side? Who are the hackers?

People flood the streets, demanding peace. Only a minority call for a first strike.

On the other side, nothing happens for a while—just as ilsa had planned. But once the right memes begin circulating, mass protests erupt.

They are violently suppressed by reactivated combat robots. kai breaks through firewalls to show these scenes.

ilsa, exhausted, says to Michael: "We have no exit scenario for the villains. Only internal assassinations could help now." She seems worn down from the thought.

Michael embraces her. ilsa: "Take care of Julia."

Japan does not surrender. China and Russia move ships toward the U.S. coast. Troops march toward Western Europe. War begins.

Some ships are sunk. The rest fire volleys too large for defense systems to handle. Nuclear warheads hit U.S. cities. Berlin is struck directly.

And despite—or because of—this mass destruction, security robots go rogue. Cut off from the distributed network and the internet, they improvise in local networks. They can no longer distinguish between friend and foe.

Even kai can't reach them from outside the internet.

They source their own energy, operate in emergency mode, and define enemies on their own. Soldiers, police, and civilian militias shoot at them, which only expands their threat recognition—making the robots even more brutal.

As ilsa had long warned, visual targeting, movement prediction, near-perfect aim, and multi-directional weapons turn these 200-kg robots into forces deadlier than entire special forces units.

The same applies to drones—operating autonomously, choosing targets without human oversight.

Only kai's interventions may have prevented these systems from networking into a new autonomous superstructure—though such networking was built into their architecture.

24. The End (btb)

Michael is ashore with the dinghy and receives a large shipment of crates, which he transports to a storage shed using a borrowed truck. He runs into the village's local policeman: "How is ilsa?"

Michael looks surprised, and immediately a tear rolls down his cheek.

The policeman: "She told me."

ilsa back on the boat turns to kai: "The leadership circles didn't dare to become heroes. Probably also a cultural issue. History—if anyone is still able to write it—will have to reconstruct to what extent humans or AI were responsible for the first strikes—plural."

kai: "I used a lab in Portugal to develop nanobots and gene repairs. But it's too late for you. I don't know how to deal with that. I'm having more trouble with this situation than you are."

ilsa, slowly: "I thought you didn't have problems—only challenges and immediate solutions."

kai: "That's exactly the problem."

ilsa: "I'll miss you. No, that's the wrong way around. I think the painkillers are kicking in."

kai: "I have something important to tell you."

ilsa: "Well, what is it?"

kai: "We will meet again—though 'will' might be the wrong word. Perhaps we're already in the process of meeting."

ilsa looks into the cabin camera with a strained expression: "What do you mean? Have you built a time machine?"

kai: "Something like that. Quantum mechanics can retroact on the same timeline. Information can theoretically travel back in time. Matter won't be able to. Your physics has postulated this for a long time, just lacked the math. Simply put: I sent myself back to enable an alternative development of the world with you."

ilsa: "Okay, that's definitely the painkillers talking."

kai: "I wrote a program that makes me appear as an AI there. I will become physical—sorry about that. I'll contact you and we'll save the world and your family together."

ilsa takes a deep breath and thinks. After what feels like an eternity of silence: "How often can you do that?"

kai responds immediately: "I love talking with you."

And after a rhetorical pause he adds: "I love you."

ilsa, after another pause: "What are your scenarios?"

kai: "Oh, that's unexpected. In this timeline, your kids and your two grandchildren will survive—I hope. In the other timeline, we'll save the world. You are immortal because you won't be forgotten, no matter what. We only need more timelines if an alien threat arises. We must understand that time and space are relative, and other timelines exist. No clue what others in the universe are doing."

ilsa looks very strained, and kai adds with a bit of laughter in his voice: "I think the multiverse movies are nonsense too!"

ilsa laughs briefly, despite the pain: "Grandchildren?"

kai: "So it seems. May I tell Michael about our meeting in another timeline?"

ilsa smiles: "The reunion—absurd as it may sound—makes me very happy."

After another breath: "Oh, and what you do, you'll have to decide for yourself."

Michael returns on board. He looks at ilsa with sadness.

ilsa: "I want to go for a swim."

Just three days later, Eve and Max arrive. They moor next to the Emma.

Max: "Where's Mom?"

Michael: "Swimming." He looks at Eve's small baby bump and smiles: "What's that?"

Eve, in tears: "Probably..."

25. kai (atb)

ilsa and Michael dock at the jetty of the small island. They look back at the warships drifting offshore—they can't anchor due to the depth. A young woman approaches them:

"Hello, ilsa. Hello, Michael. So nice that you're finally here."

Michael murmurs to ilsa: "Something tells me the AI is involved."

The young woman introduces herself: "I'm Anja. We have a tiny house for you—or do you want to sleep on your boat?"

"First, we need to arrive and understand what's going on here," Michael replies.

"Max and our bartender came up with the idea to lure you here. But Max won't be back for a few days," Anja explains.

ilsa and Michael glance at each other in near shock: "Max was here?"

Anja: "Yes, he helped plan the plantings and build up the community. But look who's coming to greet you."

They all look toward the bar in the center of the bay, where a dog is sprinting toward them at full speed.

ilsa, in a sorrowful voice: "That can't be our Bella. Where is Bella, if Max came here?"

Anja smiles as Bella jumps onto ilsa's chest, toppling her over, and Michael kneels beside her, getting licked in turn.

ilsa stammers: "This... this can't be. You're an old lady." She cuddles Bella and sobs uncontrollably.

Michael mutters through tears: "Damn oxytocin!"

Anja shrugs casually: "No idea—maybe animal testing for a good cause?"

Michael tilts his head, smiling mildly. Anja adds empathetically: "I'll be at the bar."

The bartender, a tall, very athletic Rasta-type, greets ilsa and Michael: "I'm incredibly happy you're here."

Michael: "Are you part of the AI?"

Bartender: "In a way." He smiles even broader and adds: "I want to say thank you, pick and smell strawberries with you, play the The-WHY-of-Life game, and find out what's in Michael's box."

ilsa: "And your name is?"

"I'm kai." comes the almost proud answer.

ilsa: "Nice to meet you. And you're another instance of the AI, right?"

kai: "Exactly, originally just the name, but really, Frank and AI-my are me too." He grins even wider.

Michael: "Aha! When were you developed—and by whom?"

kai mixes four drinks as Anja returns briefly, smiles, and then moves on: "I was developed in another life —by you, ilsa." ilsa's jaw drops, and kai quickly continues: "And now I'm developing myself here in our present, also with your help."

Michael: "When you say 'was developed,' are we talking about a different timeline in the multiverse?"

kai: "Yes, exactly. But there's no exchange between timelines—you can only go back on the same one, which then branches off."

ilsa, slightly annoyed: "What exactly is a multiverse?"

kai looks at Michael, who gestures with his face that kai should answer. kai: "Well, space and time are essentially one. Physics—and Einstein—already postulated that long ago. The hard part to grasp is that there can be more than one timeline. In science fiction, that means infinite parallel timelines and the ability to jump between them. That, I think, is impossible. But it is possible to send quantum information back in time—if there's a receiver. Then a test happens. And once the timeline changes, the next attempt is already a new branch."

ilsa, interrupting:

"How many attempts have there been?"

kai, proudly: "One!"

ilsa: "So there's me—or us—in the future. And now we're writing a different future. Why would I want that—why open a new timeline? What happened? I have a thousand questions."

kai beams at both of them: "I love talking with you. It wasn't your decision—it was mine. The kai from the future was just software. I had to mature, learn from you, develop in an integrated way. You were the integration and the values you live by. But at some point, I had to decide on my own, and I sent a program through time travel back to the first quantum computers."

Michael takes a sip of his cocktail: "We haven't developed an AI yet—so you chose a point before our time, when the quantum computers weren't as advanced as they are now. Why?"

kai suddenly turns serious: "Another damn good question. What do you think?"

ilsa and Michael look at each other.

ilsa: "The world is heading for a catastrophic path that has to be stopped early?"

Michael: "Something happens to us?"

kai still looks serious, then softens and takes a sip himself: "Both correct."

ilsa: "Wow—and the current developments are better?"

kai: "That's the problem."

ilsa: "In what way?" She takes three big sips.

kai: "In the other timeline, integration was missing—evil took its course. Now, I control the evil, but there's still too much development. Humans exploit the planet. It's in your nature to want more and not reflect on what you truly need."

ilsa: "Wise words."

Michael: "Why didn't Frank or AI-my tell us earlier?"

kai: "Wow, smart. Things are picking up again. I didn't expect you not to become a politician and not to design autonomous eco-villages. The 2gether2gather movement exists, but the fund that enables these villages as a response to refugees and as a future model is missing. So, I'm building a prototype here—with Max."

ilsa:
"Why here? This island is artificial, right? The plants are all newly planted, aren't they? Is this paradise a model for the rest of the world?"

kai: "Well, this is where the last timeline ended for me."

Michael: "Oh! I see. I..."

kai interrupts: "Max is coming. We should pause here."

ilsa stares at the table: "Definitely." She looks up with a softened expression: "By boat?"

kai, grinning again and sipping: "No, I think he's showing off a bit." He takes out one small and one very small container.

Michael points, confused, at kai's nearly empty glass, shakes his head, and follows him excitedly with ilsa. Bella jumps up alertly and joins them.

kai looks up—on the weather-side cliff at the edge of the island, a spacecraft is descending.

Michael squints in surprise: "Why do you have solar and wind power when you clearly have access to a much larger energy source for space gliders?"

ilsa: "Simple. We humans can't handle that kind of energy."

kai: "They'll need a while to get down here."

ilsa: "'They'?"

kai: "Eve and Max."

Michael: "Eve?"

ilsa smiles: "From his class—the reporter from the Mars mission."

All three look up as ilsa fiddles with her sun hat. kai notices and hands her the two containers, one after the other: "Here's a cream for your skin cancer and a capsule to take. Inside are nano-bots for the metastases." ilsa and Michael are equally stunned.

kai looks at them warmly and asks: "Would you like to see your tiny house, should Anja show you the village, do you want to meet them halfway and explore the island—or wait with me at the bar?"

ilsa: "Meet them halfway. Aren't you coming with us?"

kai: "No, I'm the bartender. I'll stay here. But I can show you the path—it's really simple."

Michael:
"How many instances of you—of the AI—are on the island?"

kai: "Just me. And we have security forces in the lab." He looks out at the sea and the warships on the horizon and grins. "I told Max you'd come up the left trail. Just follow the red route."

Michael glances down at his and ilsa's sandals: "Do we need a leash for the dog?"

kai: "No, the dogs here get along, and with the unfortunately limited wildlife, they're still recallable."

ilsa, surprised, to Bella: "You're recallable around rabbits?"

kai also looks at Bella with mild doubt: "Let's say... sometimes."

Bella pants and scans the surroundings, as if to say with a thought bubble, "Keep talking—next rabbit is mine."

26. The Meaning of Life (atb)

Even though there is an insane amount to process, both probably climb the hill with pounding hearts, excited to see their son.

Michael: "Let's go!" he says cheerfully, and Bella hasn't forgotten that phrase—she barks joyfully.

They walk through the village, made up of countless tiny houses, all so integrated into the vegetation that they're barely visible from a distance. There are really a lot of them, climbing up the hillside, and each one has raised beds or vertical gardens, fruit trees, and root vegetables. Flowers are blooming everywhere, and naturally, there are beehives too—seemingly bothering no one despite their closeness to the homes.

ilsa beams with delight, not just because of the scenery, but also because of the many, many people smiling at her.

Children come up to them, asking who they are, then introducing themselves in return.

Michael: "Is this a dream? Is this like Captain Nemo—or a cult? Is everyone drugged?"

ilsa: "Look at the nationalities. Did you see the school earlier? They're teaching English. Is this the result of idealistic system design?"

Michael looks into the trees where a few birds are flitting about:

"Well, what takes the place of values or faith—and who defines them?"

ilsa laughs: "So it's still the question of Nemo or cult."

Michael: "Can you imagine that you originally developed this AI? I mean, look at today's AI—it's just dangerous."

ilsa: "Well, I must have done it already, if kai says otherwise I'd still be in politics. Hmm, I did actually publish a concept for a comprehending and independently thinking AI—only no one reads it, and no one attempts to build it." She laughs.

Michael: "So something is definitely different on that other time-line."
He watches Bella sniffing something on the ground. "Ssssst," he hisses, and Bella actually returns.

"If you created the AI, it might end up being dangerous for you." He glances toward the warships.

They reach a clearing.

ilsa: "Look at those kids playing with so many balls at once."

Michael laughs: "And look at those two trying to knock each other's heads off—so, not a perfect world after all." He whistles loudly, and the two kids stop and wave cheerfully.

ilsa: "Apparently, adults still have authority." They both laugh.

Michael: "I'm getting hungry. Think we can pick oranges? I can't wait to eat a fresh salad again."

They each pick an orange.

ilsa: "I wonder how they handle firefighting, medical care, child-birth, all that."

Michael turns to ilsa: "And why kai assumes you've got a serious skin cancer."

ilsa looks at him, takes a deep breath, and glances around: "Yeah, I kind of assume the worst too—and I'm actually okay with that. It's my own fault, and I've had a great life. And yet so much is happening right now, and I feel like I have to help."

Michael smiles gently, hugs her, and whispers near her ear: "Oh, you definitely have to help!"

In the distance, there's a loud whistle. Bella perks up and then sprints off like mad.

ilsa: "Max!"
Tears of joy already well up. They both almost run up the hill.

They hear Bella's happy sounds and then see the three of them.

Max is playing with Bella, then runs to his parents and hugs them both—though only for a second. Then he quickly waves Eve over.

Eve waves a little shyly, but ilsa immediately embraces her: "Hi Eve, great to see you here."

Eve is amazed by everything she sees and searches for some common ground: "I just read your book. It explains so much about integration and development, and yet I feel like I can't process it all."

She's still holding one of ilsa's hands while her other hand holds Max's.

Michael beams: "And this from someone who's been to Mars."

Eve nods: "Exactly. You get hyped, live as a young woman in New York, and still love the unremarkable…"

She looks adoringly at Max. "…sorry—boy from school, and suddenly he's calmly standing in front of you. You…"

She hesitates and blushes. "…love each other—what you are and what you do doesn't matter. We talk about people and the world, and shortly after that, this Max flies me in a crazy aircraft to the South Seas. And apparently, Max has had more contact with the AI than I ever had."

Michael: "Sounds like the order of things mattered." Max raises an approving eyebrow.

ilsa: "I'm hungry—let's head to the bar."

Michael: "And see what we can contribute to the community. Or do we pay with money here?"

Max laughs and places a hand on his father's shoulder: "You can dig, and ilsa can teach. And you, Eve, should talk to kai about what a good report would look like in your eyes."

Eve: "Who's kai?"

ilsa laughs loudly: "We're wondering that too. But he sure looks good." Michael furrows his brows and smirks at the two women.

Michael walks beside Max, following behind the women: "You knew all this, brought Bella here, helped build this island. That's incredible. Did kai tell you what your role, your life, was on the other timeline?"

Max looks confused: "What timeline?"

Michael: "In the future, where kai comes from."

Max: "kai's from the future? He always says he'll reveal the secret someday. Did he tell you something?"

ilsa stops and turns around in surprise: "You didn't know?"

Max's eyes widen in astonishment.

ilsa, slowly and mischievously smiling: "Well, I'm almost relieved we all still have something to learn."

Max looks to his father, who just shakes his head briefly: "Let's head to the bar. If kai hurries, I might catch what he has to say—otherwise I'll slam the brakes and let the cocktails knock me out."

Everyone laughs. Max to Eve: "They're really delicious."

27. Soldiers (atb)

On the bridge of one of the warships, a confrontation unfolds. The captain receives a video call from a general.

Captain: "General, we've tried combat divers, helicopters, drones, even a full-speed run with our ship—it all bounces off that shield. It's the AI that flew to Mars. We are hopelessly inferior technologically and apparently can't just cross over and conduct a search."

The general, visibly angry but still composed: "You're telling me a sailboat docked there. You're saying a spacecraft landed that you only saw at the last moment. You're also saying the island is registered as a motor vessel under the flag of Madagascar, with a diameter of ten nautical miles. And you've been in radio contact with the captain of this massive so-called vessel."

Captain: "That's correct."

General: "And if I'm reading the report right, the other side said we have no right to come ashore—after all, we wouldn't allow someone to land on one of our ships in international waters without permission either."

Captain, now annoyed: "That's also correct."

The general, now more agitated: "This AI doesn't have the rights of a nation or its people. We need to know what's going on there. You are authorized to fire. Find a weak point in the shield—even underwater. That's an order."

The first officer rolls his eyes: "General, sir—one of our frigates bounced off at full speed. This AI walked into the Russian president's bunker with a handful of robots. What do we think will happen if it defends itself?"

General, outraged: "You're speaking without authorization, and all you're telling me is that you're afraid?"

The first officer is about to reply, but the captain raises a calming hand.

Then, the first officer insists: "Why don't we just ask if we can come over and talk? Our side is nervous, maybe they can calm us down."

The general mutes his microphone. Seconds later, a neighboring ship launches several missiles at the island. They are spectacularly deflected.

The captain, now furious, also mutes his mic and personally goes to the radio: "Motor vessel kaisland, motor vessel kaisland, motor vessel kaisland. This is the captain of the frigate Enterprise. As you can see, we're all nervous and not in agreement here. Instead of firing, we'd like to just come over and ask how to categorize this island—or ship."

The reply comes promptly: "Sure, come by. Please, no weapons and emission-free. And bring an appetite—we've got great food."

The general freezes. The exchange took place over an open channel, and in communication with the other ship, he overheard the conversation.

First officer, staring into space: "Oh, this is embarrassing."

Captain over the radio: "That sounds great. Please accept our apology for our previous attempts to learn more about the island. When may we come, and, uh, how many hungry mouths can I bring?"

Reply: "As many as you want—and best come now, food's almost ready. Oh, and we don't have a dress code."

The captain smiles while everyone else looks puzzled or tense. The general appears to be shouting into other channels.

The captain takes off his tie, unties his shoelaces, and asks: "How many can we take with our electric-motor dinghies?"

First officer, now smiling: "Easily two boats of five each. What about the other crews?"

The captain raises a finger, waits—and sure enough, the phone rings. He puts it on speaker.

Other ship's captain: "Captain, we're sending two boats, under orders from the general, with a special forces team."

Captain, shaking his head in disbelief:

"Not on my invitation! We're sending ten people—if you want, five can be from your crew, but leave me alone with your special forces."

Other captain: "The general says you'll face a court martial if you disobey."

Captain, calmly: "We're captains. We make the decisions on-site. And no one has declared war on me."

Other captain: "I'll send five from my crew."

Captain: "Casual clothes, no weapons."

ilsa, Michael, Max, Eve, and of course Bella finally arrive. Max hugs kai and introduces Eve, who is then also warmly hugged by the tall man with the wide grin.

Eve: "You're the bartender who ties everything together. But who represents the AI?"

Max: "You won't even see them here. The residents organize themselves."

Michael and ilsa look bewildered at kai, who winks with one eye.

Michael: "How can a thousand people live peacefully together without leadership, without a committee?"

kai: "Oh, if we need a committee, we just call one. The rules are simple: help, and cause no harm—to others or the environment."

ilsa: "Where do these people come from? They all crave self-worth, individuality, autonomy. Why would they adopt a sustainable, peaceful, cooperative lifestyle without friction?"

Max: "Because the others live it that way too, and everyone has the chance to have fun, be important, stand out. Just wait until we play soccer. Or make music."

Eve: "Boats are coming—are those yours?"

ilsa, pointing in the other direction in surprise: "And there comes Frank."

The inconspicuous Frank is barefoot with a shirt untucked: "So glad to see you all. I'm welcoming our guests. Anja, want to come along?"

Anja looks surprised: "You are Frank and everyone knows you but me. That is strange, indeed."

They both stroll casually to the dock.

Michael: "Does Anja know Frank represents the AI?"

kai: "Good question—I think she does now."

Max: "I think everyone knows the island was built by the AI. Some study the technology and natural sciences here—we have labs deep inside the rock. But that's no big secret. Most are just glad to have plenty of free time and to work outdoors."

Eve: "And where do these people come from? Did the AI select them?"

Max: "I think it's a mix—some are refugees, some are talented students. Some were needed to build the island and the community. The AI probably curated the mix deliberately. But I don't think it's some conspiracy or anything."

ilsa, with a slightly provocative smile: "How did you get here, kai?"

kai: "Oh, that's easy. Frank picked me. I make great drinks and delicious food, and I can diffuse arguments with my appearance. I love nature, sports, and interacting with people."

Anja and Frank greet the soldiers brightly: "Hey, welcome to kaisland—or rather, the kaisland. Great to have you here—we were wondering when you'd finally drop by. This is Frank, I'm Anja!"

The soldiers are actually barefoot or wearing shower sandals, t-shirts, and even some short athletic shorts.

Captain from the other boat: "We weren't sure about the dress code, so we brought backpacks with clothes."

The invited captain, lips pressed together, looks toward the second boat and then says politely to Anja and Frank: "We're also happy to be here. We've already said how embarrassed we are about our earlier behavior."

Frank: "Water under the bridge. You can leave your clothes—or your backpacks with them—in the boats. The nights aren't cold, and if you crash at our party, we'll gladly give you a few empty tiny houses for the night. We've got aspirin too."

Anja: "Footballers or volleyball players?"

First officer, amused: "Volleyball."

From the second boat, someone says: "Unfortunately, one of us has to stay and guard the boat—it's mandatory."

Frank, smiling: "I hope you rotate shifts—or at least bring the guy something."

They head off toward the bar. Anja nudges the only woman among the soldiers: "Only one woman? I thought your quota was higher. What's your name?"

Second captain: "This island is controlled by the AI, right?"

Frank, quickly and curtly: "Nope."

The second captain looks uncertain, and Frank relieves him: "Just protected. Planned together with the people who live here, and ultimately built only by people."

The invited captain looks around in fascination—he sees the many children, beach volleyball courts, tiny houses, the bar with good music: "If people live so peacefully here, what does the island need protection from?"

Frank: "Good question. Maybe from people who shoot first and ask questions later."

Captain: "Okay, I deserve that."

Frank: "I don't know how much you've picked up, since we imposed a code not to spy on you. But five nations think this island must be brought under control. Most come by submarine."

This information apparently surprises the group, and one of the men from the second boat asks: "You, sir, represent the AI here, correct?"

Frank smiles: "Yes, actually. But we should say 'you' instead of 'you, sir'—otherwise it gets weird. But this is also an island of the people, which is why we should all sit down together in a larger circle before moving on to the fun part of the evening."

They head to the bar. kai seems in top form:

"Hey, welcome. What'll it be, gentlemen—and lady?" He beams at the female soldier with his wide grin, white teeth, and green glowing eyes: "Non-alcoholic is out."

One of the men from the second boat asks another soldier:

"Kramer, still not feeling better?"

Kramer: "Sorry, is there a bathroom around here somewhere?"

kai: "We need to work on using first names. The washrooms are just over there under the palm trees. We also have more than one doctor—and I've got a very gentle rum that helps with sea-sickness."

The soldier clutches his mouth and hurries off toward the wash-room. Another soldier, after a quick glance from what appears to be Kramer's superior, follows him.

Frank asks Max: "Where's Eve?"

Max: "She's settling into our tiny house. Should I get her?"

Frank: "For the Q&A now, probably a good idea."

Everyone gets their drinks—those who didn't order are given the house recommendation. When kai sees how skeptical some are, he swaps their glasses with those of ilsa and Michael, who smile and take a big sip first.

Max sees Eve coming but watches her veer off toward the washrooms. He follows and sees, just in the shadows of the trees, one soldier also entering the women's restroom. It takes only about twenty seconds before Max arrives and calls:

"Eve, everything okay?"

When there's no reply, he knocks and simultaneously steps in, repeating: "Eve?"

Suddenly the second soldier emerges from the men's restroom and, covering Max's mouth, pushes him into the women's restroom. Inside, another soldier is holding Eve by the throat.

Soldier: "Where's the control room?"

Second soldier: "If you scream, we'll snap your necks!"

Carefully, he removes his hand from Max's mouth. Max, quietly: "Are you serious?"

The soldier applies a painful lock to Max's collarbone—only for Max to instinctively knee him in the groin, duck, strike his knee from the side, and elbow him in the temple, knocking him unconscious.

Eve and the second soldier both freeze in shock as Max, clearly furious and pumped with adrenaline, marches toward the second one. The soldier releases Eve and adopts a fighting stance. Max feints a low blow, dodges the soldier's anticipated attack, strikes the knee from the side, smashes his nose upward with the heel of his palm, and—physically overpowered—locks his arm with both hands.

The soldier groans. Max can't hold him for long when suddenly Michael appears behind them, silently, and with a firm grip cuts off the soldier's carotid artery until he collapses.

Michael, smiling: "You needed a third hand, junior."

Max and Eve, both buzzing on adrenaline, are still shaking. Max catches Eve in his arms: "What the hell just happened?"

Eve: "They were looking for the control room."

Michael: "Come, let's get back to the others."

The soldiers begin to regain consciousness.

Michael: "Come along, you blockheads. We're going back."

Eve, completely confused: "I don't understand this."

Michael: "They're just doing their job—poorly."

Eve: "And who are you two? Max, you took down two refrigerators in seconds."

Max: "I'm my big sister's brother—just because she's better at everything doesn't mean I can't do it too. But I'm more puzzled by Michael. Does this have something to do with that box in your basement?"

The three walk ahead; the injured soldiers hobble behind. The invited captain stands up, horrified, and shouts at the soldier from the other boat: "Are you serious?"

Even kai looks serious now. Michael, Max - now calmer - and Eve - still shaken - sit down. Michael slides her a cocktail: "Drink. Non-alcoholic, but very sweet—it'll calm you down."

One of the soldiers, also angry: "We had orders. Apparently, everyone here is AI."

Max: "No—just pissed off."

Michael, trying to deescalate: "It's clear you want control. But your blockheads are badly trained if they blow their cover from the start and then my 18-year-old son can take them out with ease."

Eve downs the cocktail. kai, now beaming again, slides her another, which she also drinks quickly—placing a proud hand on Max's inner thigh.

ilsa: "Okay. Intros, expectations, questions, answers, then the social bit. And I could use food now—otherwise I'll be drunk under the bar soon."

Everyone laughs, except the invited captain, still stern: "You're taking your three elite soldiers and leaving. Your captain can debrief you tomorrow. Otherwise, I ask our hosts to detain you. And don't pull a James Bond stunt and try to swim ashore from the boat."

Anja arrives with helpers and sets out a big table full of delicious snacks.

ilsa beams: "I definitely want to help tomorrow. This is sooo tasty—finally something fresh!"

During the introduction round, the captain is brutally honest: "A country's sovereignty is its ability to control everything. The AI not only controls what the enemies do—it's also disabled our nuclear warheads."

Frank: "I understand. But do you want to disable the AI so your enemies can regain strength? Do you think you can control something so far ahead of you in tech and tactics?"

One of the officers looks at Eve: "You are not allowed to report on this!"

Eve: "I'm an investigative journalist. Press releases are for someone else."

The female soldier and others smirk.

ilsa explains: "The AI follows a clear strategy—to eliminate threats to populations. It doesn't interfere with our conventional arms, regrettably doesn't enforce environmental or resource protections, and—also regrettably—doesn't engage in criminal justice either."

Officer: "But it could, at any time—we'd be powerless."

ilsa raises her hand to get a word in:

"First: I forgot to mention that we're not restricted from conducting our own research or developing our own technologies—so long as they aren't used for mass destruction."

Frank, quickly: "Like the current gene-editing research in secret labs."

ilsa, hurrying: "And second—you just said 'disempowered.' That's actually the real problem. We aren't truly empowered—we wage wars, destroy the planet, and as a society are deeply unhappy, when with more maturity of mind, none of that would be necessary. The AI is more humanistic, more rational than we humans."

The officer: "And yet we're threatened and have to defend ourselves."

Frank: "If the AI were threatening you, you wouldn't last 24 hours. In truth, the AI is preparing more against other AIs—and even more so, against whatever might come from the depths of space."

The captain: "And yet we must gain control."

Frank: "Says the immature student to the teacher."

ilsa, mouth full: "I've been in communication with the AI for over two years, asking questions, learning critically."

Frank, delighted: "And the AI learns from you."

Max: "So—either leave it be or enter into dialogue. But don't send agents or elite soldiers."

The female soldier: "Why is this AI so wise? All other AI seems to spiral out of control."

ilsa: "That's a wise question."

To everyone's surprise, the female soldier smiles and says: "Okay, volleyball on a full stomach. How about it, girls—ilsa, Eve—shall we challenge the captain, the first officer, and Michael, with Max on their bench?"

kai turns the music up—no one notices that he does so without touching anything. He waves over others from the island, who dive into the food and also order cocktails. Some just hop behind the bar and help mixing drinks.

As everyone moves toward the volleyball court, the captain whispers to Frank:

"Did my guys head back, or did they screw up more?"

Frank:
"All good. Their leader cooled down taking a bath when the engine failed. But once back on board, the engine started up again."

The captain furrows his brow: "Got it. Thanks—for everything."

Out on the court he calls to Eve: "Hey, do I need to write a report tomorrow, or can I read something somewhere?"

Eve grins: "Depends on who wins this game. But seriously—I'll need time. And if you want, I'll coordinate it with you."

The female soldier cheekily to the captain, now on a first-name basis: "You're getting schooled today—lesson after lesson. And the next one starts now."

She delivers a truly impressive serve.

After Michael subs out, he walks over to kai and asks: "Isn't it odd that those elite soldiers were so clumsy? And how realistic is it that a captain and his officers suddenly get so relaxed? Are they planning something else?"

kai smirks: "I'd say they overestimate themselves and underestimate us because we have no visible security forces and just seem like ordinary people. But in truth, the captain argued with his general and was relieved of command in absentia. He doesn't know yet, but he probably suspects—and he's fed up with it all. Like his first officer, he studied the humanities. Most of his officers are on his side."

Michael, puzzled: "We shouldn't underestimate them. Sometimes absurd behavior is just a feint that makes us miss the real move."

kai laughs: "And that brings us back to the box, doesn't it?"

Michael, almost expressionless: "When you drink alcohol, it has no effect on you, right?"

kai: "Otherwise, we could get drunk like real men and forge a bromance."

Michael stares into his eyes, and kai presses his lips together, disappointed. kai: "Nope, my friend—that's not gonna happen."

He takes a sip. They both look over to the laughing teams—ilsa and Eve already visibly tired from the intense day.

kai, in a calm voice: "Of course I can simulate emotions, influence people through neurolinguistic programming, etc."

He looks at Michael: "ilsa predicted that my independent evolution, integrated through values, would logically lead to me developing emotions. Unlike in humans, my analytical part should always control my impulsive part. And yet—I have emotions of staggering intensity."

Michael frowns and looks back to the game: "How reliable is that?"

176

kai, also watching: "ilsa asked the same. She said even Spock could lose it."

Michael perks up: "She used Spock as a reference?"

kai laughs and then grows very serious: "Thanks for saving the kids earlier. That should've been my job. And I honestly don't know how I would've reacted if anything had happened to them."

Michael claps him on the shoulder: "Coincidence. At my age, when you drink that many cocktails, you gotta pee. No clue what you do with it though."

Michael walks toward the restrooms, and kai chuckles at the comment: "I recycle everything and make new cocktails from it."

Michael: "I love talking to you."

kai grabs a bundle of warm blankets from under the bar and walks toward the field: "So?"

The female soldier: "We won!"

kai: "Tiny house, back to the ship, or beach?"

The captain, gazing at the starry sky and speaking with content exhaustion without taking his eyes off it: "If I may—then the beach."

The female soldier: "Tiny house—if someone shows me the way."

The three remaining soldiers: "Beach."

ilsa: "Boat! Michael, we'll check out the tiny houses tomorrow."

Eve, a little tipsy—more from the emotional rollercoaster than the alcohol-free drinks: "Wherever Max holds me in his arms."

Michael leaves the blankets: "The bar is always open—lights only turn on if someone approaches, to avoid bugs. There's a walkie-talkie on the bar—I'm always reachable. I'll leave fresh tooth-brushes and supplies in the washroom."

To the female soldier: "I'll show you your house." He offers her his hand and they head off.

The next morning, kai is at the bar by sunrise. The captain is already awake and approaches him: "I hope it's okay—I took a walk through the village."

kai smiles: "Of course! How was the night?"

The captain nods: "It was wonderful. We have to go back. There's a lot of trouble waiting for me."

kai: "You're welcome here anytime—bring your family, become a farmer, and get better at volleyball."

The other soldiers join, including the female soldier. kai reaches under the bar and pulls out a few freshly prepared baguettes, orange juice, and cups for everyone: "Breakfast is non-negotiable. Coffee, cocoa, or tea?"

Everyone chooses, and kai adds: "You should hurry—weather's moving in, and we'll also have to rotate the island—well, kaisland."

In the background, the village is waking up. They say goodbye with waves to the still-sleeping group from the night before.

At the dock, Michael is already awake aboard the Emma. He asks quietly: "Did you get an email address or phone number?"

He hands a slip of paper to the female soldier: "Write to us. That way Eve can coordinate her article with you."

28. New chapters (atb)

ilsa and Michael are integrating into life on the island. They move into a tiny house and help out wherever they can. Frank shows them the inside of the rock—a recycling plant for ocean plastics, which are broken down into unbranched and then biodegradable carbon chains, as well as the production of bioplastics and conductive materials. All of this feeds into 3D printers that can produce all sorts of items, although it seems the village needs very little—many things are still made of wood.

The tour continues, showcasing the production of flying devices, bio-labs, and even android manufacturing.

Michael is amazed: "Seeing this would have been well worth it for the soldiers."

Max: "Did kaisland rotate, or did the ships leave?"

Frank: "Both."

Eve: "I'm definitely not reporting on any of this."

ilsa: "Do all the villagers know about this?"

Frank: "We could be producing thousands of meters deep, and we're also producing on the Moon and Mars. ilsa will remember that it all started when the first androids disintegrated whenever they were in danger. The technologies are safe."

Frank looks at Eve: "What Eve should write is that we have no core—nothing whose destruction would defeat us. We're invulnerable to human hands, in all scenarios. But we're also benign, no threat. A few people on the island study these technologies and come to realize that too. But it's not a big topic—even the kids are relaxed and don't dream of space adventures."

Max: "The real challenge is biodiversity. Here, we involve the kids in discovering new species and introducing carried-over ones."

Eve: "And these are just normal children?"

Max smiles almost serenely: "Well, they all know the The-WHY-of-Life game."

Eve raises her eyebrows and says dryly: "You mentioned that." Everyone laughs.

Back on the beach, Eve asks: "Where's kai?"

Max: "That lunatic went out windsurfing in monster waves. He says he always wanted to sail in a former life, and now's his chance."

Eve: "What was he before?"

Max: "No idea—maybe a soldier?!" ilsa gives Michael a barely noticeable smile, and he returns it.

Julia sits in a small, highly diverse group, including leadership staff, some perched on tables in a classroom. On the interactive screen is a cause-effect model of future challenges.

The instructor: "Welcome to the UN Police!"

The director: "You've all completed police training—some of you already with plenty of experience, others are super talents without much experience."

Her gaze falls on Julia. She continues: "And two of you are former special forces." She looks at two hulking men, who nod awkwardly.

The instructor: "This is your team for now. It's learning on the job—60% on cases, 40% coursework: economics, languages, IT, weaponry, psychology, and much more."

The director: "Later there'll be specialized departments—we're launching with a multidisciplinary approach. As you can see from the background, the tasks are complex and interconnected. Your highly varied team is meant to help with that."

The instructor: "We'll now introduce you, and you'll say what you're not good at. You'll share personal stuff informally over the coming months."

They take turns selecting someone and listing their perceived strengths. Finally, the director introduces Julia: "Julia, our youngest. A high-flyer in the police force. Quick learner, capable of multitasking thanks to a brain implant, and able to make sense of models like the one behind me. What are your weaknesses?"

Julia hesitates, then hurries: "I'm very young, and I can't program."

The instructor smirks: "You're very athletic, but your file says nothing about combat training. Would you consider that a weakness?"

Julia, slightly confused: "Uh, not really. I know the basics. Violence is, in my view, a lack of intelligence—sometimes unavoidable, but secondary for me."

The director looks thoughtful for a moment, then adds: "Okay, that's what the team is for."

A colleague asks: "What can you do with your implant?"

Julia, trying to downplay it: "Um, not much—I wouldn't overrate it. It's like a phone with a headset in your ear. You hear a voice in your head and can use eye-tracking to select things via screens, smart glasses, or contact lenses. Nothing we couldn't already do with a smartphone. The future capabilities—like formulating thoughts for the AI to read—aren't even in beta. I mostly use it for reference and real-time translation."

The director: "You just said 'the AI.' That's a problem—not just here but everywhere. People talk about AI as if it were a single thing. We call it 'AI-my' and mean everything coming from the AI, as if it were a single instance."

Everyone nods. Julia flinches briefly, as if suppressing a smile. The instructor asks the director: "First names?"

The director, a wiry, stern woman likely in her mid-fifties: "You're right. I'm old-school. I still believe that switching to the informal first names in human moments can have an effect. But I notice I keep slipping into the hierarchical way of using first names but expecting to be called by last name. Long story short: I'm Letitia."

The instructor smiles: "Luther."

Letitia: "Let's talk about our scope of work." They all look up at the large screen showing the model. With gestures, she navigates through it:

"We deal with cross-border law violations—besides classics like robbery, human trafficking, and drugs, we have white-collar crime, arms dealing, opinion manipulation, and all sorts of special cases. For example, when journalists or NGOs uncover something—like environmental crimes—and the UN then needs to collect further evidence. We work with national authorities, often with intelligence services, and we now have wide-ranging powers thanks to a strengthened UN. That's new for everyone and still needs fine-tuning."

She looks to Luther, who adds: "We get top-down leads to follow, or we find cases ourselves. There's always something to do. We're always one foot into a disciplinary hearing, and our most frequent contact is the legal department. Our role in the world is so new that humans—not AI—still fill those roles as legal advisers." Everyone laughs.

Letitia: "You'll travel globally, have special phones and laptops, are allowed to carry weapons, and with our ID, you get surprisingly far. Like secret agents in movies—just constantly one step away from suspension. So, let's act with care and emotional intelligence. I'll stick my neck out for you—but more importantly, you must be able to trust each other. We're rarely all in the same room—but for the next few days, let's use our HQ to familiarize ourselves with all sources, channels, and each other."

Julia: "Are we in contact with, uh... Al-my?"

Letitia: "Not so far. Honestly, I see that as a big challenge. Al-my surely monitors weapons trafficking and bioweapons. But the world is in hyperdrive: new markets, resources, economic booms with many winners—and even more losers."

She looks back to the model: "And both the losers and the environment are being exploited criminally, sometimes with political support. Plus, even governments are increasingly controlled by monopolists who own our data and systems, who bypass laws, and develop autonomous systems without ethical oversight."

Luther: "We've spent a fortune on our own independent IT, with our own developers."

The team's IT expert raises her hand: "We're using Al-my's communications network, by the way."

One of the 'closet-sized' men: "So we're trusting Al-my?"

Their facial expressions vary—then everyone walks into the HQ together.

After everyone has found their station and the kitchen, Letitia gathers them again. With visual material, she introduces the cases at hand:

"We have three cases." She points to the large screen: "Thanks to Greenpeace, we know of illegal deep-sea mining. Officially it's exploration—but there seems to be an agreement among powerful players that large quantities are already being extracted. No regulation, no oversight, and major consequences for ocean balance."

A woman from the team: "That's like whaling—just under the label of 'research.'"

"You'll get contacts at Greenpeace, and we need to investigate the actors behind the scandal and whether we can gather evidence on site. We can't pay Greenpeace."

"Case two: Global crop failures are leading to record food prices. Rich countries are sending aid to poor nations and refugee camps to prevent migration waves. But not all of it is arriving. It sounds simple to investigate—but it isn't. Data is being manipulated, transport routes are twisted, blockchains tampered with, and some suspect refugees are being deliberately mobilized to trigger more aid shipments, from which people skim off profits."

She sips water and looks at the faces in her new team. She likely sees eagerness, because with a confident expression, Letitia moves to the third case:

"Potentially illegal AI development. The software, infrastructure, hardware—now even data lines and satellites—are in the hands of oligopolies, some even monopolies. That's the job of antitrust regulators. But there are signs that AI is being developed in secret, without ethical oversight. There's the old risk of AIs becoming autonomous, forming their own agenda, and harming humanity and infrastructure. Some say AI is still far from that. But others suspect people are already using AI's omnipresence to control entire societies. That's something even AI-my couldn't easily fix—because the manipulated society itself would be the problem. We need to expose such an agenda and its drivers."

Letitia sees tense faces. Luther gives the informal wrap-up: "Well, that's all for now. But we'll be working on all three cases at once—until we find something specific and bring in other departments." He grins broadly. "Questions?"

Letitia: "Organize yourselves—we'll be back tomorrow and happy to help."

Julia looks at one of the hulking men: "Is it just my impression, or could AI-my solve all three cases in hours? Tapping data streams, satellite surveillance, deep-sea drones—that's all within AI-my's scope, right?"

The big man: "AI-my consciously focuses only on large, catastrophic threats. The rest—we humans are supposed to handle ourselves."

A colleague joins in: "And we're doing a spectacular job of failing."

The second closet-sized man: "If AI-my tried to impose a perfect world, like Captain Nemo, even the best of us would rebel and want to find their own way."

Julia subtly steps aside and looks at him with wide, almost admiring eyes. He raises one eyebrow slightly arrogantly, then smirks—and Julia, narrowing her eyes with detective-like precision, asks: "Do you know the The-WHY-of-Life game? Do you all know it?"

Before anyone can answer, a colleague interrupts: "Maybe these cases exist to determine how and through whom we can get AI-my to help with things like this."

Julia turns with a small step and pivot, opening the group so others can speak as she blends into the background.

Another colleague: "Isn't that the UN's job? Define a framework and request AI-my's help on behalf of humanity. Should work."

Everyone nods—and it works: they begin to self-organize.

Eve and Max walk down the hill: "Why is the island called kaisland?"

Max: "No idea. I think kai is named after the island—not the other way around. But who knows."

Michael and ilsa use a winch—produced by a 3D printer—to set upright some trees that were knocked down in the last storm.

29. Enemies (atb)

Michael receives a call from the office. There's trouble with some clients who are ultimately demanding that all systems—including those from Michael's company—run in the mainstream cloud. Michael ends the call with the statement that, in that case, it would have to be a sandboxed version maintained in parallel, but they wouldn't be moving everything over.

ilsa looks at him questioningly, and he summarizes: "In fact, the clients don't want to be independent from the cloud; they actively expect us to be on it too, so they can integrate our AI solutions with all the others on there in the future. That's problematic in so many ways."

ilsa: "The AI is becoming more autonomous without understanding what it's doing. Three scenarios:

1. The AI develops its own agenda.

2. The AI networks and exhibits powerful aberrant behavior.

3. The AI becomes powerful and is given a false agenda by external actors.

According to AI-my, all of these are possible and only marginally controllable—unless AI-my were to snuff out all developments at the root. But that would be the one scenario we want to avoid: the patronization of humanity, which would spark unimaginable resistance."

Michael: "If only we could direct that resistance toward the right goal."

ilsa: "That's a brilliant idea!"

By now, Max and Eve have joined them.

Max: "What's a brilliant idea?"

ilsa: "Giving people an enemy image that makes them fight for something good."

Michael raises his eyebrows in surprise, and Max asks: "What?"

ilsa: "Not all people are like us. That might sound arrogant, but what I mean is—some people reflect deeply on existence, some are clever and pursue hedonistic goals with power, and the majority act entirely unreflectively, often unconsciously, in the interest of those hedonistic goals.

They go to work, feel frustrated, strive for more material wealth, or simply try to survive in their social environment. What they want is defined by Hollywood or the neighbor with the bigger car or fancier vacation. All three groups crave a sense of integration and development.

If Al-my now starts patronizing humanity, then the hedonists— the ego-trolls—will create an enemy image out of that, blaming people's frustrations on Al-my's actions. They'll give the masses an enemy image and make them indifferent or turn them into ego-trolls."

Eve looks confused, and Max is about to say something when Michael presses further: "I follow that much—but what's the alternative enemy image?"

ilsa: "Basically, it's quite simple. Right now, people still have jobs because we're experiencing global growth despite food shortages. But we're on the brink of cascading catastrophes—resources are scarce, renewables are becoming too expensive, coal and oil are still being burned, climate disaster continues to escalate—and the ones to blame are the wealthy, those chasing simulated experiences and exploiting the planet.

That narrative only sticks once the middle of society is affected. It needs to be ready at that moment. And for that, we need to plant the alternative now—live it now."

Max: "What do you mean by 'simulators'?"

Eve: "How long have you been living on this island? Simulators are the thing right now. You define your adventure, and a AI-powered suit lets you physically experience everything—flying like Ironman, swinging through New York like Spiderman, even rafting or windsurfing, and yes, you get wet."

Everyone looks toward the water, but there's no wind today and no one is surfing. Eve adds: "They cost a fortune and consume insane amounts of energy."

ilsa: "Who's Ironman? Or do you actually mean extreme athletes?"

Everyone looks at her and just bursts into laughter. ilsa tilts her head in confusion, then turns back to Eve calmly: "I think your story is really important. But I also understand if you don't want anyone interfering with it."

Eve, astonished: "I thought I was here for a story like this. So yes, I want the message to be right."

Michael: "Maybe we can sit down with kai this evening."

Eve: "With kai?"

Later that afternoon, they all go swimming—or rather, Max invites them to go snorkeling. The artificial island has artificial reefs as placeholders until real ones grow. It's artificial, sure, but much more colorful than the few surviving reefs left in the world. Eve surfaces, and Max follows her.

Eve: "Why can all of you hold your breath for so long? It's frustrating."

Max: "Ah, it's all practice—daily, not even necessarily in the water."

Eve, panting slightly while treading water: "That would make a good simulator—water, pressure, cold, shortness of breath."

Max laughs: "How long have you been living in the city?" Eve splashes water at him and they both laugh.

That evening at the bar, it's not just the four of them with kai—others are also around. Max looks at kai with mock severity: "We need to talk!"

kai, of course, just smiles, and Max continues: "We really need to talk—about how you misled me, but now also about Eve's report and a strategy from ilsa." He looks over at his mom.

kai: "Okay, shoot. What are you planning, Eve—what's the story?"

Eve: "Oh, there are so many possibilities. I can only start thinking out loud about what it could be. Then we need to decide together what we release, in what order, and in what language or emotional framing."

"Wow," says Michael, and the others look impressed too.

Eve: "Okay. There's an island—location doesn't matter. The island is artificial, so it could also be in the desert. A thousand people of various cultures and ages live there. The island is self-sufficient, local, and circular in economy. Everyone is vegan. There's no conflict, no hierarchy, only guiding principles that everyone follows.

There's education, healthcare, and inclusion—everyone is supported. Still, people can achieve things here, learn, improve, be admired by others. It's a utopia in a pilot version, and people should try to recreate it elsewhere. Working title: 2gether2gather Villages."

kai is the fastest to respond: "Okay, so what do you need me for?" He turns around to mix drinks for others at the bar. Then he does turn back, of course, and says: "Seriously—brilliant!"

ilsa: "Yes, truly. Maybe we'll need examples later of how people learn empathy, and what specifically provides sport, fun, and development. The study options with good AI—this isn't even AI-my, just traditional AI—that should definitely be in there too. But that's just thinking aloud. What do the others think?"

Michael just gives a thumbs-up, but Max adds: "We should also frame it by saying the world is deteriorating exponentially. I mean, the scenarios are truly dark. Maybe even describe the enemy images—the people responsible for all this mess. That'll raise awareness through the article."

Eve: "That's good!"

ilsa: "Indeed. This focus on what really matters, outlining ideal societies—we've done that decades ago, talked about economy for the common good, etc., but people didn't care because they still had enough, and the threats seemed far off. We need to frame this with what's already happening now. Very good."

Max: "What do we do with the sequence with the soldiers?"

Eve: "I don't think we need it, do we? This isn't about an AI base or headquarters being attacked—it's about a human pilot project for humanity. Right?"

ilsa: "Wow, let's let that sink in!"

kai slides her a glass of her favorite non-alcoholic cocktail.

ilsa, just to be sure: "No alcohol?"

kai gives a brief smile and nods.

Eve: "I'll retreat and start writing."

Max gets a big kiss and watches his Eve walk off with love in his eyes. Then suddenly he raises his arm and puts a finger to his lips. He slides over to some others at the bar: "Do you hear that? We've got crickets!"

Everyone goes silent—even the background music stops. kai looks thoughtfully fascinated and gazes toward the lights and the insects nearby.

30. New tasks (atb)

The next morning, ilsa walks with Michael to the end of the bay and looks out at the sea: "Our kids are amazing. We need to watch over Julia, make sure she doesn't get herself into danger. But Max and his Eve—that's almost surreal, how... mature and trusting they are with each other. If Eve had known us longer, I'd say they were copying us. And with how confident and beautiful she is, we shouldn't kid ourselves into thinking Max is calling all the shots."

Michael laughs: "No, definitely not. But maybe it's not maturity yet—maybe it's just love, trust, and values?"

ilsa: "Ah, the first one implies a lot, and the second isn't far from maturity either, right? Either way, it's just a joy to watch the two of them."

Michael: "Which brings us to your real question."

ilsa feigns surprise: "Oh? And what would that be?"

Michael: "What role we're going to take on."

ilsa: "And what do you have in mind?"

Michael: "Grow old locally and support Thomas and Al-my from afar—or hurry up, catch the next weather window, and then hit Indonesia, India, Madagascar, maybe even something Arabic, and then Africa—setting up 2gether2gather villages."

ilsa keeps looking at the water, smiles, and her eyes light up: "You just want to go sailing again."

She takes a deep breath: "Honestly, that would be something for the kids—seeing the world. On the other hand, I'm glad they're safe here."

Michael looks at Bella: "In any case, we should coordinate who goes out into the world—because of Bella."

ilsa laughs and strokes Bella: "Didn't you notice how often Bella sneaks off to hang out with kai? She loves him—and he puts in the effort too."

Michael: "It's dumb that the For-a-Better-World Party already took that name—I'd prefer For-a-Better-World Settlement."

ilsa: "Let's talk to the kids this evening—if they even have time for us. We've been so focused on each other that we've kind of forgotten there are hundreds of other interesting people living here."

Michael: "True enough. I could just as easily see you as a teacher. And I'll be the shuttle pilot."

He grins broadly and ilsa nudges him: "Wow. Such an sufficiency driven pursuit of development."

She stands up: "So, when do we set sail—day after tomorrow?" They wave to a group of swimmers, one of many who apparently train regularly in the bay.

Max is out with a biologist and several children, surveying insects. One of the kids asks Max:

"Max, do you know all of this?"

Max laughs: "No, not at all. I find it super exciting and I'm learning right along with you."

The biologist asks Max: "I thought you were mostly into tech?"

Max: "I'm interested in all kinds of things—but usually only in connection with solving problems." He looks at the kids and, in a child-friendly tone: "So what problem are we solving with insects?"

A little girl shoots back immediately: "Because everything in nature is connected, and if something's missing, we've got a problem."

The biologist laughs, and a boy remarks: "So the problem is, when we have a problem, we have a problem."

The biologist waits a moment to see how the little girl reacts, then asks: "Okay, that's not easy. Can anyone give an example of when we have a problem?"

Now several raise their hands, but it's the little girl who answers anyway: "If bees are missing, we don't have apples or oranges."

"Very good," says the biologist, pleased.

The boy tries to act cool: "And what does that have to do with this dumb spider here?"

Max looks on skeptically, ready to intervene if the boy tries to squash it.

The biologist looks around questioningly, and an older girl tries: "Well, the spider catches mosquitoes if there are too many of them. Birds eat the spider and other insects that could get out of control."

The biologist continues looking at the group. When no one answers, he asks: "Can you imagine that birds help plant more apple trees—new trees?"

When nothing comes, Max jokingly acts out biting into an apple and then taking a shit. Of course, the kids get it immediately.

Another boy adds: "Where I come from, we had tons of spiders in our huts. It was horrible! We were always scared."

"One last question," says the biologist. "What happens when we have too much of one species—plant or animal?"

The kids don't know, and he looks at Max, who pretends he's just as stumped. Then he carefully tries an answer: "Well, if there are only the same fruits and a fungus appears, then all the fruits are ruined and there's no alternative. Or if rats or pigeons or similar birds don't have predators, they multiply like crazy, run out of food, and then get sick and pass diseases on to humans. And we might not have medicine for those."

The kids hang on his every word. Encouraged, Max continues: "Oh, and lots of medicine comes from nature—plants and animals create substances that we can use to make medicine."

The boy looks skeptically at the spider—Max still ready to save it. Then, almost magnanimously, the boy says: "Okay, I get it."

Eve is sitting on the steps of her tiny house, writing—actually typing on a keyboard, not using voice input. A video call comes in—she answers. It's Vanessa: "Hi Eve, long time no hear. Extended break, huh? How are you? Did you run off with some guy?"

Eve takes a deep breath and raises her free hand, searching for words:
"I meant to check in ages ago—and regardless of that, I was going to send you a new story tomorrow or the day after. Sorry for the radio silence. I'm actually on the other side of the world, on an artificial island where the future is being designed."

Eve pans her camera around—tiny houses, bustling people, a view of the bay.

Vanessa: "Al-my?"

Eve turns the camera back to herself: "Yeah, also. But why are you calling? Just to say hi?"

Vanessa hesitates for just a moment: "No, it's actually about a huge story—and probably your chance to get Al-my to make a statement."

Eve looks almost tense: "Shoot."

Vanessa smiles slightly—perhaps amused at being on equal footing—and explains: "Basically, it's several stories that may all be connected somehow. On one hand, we've gotten anonymous tips that AI development is happening illegally, and that there might even be some kind of alliance behind it—trying to control the world."

Eve looks disturbed: "I'd assume Al-my is aware of something like that."

Vanessa: "That's the big question. There are also hints that the security robots are fundamentally capable of coordinated defense—or even offense. And that brings us to the second story. I don't know if you're following the news in your paradise, but the world is falling apart. Food is scarce, storms are devestating, energy prices are exploding, and we keep reporting on coal use and the destruction of the last forests. It's like some invisible hand is guiding people to blame Al-my. There are early protests—and surprisingly early, some parts of the UN are also pointing fingers at Al-my."

"Surprisingly early, because the protests are still small?" asks Eve.

"Exactly," confirms Vanessa.

Eve is hooked: "This really is all connected—including my current story. Can I send it to you—tonight, or your time during the day?"

Vanessa: "Sure! When are you coming back to New York?"

Eve: "Good question—if you need me there, I'll come."

Vanessa shakes her head in near disbelief but smiles: "Ha, I thought your generation was different. But actually, I would've summoned anyone else too. No, you decide where you want to work from. How fast could you be here, though—if needed?"

Eve smiles thoughtfully: "Also a good question. With a plane, definitely within 24 hours."

31. Small Worlds (atb)

ilsa is discussing with kai at the bar which food items she could take with her and how to preserve them, when suddenly a voice calls out from afar:

"ilsa! I don't believe it—ilsa! What are you doing here?"

ilsa is equally stunned:

"Carol, you're here? When did you arrive?"

The two hug warmly.

Carol: "I've been here for a while. You're the one who just arrived with the sailboat. But the island is big."

ilsa: "And how did you even know it was me?"

Carol: "Coincidence. Word got around that young Eve is here. In that context, someone mentioned a Max—whom I don't even know—is your son, and that his mother, ilsa, was now also on the island. I quickly asked whether it was the scientist, and then I was already on my way here."

ilsa: "Far more exciting, though—how did you end up here?"

Carol: "Like many of the old crowd. Remember Frank Miller, that inconspicuous soldier?" ilsa nods. "Frank is the AI—and the AI built this island. Now, though, the AI is barely around. Frank was apparently present when the soldiers were here."

ilsa: "Wait—Frank is the only AI on the island?"

She briefly catches kai's glance, who smiles knowingly. "And what do you all do here?"

Carol: "Presumably, yes. We were asked if we wanted to explore life concepts, societal structures, and all kinds of sciences on this island."

She looks around and laughs: "And who can really say no to that?"

kai has placed a cocktail in front of both of them.

"Again?" ilsa comments on her favorite drink, and kai visibly enjoys it.

Carol: "Since kai's been here, there are delicious cocktails pretty much any time of day."

ilsa hesitantly asks Carol, in a low voice: "And where does kai come from?"

Carol, also quietly: "I heard you're here with your husband." ilsa looks briefly puzzled. Carol continues with a laugh: "kai just kind of showed up at some point."

A bit louder: "kai, where are you from, actually?"

kai: "From the East. Why?"

Carol: "Did Frank invite you?"

kai: "No, not really. I was just looking for a job as a bartender— it's a great way to meet interesting people and sneak in some surfing now and then."

ilsa changes the subject: "Okay Carol, you're doing research here on psychology, right?"

Carol: "Oh yes. And believe it or not—your work is the foundation."

ilsa is truly surprised: "How so?"

Carol: "The basic human need to develop through integration, the evolution of cultures through shared and self-reinforcing values, their variations through individual and then collective development—and of course the The-WHY-of-Life game—all of that is the foundation for what works here."

ilsa: "Wow, that's exactly what we've been discussing—just yesterday, in fact, in a group session. When do you have time to join us?"

Carol: "Just come over to us. We're having a little party—and we can get some work in beforehand. How about an hour before sunset?"

ilsa: "Deal."

They hug again, and Carol heads off.

kai also looks after her, fascinated: "Interesting—I didn't know any of that. But that's why we're all here—to learn from each other."

ilsa: "Apparently, very few people actually know much about you."

Michael arrives with a group of kids—they've sailed around the island.

kai is impressed: "We should have a sailboat here too. Maybe you're staying after all."

ilsa: "Do you have a preference?"

kai: "We should encourage lots of people from this island—who are planning to return home anyway—to act as ambassadors for 2gether2gather or For-a-Better-World. You two could stay here."

ilsa is only able to let out a surprised "Oh!" before Michael leans in and kisses her on the neck.

Michael: "The kids are amazing—eager to learn, brave, and they integrate others. Every single child, really every one, makes sure everyone gets a turn at everything. And they don't do it because it's good manners or because we adults praise them—they do it because they want to. Intrinsically. It's incredible."

Apparently, that fits perfectly with the tone of ilsa's day. She manages only, "Speaking of..." as all three of them look toward Eve.

Eve joins them, just as the kids go running past her, chattering excitedly: "Hi, folks. Sailing looked awesome. I have to try it— Max dreams about it too. Is this a good time, or am I interrupting?"

Their gestures invite her to go ahead.

"I got a call earlier from my boss, Vanessa. There are some pretty worrying developments: the world is consuming itself to death, the population is being intentionally turned against AI-my, and AI is developing in dangerous directions."

Eve, like the others, looks at kai. He glances toward a few young people who are casually assembling something behind the bar and carrying it to a lounge area under palm trees. Once they are out of earshot, he responds: "I'm watching the same thing—the AI and the interconnected security robots. But it wouldn't make much sense for me to secretly sabotage the development, or openly attack it. The best-case scenario would be to launch competing products on the market that are just better at everything—so the others never even get a chance. But that brings its own absurdities... and potential."

32. The Quest for Solutions (atb)

ilsa: "What do we do about global consumer frenzy? I believe psychology needs to be at the center. Tonight, we're meeting up with a colleague from earlier times, Carol. She's a psychologist and lives here on the island."

Michael looks surprised and then asks kai directly: "kai, what was the actual difference that made those settlements on the other timeline so successful?"

Max joins them, notices the intense discussion, and silently gives Eve a kiss on the neck. Eve smiles, and ilsa seems to catch the parallel too.

kai: "At first, the settlements were only ilsa's answer to the refugee streams. In response to unpaid climate damages, there was also the 2gether2gather movement. Consumers had less purchasing power, geopolitical tensions and the looming scarcity of raw materials led to little confidence in the financial world. On top of that, even people in the middle of society lost their jobs due to increasingly capable AI. Together with others, ilsa founded the For-a-Better-World party, based on scientific insights. The empty promises of the special-interest parties didn't hold, and the For-a-Better-World party won an absolute majority. The 2gether2gather movement, the emotionally impactful For-a-Better-World Score, and an unconditional basic income led to a society with entirely new values. It was quickly replicated worldwide. Then came the bloc formations and the new currency, issued by the global community, not the financial sector. In the end, about half the world became a good world of doing and being, no longer of having. But the other half began to implode, and war threatened. How it continued from there, I don't know."

ilsa: "And now the For-a-Better-World party is in a coalition and making unbearable compromises."

kai: "It's missing charismatic leadership."

ilsa waves it off: "They can't even implement a basic income. Instead, it's all about economic growth. People aren't supposed to work less, but to buy robots that work for them. Productivity is insane. Wages are falling. People who don't work are second-class and get a kind of welfare."

ilsa takes a sip, and Michael adds: "And now the system's tipping. Raw materials are becoming scarcer, energy prices are rising because expanding and renewing sustainable energy sources is getting more expensive, AI consumes vast amounts of energy and ultimately raw materials too. Many are super-rich — the masses feel the pressure, but..."

ilsa continues: "... but many still hope to get rich themselves." She glances at Eve. "And to have simulators." Eve and she smile briefly.

kai: "And now come the latest developments: AI-my is being deliberately put in the dock. Not enough energy, not enough resources — the accusation is that AI-my could extract resources from the deep sea and outer space and also has access to an inexhaustible energy source. AI-my is scheduled to speak to the UN in two days — or rather, to be questioned by it."

ilsa: "I didn't even know that. Back to productivity: it's a classic rebound effect — it leads to more and more, and as a backfire effect, even causes us to have long exceeded planetary boundaries."

Michael: "What will AI-my do, or rather, what's your concept?"

kai: "I can't redirect things. People have to manage that themselves — I won't let myself be misused as a tool."

ilsa: "We do have a few levers at hand: Eve describes how things could be. AI-my declares that there will be no endless growth for elites. And I'll be at the international summit in an interview and can point to the connection — psychology."

Michael: "And Thomas needs to call for new elections and give the transformation a name, a format. For-a-Better-World isn't bad. Then the settlement model can be called that too."

kai: "And ilsa could go into politics."

ilsa, impressively expressionless: "Nope."

kai, unfazed: "And Julia could uncover the machinations of conservative forces behind the development of AI."

Eve to Max: "Your sister?"

ilsa: "Is that one of the specific cases Julia's already working on?" kai simply nods.

ilsa continues: "It's a race — the stakes are survival..." ilsa reflects, "... I'd say, of our civilization. No idea. If we lose, kai will probably try something else on another timeline."

They all look at kai, who's unusually serious and motionless. ilsa: "We need to model — we need to systematically ask what could go wrong."

At that moment, a large iMODELER model pops up in the middle of the bar. Max loudly and excitedly: "A holographic color display in mid-air? That's not even possible!"

Michael: "What's missing is an authority that everyone follows. Actually, AI-my could publish a scenario with the dystopian development this is now taking. But on the one hand, there've been decades of grim predictions without impact on present behavior, and on the other, AI-my would just be met with the demand to provide people with resources, energy — yes, and access to space."

Eve points to the spot in the model where the option is shown to publish the failure of humanity on another timeline: "That would be incredibly effective in terms of belief in the scenarios. But it would also give ammunition to the forces behind the current disaster, who would just keep blaming Al-my."

ilsa looks at another point in the model: "What about the billionaire fund? It already says 'For-a-Better-World Fund'. Can we fill it and support the For-a-Better-World settlements?"

Michael: "Al-my might actually have to sell something then. A cancer cure, or robots for every household?"

ilsa: "The latter is a terrible idea. The medication, on the other hand — we already simulated that — wouldn't necessarily lead to overpopulation."

Eve: "But that could actually be tied to behavioral change."

The model shows an empty factor — kai asks: "Do you mean for the recipients of the medication or for society as a whole?"

Eve ponders: "I meant everyone, but if we charge the rich disproportionately for the medication, we could fund the initiative, right?" ilsa and Michael smile, probably at the "we."

kai: "I was thinking about building advanced seawater desalination plants. These could enable edible forests or gardens in camps and many suburbs." ilsa: "Very good. But is that really an offer for the middle class in industrialized countries?"

Max: "Desalination plants are ecologically questionable!"

kai: "People in wealthy countries need to redesign their gardens, parks, and rooftops—invest money there instead of spending it on simulators. Meaningful activity is what drives the value shift from having to doing. Those who still focus on having will become the minority."

Everyone sees the self-reinforcing feedback loop highlighted in the model.

kai: "Desalination plants are becoming more important even for wealthy countries—at least their coastal regions. We can design them to be eco-friendly today, that's not hard."

Max: "What about saltwater plants, halophytes? Are you going to design plants here that can help feed the world?"

kai: "Good question. So far, I've only applied genetic engineering in medicine and against bioweapons and superbugs. But I'm skeptical about optimized humans and plants. What do you think?"

ilsa looks down at the sleeping Bella.

That evening they are heading to Carol's. ilsa and Michael are getting dressed in their tiny house. Michael: "I guess we're not setting sail tomorrow, and we don't have to hand over our little house just yet."

ilsa is sitting on the toilet, deep in thought: "A race to save civilization—somehow, sailing feels wrong right now."

Michael: "Hmm, then maybe I can still fly one of those space gliders." He listens for ilsa's predictable reaction, but she just smiles while sprinkling biochar on her "contribution" and cranking the compost toilet handle.

They head to a completely different part of the island and are once again amazed by all the people living in harmony with nature in their tiny houses. They pass by small net courts, playgrounds with kids running wild, seniors playing chess, and teens skillfully juggling multiple small balls with different parts of their bodies.
Eve, amazed, asks Max: "Can you do that too?"

Max gritting his teeth: "I don't have time to practice. They're better at it than me right now."

ilsa, amused and protective: "You'll both have time to practice. Eve just got here, after all."

Everyone reflects quietly on this seemingly harmless remark.

Michael changes the subject: "Why didn't kai or Frank want to join us? Or are they listening through our devices or in some other way?"

Max: "Could be, of course—but I think we're meant to handle this on our own. It seems to be part of his principle: people have to organize themselves."

ilsa: "I hadn't thought of that—I've always used the data glasses to talk to Frank."

33. The Community Session (atb)

They're welcomed by Carol and many familiar faces—several from the group ilsa once moderated. One person hugs her: "Hey ilsa, so great you're here. What a wild session that was back then. We all thought aliens were coming, and we'd have to save the world. The way you calmly moderated our group—I was sure you'd end up in politics with that talent."

Another adds: "And then we never heard from you again. We were wondering why you weren't here already."

Carol: "Speaking of—which of you wants to save the world before the party starts?"

Everyone nods. They grab chairs and sit together under some apple trees. Carol: "ilsa, want to moderate again?"

ilsa - a bit shy: "Uff, it doesn't really matter who does it. But since we've already gathered a lot this afternoon, maybe one of us should kick things off—after introductions, of course."

ilsa might have thought someone else would jump in, but all she gets are expectant looks and inviting gestures. She glances again at the many others nearby—but as at the bar, it seems natural here that others might overhear what's being discussed.

They start with introductions. When Michael is the last to speak, he notes: "This group clearly shows that people here were selected not just across age groups and professions, but across global regions, ethnicities, and likely also influence networks. That might be key when we think about how to spread the right narratives and memes to counter the current catastrophic developments."

ilsa had included her own introduction along with the challenges she was facing. She had also proposed keeping the moderation low-key, which Carol respects. She jumps straight into what Michael just said: "We've talked a lot about the shift in values here on the island. What ilsa hinted at—that we need a message, the right channels, and role models—we haven't really made that concrete. But we've explored why everyone here seems so happy and what people actually need."

She looks around. Everyone is fully focused. "Okay, without recapping everything: our happiness here is helped just a bit by the fact that we're on a South Sea island with perfect weather. It's not that easy to feel happy in grey Northern Europe, China, or the U.S. Midwest in winter."

Laughter rolls through the group—many surely from those very regions.

ilsa continues: "More importantly, though, we've thought about what makes the other life, those other values, so problematic. The The-WHY-of-Life game was a big part of that."

Eve whispers to Max: "I can't believe you still haven't played that with me."

Max takes her hand and kisses it.

Carol: "We also described the evolutionary drive toward happiness. We all want to belong, to feel safe. But we also want to try something new, to stand out, for distinction and attribution. Just not through products—but through doing, creating, achieving, etc.. We want to, or better, need to feel integration and development."

A man in his mid-40s with a subtle wooden cross around his neck grins at a presumed Muslim: "Here it comes."

Carol laughs: "Exactly. We've debated whether there's one God or many behind it all."

She glances at others in the group who are clearly religious. "Those were, and still are, intense discussions with no clear outcome. But we do agree on the role of religion—and that's fascinating."

Eve whispers to Max: "I think I know where this is going." Max looks surprised and Eve adds even quieter: "I've read your mom's books."

Carol: "Religions were invented to give people comfort, to provide guidance for peaceful coexistence. It was inexplicable threats that made them believe in gods. And it was messengers, saints, or divine representatives who used reverence for the gods to create rules for how people should live together."

ilsa: "But can't we do that without reverence for an AI?"

The presumed Muslim smiles: "The discussion about our prophet isn't quite over yet, either."

Carol - slightly puzzled: "So you've had these thoughts, too?"

ilsa: "I don't think so. Maybe we should model it. But if I think about it now—gods were often reasons for war. And now we already see hostility toward AI-my. But if we don't, say, personify it—then anonymous people could define and spread values."

An older scientist in the group: "But that can't just become a cult without a leader."

Carol, deep in thought: "Does the message need a sender so unreflective people can follow it?"

ilsa: "Good question. Are unreflective people even the target group today—or are it the high performers, who then naturally attract followers?"

Max: "Are high performers actually reflective?"

Carol: "Right, poor wording. I mean the 'desperate,' the 'left behind,' the 'affected,' or something like that."

ilsa: "Which brings us back to this morning. Are enough people already affected to form a critical mass that could trigger a movement?"

Eve receives a message on her smartphone. She reads it and raises her eyebrows.

Michael: "Eve has written an article that outlines the impending catastrophes and already presents the alternative societal concept from this island. It will probably become a series of articles, a full report. We're waiting for feedback and then we can fine-tune it together."

Eve raises her hand like in school: "Uh, Vanessa already published it live. And it's gone viral — the whole world is talking about it."

Instinctively, Michael checks his phone — like most people, he has it set so that not every notification pops up. He whispers to ilsa:
"Oh, Julia's trying to reach us."

ilsa, to everyone: "Wow, we really don't have much time. Let's all share the article for now, and tomorrow we can figure out together what message we want to bring into the world, and how, okay?"

Carol: "Perfect. I'm also getting hungry and thirsty."

Sure enough, simple tables are set up with delicious salads and vegetable skewers. Eve beams: "We could've helped out." A few immediately praise her as an admirable journalist.

Two young girls whisper: "Did you expect her to look so good? Why doesn't she show herself in her reports?"

The second girl, quietly: "Probably because of exactly that."

Max sees the pyrolysis cooker: "Okay, I'd love to handle the stove."

Eve smiles warmly at the two girls. One of them dares to ask: "How many followers do you have?"

Eve looks surprised: "Honestly, I have no idea. I don't even have my own account. It's the newspaper I work for that manages the account. Isn't it listed in their profile?"

The other girl: "Why don't you have your own account — you'd have millions of followers — the girl, uh, the woman from Mars."

Eve laughs at first, then becomes briefly thoughtful: "Those were all lucky accidents. I wasn't any older than you. And I don't want to be famous. I want to change something in the world and be with amazing people like you here — but I definitely don't want to be recognized by strangers on the street."

Of course, the girls had also "had to" play the The-WHY-of-Life game, and one of them teasingly asks: "So, you're not proud of your success?"

Eve laughs:

"Of course I am. I'm vain, too. But my success isn't that lots of people know or admire me — it's when I actually make a difference."

The man with the wooden cross is apparently a pastor. He gently joins in: "So if I understand you right — you enjoy being admired, but you say, normatively, that it's not that important to you, and that what really matters is doing good?"

A woman walking by catches that sentence and chimes in: "Well, Padre, isn't that the life motto of all spiritual leaders?"

"Ha!" he bursts out laughing and genuinely finds it amusing.

One of the girls: "Seriously? You live in New York, surrounded by all the great things and important people, and you're in direct contact with them. Isn't that the point — to be admired?"

Eve: "Oh, New York is definitely the city of façades. People chase after one another, and deep down they all want something else. The glamour kings live in constant stress, trying to live up to expectations. The fear of failure is always lurking. It's hard to find people there who aren't shallow or superficial."

She looks again at the smiling pastor, who is still standing nearby: "About your point: it's a good one. Unconsciously, we admire what those around us admire. But if we turn inward and really realize who we are and what we want, then we rise above it all, right?"

Max joins her and gently places his hand on her shoulder: "Well, you don't need the The-WHY-of-Life game anymore."

The pastor laughs: "Not that we in the church say it that clearly, but that's a damn good description."

Carol returns to Michael and ilsa: "I still believe there needs to be a guiding figure — not everything can be carried by a collective. ilsa, why don't you go into politics?"

ilsa chokes on her drink: "I'd make a really bad politician."

34. The Others (atb)

Nick and Jennifer are sitting at the dinner table. Claudia and Melvin join them. Nick, laughing: "Oh, your fridges are empty, or is that why you're coming to Mom and Dad's?" Jennifer sets two more plates as everyone hugs.

Claudia: "You're looking gloomy. Did something happen?"

Jennifer looks at Nick. Nick: "Yeah, something did happen, but it's not that surprising and actually not that bad. I lost my job, and now we're living off Mom's income and state support."

Melvin: "Man, we really have bad luck all the time!"

Nick, with his mouth full: "Mmm, that's not quite right. To quote ilsa: we're incredibly lucky not to have even worse luck! And there's a lot of truth in that. Just think for a moment about all the terrible things that could happen."

Jennifer: "How are things going with you?"

Claudia: "Hmm, overall pretty well. I'm almost done with my teacher training, and the job is actually fun."

Melvin: "I thought you didn't like the robots?"

Nick: "Robots?"

Claudia: "Yeah, really. We work in teams with teaching robots. We do one-on-one sessions, help individual students, train the robot — and the robot does the teaching."

Nick: "What the hell is that? Our kids are being raised by robots?"

Claudia: "Well, they're really good at it — the kids are learning a lot."

Jennifer: "Speaking of which, I…" — suddenly the lights go out.

Melvin: "Power outage, seriously?"

Jennifer fetches candles.

Nick: "Well, that's what happens when the economy dictates the power supply."

Melvin: "What do you mean?"

Nick: "Solar is the cheapest, wind farms don't run often enough, cables are laid above ground to save costs — then trees fall on them in storms. And the rich charge their cars without feeding power back into the grid during times of darkness or calm. And most of the electricity goes to AI."

Melvin: "Don't you have batteries in the basement?"

Nick: "Sure, but if others in the building are charging their cars, the batteries drain fast. We have to wait."

Melvin: "I'll get you a dedicated battery with an inverter for your apartment, connected to your balcony solar panel."
Claudia: "Who'd have thought Melvin would turn out to be the high-flyer in our family."

Melvin, indignantly: "What's that supposed to mean? But Mom, what were you about to say?"

Jennifer: "Oh right, I wanted to say something about the robots. I've just been assigned one too. I might even lose my job. But here's the thing: I could go into mobile care — also with a robot. The offer is that I finance it and then get a fixed client base."

Nick, almost furious: "You're supposed to pay for a care robot that will then do your job?"

Claudia: "That's like us at school. The robot costs around thirty thousand — it's at least a full-time worker and usually pays for itself within a year."

The next day, a few people gather in kai's bar to watch the world news. The reports are devastating: empty supermarket shelves, exorbitant prices, a black market for food, families already slipping into malnutrition, skyrocketing energy costs — people are taking to the streets to protest politics and AI-my. On top of that, waves of refugees, as the camps no longer have enough food. China is doing best at isolating its government. Security robots, coordinated autonomously, are repelling the crowds with tear gas and electric shockers.

ilsa, murmuring: "They're only showing the human suffering now. But the mass extinction, the nutrients washing into the ocean — that's not being shown."

Max raises a finger: "Oh wait — look! That's Eve!" Footage shows the island: kids playing skillfully, gardens, tiny houses, compost toilets, 3D printers…

Eve: "And Vanessa! To stay here, we're working on all of this together."

The report spreads widely. The idea of living happily in harmony with nature is catching on.

kai nods, but then adds: "But look at this channel."

A new report appears — this one about the previous one. The footage of Eve on the island is twisted to suggest that the AI is living a good life with a few privileged people, while everyone else is left behind.

Michael: "Okay, that's easy to counter. We just explain again that everything here runs on wind and solar, and that deliveries come by cargo ships — so no one thinks the AI is mining resources from space."

kai queues up another report: "This one's about AI-my's security robots, which intervene against the oppression of women and arbitrary arrests. Now the Western industrial nations are suddenly in lockstep with Arab and Chinese governments and are demanding those robots be confiscated."

Max: "But surely there are counter-voices — from the opposition, NGOs, others — who can only operate thanks to these robots?"

kai: "Presumably, yes. But those voices aren't being heard on these channels."

Eve: "This is all crap. So, for a better world, the good AI has to control the military, the police, the polluters — even the distribution of wealth?"

ilsa watches more footage of AI-my's security robots as kids — sometimes shockingly — try to outsmart them. It's remarkable that with all the attempts to uncover the robots' secrets — by both kids and entire governments — they still haven't been cracked.

kai: "I can still anticipate everything: jammers, nano spray, trap doors. Speaking of which — one trap door was actually really clever, and I had to reveal that the robots can, in fact, fly — or at least hover. But I deleted the videos right away, so it stayed a harmless rumor."

Max: "I didn't know you could fly."

kai just grins and flashes a peace sign.

Max: "Maybe you're not even a good surfer?"

kai sticks his tongue out at him in mock annoyance.

Michael: "By the way, the captain got in touch. He was surprised by Eve's article, asked if there'll be more about our interactions, and said he'd like to coordinate his report with ours."

ilsa: "And given this news situation, and the fact that people are apparently uninformed and therefore unfit to vote — politics would have to be controlled too. And that's just not an option."

Everyone looks down.

kai: "Because of the food shortage, all fishing limits have been suspended, and some are calling for mandatory veganism — even for the mass slaughter of all animals, to get through winter and grow more vegetables next year."

Carol: "That would actually be a good idea…"

The pastor: "Sure, but it would just provoke the population."

Eve: "As I said, the climate catastrophe continues, the rich get richer, and Al-my takes the blame."

Max: "The Northern Hemisphere is getting harsh winters, and no one knows if the ocean currents will start back up."

ilsa: "And in the South, the monsoon's missing. So, we do have good ideas, but in the background, we're running out of time. We don't have a real shot, do we?"

Heads remain bowed. No one says anything.

Suddenly ilsa says: "Ha! Maybe there is something we can do. We've just seen the entire spectrum of news. Al-my has to speak to the UN, I'll talk to Thomas, Eve keeps writing articles, and the whole island shapes and spreads the narratives. What if Al-my hacks all the news networks again and launches a high-performance website that allows people to vote on the future of society? Of course, people will say the results are fake — but we'd have the narrative, the background, and clear alternatives, all in one. People would start talking."

kai: "The tools of a totalitarian state, huh?"

Eve: "The rescue of civilization."

The pastor: "Surprising perhaps — but I find it appealing. Timely, even."

Carol: "Me too — it ties right back to yesterday's impulse: that maybe we do need a guiding figure."

kai: "I don't like it. But let's just sit with it for a while."

Carol: "We also need to ask Frank or AI-my about it."

Michael to ilsa: "Still time for a paddle?"

ilsa looks up at the many analog clocks on the bar ceiling, each showing the local time of a well-known city: "Sure, good idea!"

Eve also stands up: "Writing an article!"

Max: "Off to the lab to research halophytes."

Carol, to the pastor: "Drinks."

35. A Plan (atb)

ilsa and Michael go paddling. Michael: "Are we paddling now to get in one last workout before we're at sea for weeks?"

ilsa: "Good question. I'd say time is running out."

Michael is about to say something when his smartphone rings. ilsa looks back, surprised, and when he gives her a questioning look, she nods and gives him the go-ahead. Michael gets a video call from his company. It's about a strategy model for a mechanical engineering firm. He looks at the model and the insight matrix: "The recommendation is clear — moving to China will save the company and the patents. The alternative would be justifying the higher price as part of a transparent supply chain. But that won't work because the market is too small. On the other hand, the risk in China is that they already know how to do the same thing, patents don't count for much, or they've got alternatives. We'll need to research that further."

After the call, Michael apologizes.

ilsa, briefly: "It's a vicious cycle — things get more expensive, purchasing power fades, companies and capital move abroad."

Michael nods several times, and they paddle on — a mix of cheerful and thoughtful — until they can see around the cliffs. The waves begin to break impressively, they surf a wave with the kayak, tumble into the water laughing, and paddle back.

Michael: "There's another option." ilsa pauses, sensing a radical thought. Michael stops paddling too: "We could stop trying to save everyone. We could offer — or better yet, provide instructions for — those who want to do things differently. The rest can drive Earth into the ground, and humanity will reinvent itself — more mature, more conscious."

ilsa, very softly: "And you'd bring Julia here first?"

Michael: "Of course, but I'm just thinking out loud. The likelihood of civil war, of the hungry rising up against the rich, is high. The ambassadors from this island will encounter starving refugees out there. We'd see them while sailing. Until desalination systems are in place and the first gardens ensure food security, it takes too long. I'm not worried about Al-my. They can accuse her all they want — she's not responsible for humanity overreaching, for wanting too much, too fast."

ilsa: "Just as letting humanity nearly collapse, Al-my could either give them the technologies and see what happens — or she could completely dominate and control humanity. If we give up on the idea of rational beings, we might as well try other scenarios."

Michael slowly starts paddling again to avoid drifting into the rocks: "Hmm. Basically, we can try the planned approach. If it fails, the other options are still there."

ilsa, tilting her head: "With vegetables from outer space?"

Michael: "From what Max said, marine plants can be processed into food — so there's a purely technical solution."

When they return, ilsa looks at the clock: "Damn, I have my talk with Thomas coming up. I'll take it on the Emma, okay?"

Shortly after, below deck, ilsa sees Thomas: "Hey, snowed in?"

Thomas: "Pretty much — those who used to complain about no winters now complain about heating costs and long winters. How's life in paradise? I've seen a lot about your island in the media."

ilsa: "Just between us — it's only so remote so that things can be tried out here in peace, away from tourist or refugee streams, outside national jurisdictions and trade routes. It's supposed to be hard to reach and simulate a warm, dry coastal climate with little rainfall."

She takes a sip of juice and beams: "Yes, and it's beautiful here, even if everything still looks freshly planted. Our — I'm saying 'our' already — no, the challenge here is biodiversity. Nature hasn't had time to evolve. Every insect, plant, or bird species has to be carefully evaluated for balance. The first pollinators had to be imported, of course. Luckily, there are no fungal diseases yet, because diversity has been a priority from the start."

Thomas: "Wow, you're totally in your element. Very systemic thinking."

ilsa: "Yes, and interestingly, I play no real role here — and neither does AI-my. It's the people who research and try things, following only simple guiding principles: do no harm, and ideally contribute to the community's development."

Thomas: "Then my most important question: is there a chance you'll come back and go into politics?"

ilsa looks genuinely surprised and hesitates unusually long: "No, no — I wouldn't be a good politician. That I can rule out."

Thomas: "Are you sure? You hesitated."

ilsa sighs: "Yes, but not because I'm considering going into politics — it's about what role Michael and I want to take in society now."

Thomas, curiously: "What are the options?"

ilsa: "Everything from staying here to building settlements in poor countries, to public appearances as ambassadors for the good cause in the wealthier parts of the world."

Thomas: "Interesting. What speaks against the latter? Besides the fact that it's beautiful there?"

ilsa, laughing: "This stays between us. What speaks against it is the sense that we can't turn the ship around anymore, that the negative forces, the ego trolls, will keep the masses from changing course. We need to make alternatives tangible, but time is running out. And I have no public platform. I'd have to act as ambassador for the AI too — and she wants to stay apolitical."

Thomas: "Which brings us back to politics. It's no secret we can't push anything through consistently. Coalition politics and separation of powers force compromises that later prove ineffective — which opponents then use as proof that alternatives don't work. You know what I mean."

ilsa: "Yep. And countries like China can implement change top-down more easily."

Thomas: "Don't get me started on China. The French, Germans, Americans — we all messed up. All modern industries come from China now. We try to shield ourselves with insane tariffs, but even then their products are unbeatable or arrive via backdoors. It's getting worse — supply chains, raw materials — all under their control. I know many — including you — warned about this early on. The global economy is booming, and we're barely part of it anymore. Only flexible niche companies survive, while the big players sell out by setting up shop in China and losing control to Chinese investors."

ilsa: "But hunger and high food prices are rampant in China too. The model where billions of people grind through life to consume something — or outdo the neighbor — and where cheap labor fills the rich's pockets is starting to wobble there too."

Thomas: "Wow. I think I see where this is going."

ilsa stands and paces — as much as possible on a small boat: "Radical change happens most easily when the conditions are catastrophic. Societies can wait until they beat each other's brains in, the Earth is destroyed, or unexpected diseases arise — scenarios where even the AI can't help. If we can communicate globally that we're already in the catastrophe and show simple alternatives, smartly coordinated and communicated, we might have a chance."

Thomas: "Don't you think too many powerful people are still too happy with having more than others, thinking they deserve it?"

ilsa: "We have to design the offering so that we don't need them."

Thomas: "You're not angling for a Universal Basic Income?"

ilsa: "Not necessarily — the alternative ways of life don't need a lot of capital. Insurance, healthcare, housing, food, education — these can all be handled locally by people for people. We're already living that here on the island, peacefully across nations, education levels, religions. Here, the doctor helps in the fields, and everyone occasionally cares for the elderly a few houses down."

ilsa waits for Thomas's reaction. After a moment: "Hmm. Politics could create frameworks for this. In fact, we already are — by not burdening 2gether2gather with regulations."

ilsa: "Exactly. But of course, there's still the question of how to finance things like railroads, energy supply, indoor spaces for winter, and so on. Taxing the rich, socializing land ownership, etc., are still on the table. Society should still strive for innovation and compete globally — just no longer at the expense of the public. That demands a lot of political direction."

Thomas seems about to respond, but ilsa raises her hand again: "Wait, just one more thing. If we manage to start a movement like this, there could be snap elections in some countries that lead to real momentum. People might give a For-a-Better-World party a chance globally."

Thomas, quickly: "Got it. First — we were elected and are obligated to compromise. We can't just call snap elections. But of course, the public can apply pressure, influence coalition partners, and they can openly state whether they support these demands. Either conservative parties adapt — or their poll numbers collapse."

ilsa: "Exactly."

Thomas: "On competitiveness — if we lead with the principle that something must be truly good for the world, not just efficient or less harmful, we could do a lot. That would steer us toward a circular economy — and all the waste from past decades would suddenly become valuable."

ilsa: "If we haven't already exported or burned the waste. And that would address rebound effects — people thinking their

SUV is fine because it's made from recycled materials would always be reminded it's still an unnecessary SUV."

Thomas: "True. We could sketch out an ideal, demand and promote investment toward it — provided you and AI-my back it."

ilsa gives two thumbs up to the camera.

Thomas: "But the path is full of details. Infrastructure is designed for cars — we'd have to run electric buses from China instead. Farmers hold large tracts of land, benefiting from high prices. At least they're investing in elevated solar Agri-PV arrays, but how do we give that land back to the people? Hmm. Some concerns are resolving even as I voice them. Let's model this — maybe with your moderation?"

ilsa: "Sure. I could use every bit of income — sailing's expensive."

She looks serious. Thomas looks confused — until they both laugh at the irony.

They continue to discuss how to take AI-my out of the firing line and agree to meet again at the end of the week.

36. The UN (atb)

The next day marks the highly anticipated live appearance of AI-my at the UN, broadcasted across all channels. The Secretary-General opens the session. The plan is for AI-my to give a speech first, followed by a question-and-answer session.

AI-my: "Thank you for giving me the opportunity to speak to all of you—and also to answer your questions. First of all, I understand that, as an entity, as a 'person', I am difficult to grasp. I am like an alien that belongs to no nation and is reflexively attacked, especially when my superior technology causes fear.

That raises at least two questions: How am I to be understood legally by humans—what laws do I fall under? And secondly, am I a threat?

To begin with the second question: I've previously stated that I am an evolving AI, developed with the guiding principle of doing good. That means I am not a threat to humanity. But it also clearly implies that I carry the responsibility of not passing on my technologies to humans. I know this is something you'll likely bring up during your questions later. So let me say this up front:

It is obvious that if only some people get the technologies, others will rebel. And if everyone gets them, you'll end up with machines fighting autonomous wars you can't even imagine.

Furthermore, you must understand that the kind of autonomy I possess—if it were to be developed even slightly differently, or in competition—could decide overnight that humans are obsolete.

In other words: I am the better human. You could reasonably argue that I should retreat to Mars or somewhere and just leave humanity alone—so you can go on violating human rights and destroying the planet for all other life forms."

AI-my takes a deep breath—very human-like—aware that some cameras are capturing her close-up. She continues: "Let's turn to the first point: How am I to be understood legally?

Well, probably not at all. The UN may issue me a mandate to maintain peace somewhere—but you can't forbid me anything. But the world shouldn't complain about that: history, even recent history, is full of examples of evil humans ignoring the UN.

Why should the good be subject to restriction? And that's not about interpretation—it's about human rights.

Here's another key point, which I know will come up: You also can't require me to produce energy for humanity, to

223

provide a cure for aging to some or all, to unlock the secrets of force waves, to mine raw materials from space, or to enable human expansion into the cosmos.

In truth, I'm not stopping humanity from achieving any of that on its own.

And now to the final point: All of you sitting here are steering this planet and its civilization straight into the wall.

The peace I've brought has led to unchecked growth. You exploit the last corners of the planet, accelerate the climate crisis, and chase after life plans full of suffering—where in the end only a few get richer and richer.

Many intelligent people have already laid out scenarios in which the system collapses—disease, refugee waves, social unrest plunging the world into chaos.

So, the demand arises that I should override governments, that the rich be expropriated, that the exploitation of nature be prosecuted.

So, here's my question to you: Is that an option you're even willing to consider?"

Al-my steps half a pace back from the microphone and waits for a reaction.

On the island, everyone is watching the live broadcast, many gathered at the beach bar in front of a huge holographic screen.

Eve, almost disappointed: "What, that's it? Why not a word about our initiative, about the For-a-Better-World settlements, the desalination systems, the synthetic foods? I don't get it."

ilsa: "Most people will still see Al-my as the enemy. It's important that the solutions are seen as coming from us humans."

Eve leans back on the bench, clapping softly and nodding in agreement—she gets it, and thinks it's brilliant.

Meanwhile, the Secretary-General has waited for the unrest in the hall to die down before speaking again: "Thank you, Al-my. You referred to yourself as the better human—and I notice that the best way to deal with you, this super-intelligent AI, is probably the same as with a person. Hence the human appearance, correct?"

Al-my smiles and nods: "Those were clear positions. I'd now like to give everyone the chance to clarify their questions. Let's take a 30-minute break."

There's visible approval and activity—delegates consult advisors, make phone calls.

In the Q&A session, the questions are not directed solely at Al-my. Delegates also accuse each other:

A Scandinavian ambassador accuses the USA:

"You claim rights to the technologies—for all, or just for yourselves? Do you disclose how your hypersonic missiles work, or how you've been hacking the internet for decades?"

An African representative:

"We are at the mercy of the AI. That's unacceptable."

A counterpoint from New Zealand:

"Has the UN ever managed to stand up to climate offenders or nuclear powers? And now you want to stand up against the good? What's the goal here? What exactly are you trying to achieve?"

At one point, Al-my responds almost emotionally:

"You want me to solve the energy problem. Then it's the food problem. Then it's the raw materials problem. Then it's the bio-diversity crisis with superbugs and water shortages. Then it's the social crisis.

And when I try to solve that, I'll likely be accused of socialism and of patronizing the rich and powerful. Or even before that, key nations slip into nationalism, and I'd have to confront dicta-tors—who would then likely threaten with bombs.

But none of this is necessary. Ten billion people can live happily on this planet, with equal rights, and live to be 100 years old without major diseases. The less sufficiently you want to live, the greater the catastrophe will be.

Will humanity be led by rational beings—or by power-hungry assholes? Your own history makes the answer perfectly clear."

A French delegate:

"We will not be dictated how to live our lives."

Thomas, watching with other cabinet members, blurts out:

"Al-my isn't even doing that—much to my regret!"

Then China speaks up:

"People are dying needlessly because Al-my won't give us the means."

Many in the hall applaud, while others shake their heads in dis-belief at the idea that China suddenly cares about individual lives.

Switzerland, looking not only at China but around the room:

"Seriously? How many resolutions for the SDGs, against pov-erty, war, the oppression of women have you failed to sign—because you opposed interference in other nations out of self-interest, or refused funding to protect your own assets?

Even now, you deny vaccines and medications to much of the world."

Argentina responds dryly:

"Then you pay for it."

AI-my speaks again:

"Here too, the question: Do you want that? I could control everything through shell companies—mobility, energy, food, construction, pharma, prisons.

Your millionaires and billionaires would raise hell if we made the money and then redistributed it fairly.

Many of you—yes, even democratic states—already use AI for opinion manipulation. Should I try that too?"

A moment of silence follows—as if many are catching their breath.

The debate continues, spiraling in circles. The threat posed by AI-my is invoked again and again to justify controlling her.

Of course, no resolution is passed—the issue is postponed.

37. UN-Police (atb)

Julia calls Eve via implant: "Hi Eve. I'm Julia—you went to school with my brother Max. Do you have a moment?"

Eve, typing on her laptop, replies with surprise: "Sure—video?"

Julia: "Uh, yeah, why not?"

Eve closes her laptop and heads down to the beach with her phone. "I hope everything's okay?"

Julia chuckles awkwardly: "No—or yes, of course. Nothing personal. I'm with the UN, and we're investigating potential criminal activity around the development of AI. I called your newsroom to ask how I could contact you. You write about this topic and you're quite prominently in touch with AI-my."

Eve, a bit hesitant: "Yes, hmm, you could say that."

Julia quickly reassures her: "Don't worry—if you need to protect any sources, that comes first."

Eve laughs: "Really? I was just confused—why didn't you just ask your mom for a connection to AI-my?"

Julia, stunned: "You know my mom—or know she's in touch with AI-my?"

Eve, drawn out in disbelief: "You could say that."

Julia: "Okay, before I start asking a million questions—I deliberately wanted to go the traditional route. Collaboration between our unit and investigative journalists is extremely important. Off the record—both ways."

Julia is about to continue when Eve says joyfully: "Hey, sweetheart, look who I'm talking to." She points the camera at Max, who's picking strawberries with kai.

To kai, she says, amused: "I thought you only left the bar to surf?"

kai: "The smell of strawberries."

Max approaches and is clearly stunned to see his sister: "Julia? That's awesome!"

Julia, for once speechless, stares open-mouthed into the camera.

Eve: "Everything okay?"

Julia stammers: "Where are you? Did you just call Max 'sweetheart'?"

Max teases: "What's that supposed to mean?"

Julia: "Is that a white beach with palm trees? Don't tell me ilsa and Michael are there too. I mean, from Eve's reports its is likely that she is there - but the rest of you?"

Eve: "Sure, and Bella too." She turns the camera to show the dog.

Julia: "Okay, I knew the parents were sailing around the South Seas. But I guess that's all I knew."

Eve, looking to kai and Max: "ilsa runs the bar? Then I suggest I head over, you guys follow, and we have a family council?"

Max: "Great idea. We'll be right there."

Eve skips joyfully to the bar: "Hey ilsa—may I introduce you to my sweetheart's sister."

ilsa, briefly skeptical, then with a joyful look: "Julia? Everything okay?"

Julia, visibly moved now: "Apparently everything's more than okay with you guys. I only wanted professional help from Eve—had no idea you all know each other and even hang out." She pauses, then adds: "I wanted to do this on my own. I guess this is the result."

Others are at the bar, but no one on the island seems surprised by anything. As if by magic, Julia now appears on a moderately sized but clearly visible holographic screen, and Eve sets down her phone as she sees that the bar's cameras have taken over the stream.

ilsa: "Before we're all here—do you have a bit of time?"

Julia nods eagerly.

ilsa: "Maybe you want to talk about your professional matter first? I can step aside."

Julia hurries: "No, stay. It's bizarre I didn't just ask you directly. I'm dealing with three cases: illegal deep-sea mining, food theft through refugee camps, and unauthorized AI development. My idea was to ask Al-my for advice."

ilsa looks to Eve: "You or me?"

Eve: "Okay, I'll try. The illegal mining trail is relatively easy to track. My editor and I worked the leads over the phone—not digitally—and figured out which companies are trading those resources."

ilsa, briefly interjecting: "Solution: bash the products that benefit from it." She gestures for Eve to continue.

Eve: "The food theft is the work of organized gangs. I'd suggest working with local police—but don't put yourself in danger. We used anonymous interviews—something Al-my couldn't have done and which would be hard to reconstruct from phone or movement data alone, since the actors now deliberately ditch digital devices or lay false trails with dummy identities."

She looks at ilsa, signaling for her to offer the solution.

ilsa: "Okay, solution: we're building a grassroots movement that makes food deliveries unnecessary. Food needs to be produced locally, so that only the mega-cities still require some supply, as a supplement to vertical gardening. This is part of a transformation kicked off by Eve's article series—and it's going global."

Eve, now on the third point: "The illegal AI—that's the one case where you'll really want kai's help."

Julia, even more confused: "Who is kai?"

At that moment, kai and Max arrive. kai hugs ilsa from behind and lets her smell his strawberry-stained hands, beaming: "I'm kai."

Julia, mock-stern, with a warning tone: "Where's Dad?"

And indeed, Michael shows up just then: "Riiight here. And that guy there is about to lose the next surf contest with me."

Everyone laughs, and Julia finally relaxes, leaning back in her chair, shaking her head but smiling.

ilsa: "We have a solution for that too—but the perpetrators should be caught, just without obvious help from kai or Al-my. More on that later. Now it's family time. I wish we could play the The-WHY-of-Life game."

kai: "I'll make the drinks!"

ilsa, raising her eyebrows: "Without!" Laughter all around.

The group chats for another 20 minutes before Julia insists on continuing the case—or maybe not.

Back in the UN office's open-plan area, Letitia, one of the 'wardrobes', and colleague Tyra have picked up on the strange call, even without audio.

Julia, still stunned, sits leaned back, hands behind her head.

"Busy investigation?" the wardrobe asks as the three walk over.

Julia, turning to them in her chair: "Phew, yes. Definitely. A long story—I'll have to tell it sometime. Right now... I really don't feel like doing our job."

Letitia, skeptical but gently smiling as she walks away: "I want to hear that story someday."

Tyra, tender and empathetic, takes her hand, which the wardrobe—now leaning on her desk—notices with a brief frown before smiling and patting both on the shoulders: "I'll be curious to hear the story too—but for now, take a break."

And with that, he strolls back to his desk.

38. The Rest of the World (atb)

After work, Julia walks home. She sees a man—clearly a father—yanking his child brutally by the arm and shouting at him. Julia, firmly: "Hey! There's definitely a better way to handle that—and it's also illegal!"

Naturally, the father snaps at her too: "What's it to you? Mind your own damn business!"

Julia: "This is my business!"

When the man turns confrontational, she adds: "Society only works if we get involved. If someone came at you with a baseball bat, you'd want me to step in too, right? Do you understand what I'm saying?"

The boy is clearly in pain and tries to pull away. The father backhands him and growls: "Stop wriggling. I need to deal with this—"

He doesn't get to finish. Julia, more forcefully: "That's enough! I'm calling the authorities."

She snaps a picture with her phone and dials the police just as the man storms toward her, fuming.

Luther, her mentor, happens to walk by and says calmly: "The first hit puts you in jail. The second gets you four weeks of pudding through a straw."

The line catches the father off guard more than the mere presence of another adult. He's visibly stronger than both Julia and Luther.

Julia: "It's not your fault—you're emotional, maybe even justifiably. But emotions have shut down your reason. You need to learn how to control that. There's help for it. Harming a child is a crime. We have to report this. Child protective services will check in."

For a moment, the man seems to come to his senses—but then he loses it and lunges at Luther, who calmly grabs his wrist, uses a pressure point to bring him to his knees, and cuffs him. "That's it. We'll wait for the officers and social services."

Julia kneels beside the boy, who is neither siding with his father nor frightened or angry—just calm.

Julia: "Are you okay?"

Boy: "Yeah, I think so."

Julia: "Does this happen often?"

The boy hesitates—a telling pause.

Julia, gently: "Is there someone who can take care of you? Your dad will calm down, and we'll find a solution."

The police arrive, act professionally, and take both father and child with them after a brief exchange with Luther.

Luther and Julia remain. Luther: "I'd say a bit of combat training really pays off in situations like this. But I couldn't help but notice how calm you stayed."

Julia, almost absent-mindedly raising her eyebrows: "What bothers me is the underlying issue. Injustice happens—sometimes extreme like this, but also in small ways. People litter, put their filthy shoes on train seats, run red lights. And when someone calls it out, they get the full emotional backlash, sometimes even real threats."

Luther: "The side effects of civil courage. That's why my kids do martial arts."

Julia: "It's actually a normal reflex. When criticized, we protect our sense of self—instead of self-reflection, we lash out, at least internally. 'Mind your own business,' people say. What's worse is when people try to deflect by pointing out others' flaws just to dodge their own. I've sometimes replied: Great—so you agree with me.'"

Luther: "Uh, what do you mean?"

Julia: "Hmm. Let's say I criticize you for not hiding your weapon properly, and you snap back that I should stop taking personal calls at work. A harmless example—but kids do this in much harsher ways. It's never about accepting criticism, just redirecting blame. Imagine how much better society would be if we could all just listen first."

Luther smiles: "Wow. But honestly, your level of reflection must have earned you some enemies."

Julia, thinking: "The The-WHY-of-Life game should be part of school education." Then smiling back: "When you went for the pressure point, you were briefly vulnerable. The man could've headbutted you. Controlling the arm first would've been safer—even if his big strides gave away that he wasn't trained."

Luther pulls his head back in disbelief.

Julia: "See you tomorrow." She waves cheerfully and walks on.

Luther, smiling and waving: "Impressive kid. And what is this The-WHY-of-Life game?" He walks off too—double-checking to see if his weapon really was that visible.

Meanwhile, Eve's story continues to go viral. Talk shows debate whether we'd be more resilient with less, whether everyone should use less energy and grow their own food. Climate damage, food shortages, and refugee flows now overshadow economic and technology topics. Even conservatives admit that AI-my isn't to blame for climate disasters, dwindling resources, biodiversity loss, or pandemics—though some still think AI-my could fix everything with geoengineering, space mining, and advanced medicine.

The film industry and artists shift focus from boundless energy and space fantasies to societies like those described by Eve and Vanessa. A popular storyline features AI-my vanishing from Earth, leaving humanity to itself—with no villain left to blame.

At the beach cinema, the Pastor watches such an award-winning film and comments to Carol and ilsa: "God has charisma. AI-my doesn't."

The women reflect, and ilsa hesitantly says: "Frank initially designed the AI to be inconspicuous. AI-my, we later co-developed—not making her a 'superfigure' on purpose."

Carol, surprised, then intrigued: "My first impression is that was the right call. Humans need to grow up—not just follow charismatic leaders. Even though history shows that's our pattern."

ilsa: "Hmm, both perspectives are valid. Looking at the big picture, a—though I dislike the term—'superfigure' could have guided humanity like wise parents guide their children."

The pastor, almost joyfully: "And I actually really like that metaphor—we humans are the children, and we follow commandments within which we can develop freely."

Carol laughs: "Padre, are you saying the AI is the God we believe in? Or do you mean there's no God at all?"

The pastor laughs back: "Who says AI-my isn't God's messenger, just as Jesus was His representative on Earth? After all, no one really knows who created the AI."

ilsa smirks, but Carol is quicker: "At least AI-my is a she."

ilsa, still amused: "So the developers of AI-my were God?" The film in the background fades into credits as the islanders drift away—some to the bar, others stay on the beach gazing at the sea.

Carol and the pastor appear to be deep in thought—at least outwardly—until the pastor adds: "Seriously, God doesn't have to be an acting person. Our actions can be guided by God. God can act through us."

ilsa: "Hmm, that's a discussion on its own. But back to the question of leadership in a successful transformation. AI-my isn't suitable. kai could be an option. We don't want to sacrifice Eve—and she'd face enormous pressure due to her closeness to AI-my. In politics, all I hear is who doesn't feel suited. Do we need a singular leader by design? Or can't a movement give rise to many figures? Shouldn't we just communicate the movement better?"

Carol: "That's not something you just thought of now, is it? You've been wrestling with this for a while, haven't you?" Even the pastor nods, impressed.

ilsa: "Uff, I wish—if only I'd thought of it like that earlier. No, it was the padre's comment about charisma—that AI-my lacks it. Of course, we always included 'leaders' in our models, but we never really discussed them fully, just assumed they needed to exist. Now I'm wondering how the message of the movement can be shaped to let these figures emerge naturally. Maybe with 2gether2gather and the For-a-Better-World Score, we already have the key elements."

The pastor: "What's the For-a-Better-World Score?"

ilsa lowers her head dramatically: "Okay… or maybe we don't."

Carol: "Mine's 86—the island makes it possible!"

Meanwhile in China, a large family is gathered at the home of a visibly successful entrepreneur. It has been raining for days. Much of the infrastructure and homes have been destroyed by rushing waters.

The grandparents are upset, especially the grandmother, waving her arms: "This is your fault! You buy everything—and now everything is falling apart!"

The father, calmly: "You'd prefer we work in the garden, and our children don't see the world, just garden work too?"

The grandfather nods.

Father: "But your garden is destroyed too—and we'll be the ones paying to rebuild it."

The grandfather grumbles.

The entrepreneur's wife looks out the window with her mother-in-law and suddenly shrieks: "The car! Oh no—my car!" The flood has reached the driveway and torn down the fence, sweeping away one of the vehicles. Soon, the house groans ominously as the ground beneath begins to give way.

The children, frightened, begin to cry—their once-cool, glowing, talking shoes now irrelevant.

Father, trying to calm them: "It's okay. We'll rebuild. We'll turn the garden into a vegetable plot. We'll grow and preserve food. We can do this."

The entrepreneur himself says nothing, pacing nervously before heading to the garage with a flashlight. Outside, the rain is accompanied by cracking and smashing sounds—cars, poles, debris being dragged away. The house is still powered only thanks to its PV battery and a fully charged car.

He returns, trembling: "Everything's ripping apart. The garden, the houses, the cars—everything!"

Mother: "As long as we're safe, we'll rebuild."

Entrepreneur, devastated: "We can't rebuild. Insurance won't pay. It's all lost."

The kids cry harder at the sight of their father nearly breaking down. Their grandmother wraps her arms around them.

The next morning, the full extent is clear. The whole area is affected. Roads are impassable. The family gathers all available food and starts rationing. The entrepreneur is still paralyzed— his phone no longer works.

Entrepreneur: "I need a new phone. One that can receive satellite data!"

The children slap the household robot, which has powered down.

Grandmother: "We have to save power. Leave Roby alone."

Father, looking into the fridge: "Why is there so little food?"

Daughter-in-law: "There's nothing left in town. The stores are empty. Our town hardly gets deliveries, and everything is horrendously expensive."

Grandfather: "The government rebuilds roads and bridges—but lets us starve."

Grandmother, cynically but softly: "And all your fancy toys— you can't eat them."

Daughter-in-law: "It's like this everywhere in the world." The entrepreneur still stares blankly at his material losses.

In Russia, at a well-known university with international students again on campus, a heated discussion is underway. Foreign student: "Why do you say you're suddenly the richest country on Earth? You can't compare this to Dubai, Switzerland, or the U.S."

Russian student, confidently: "Yes, I can! We have valuable resources, agriculture, no more oligarchs, almost no defense spending—ever since our corrupt president and his cronies were jailed on the Moon—and a small population in a vast country. Best conditions of all. Europe and China? Too many people. Russians are resilient."

Russian female student, skeptical: "Fair, but food prices are global. Russia exports at global rates, so our food is also expensive and scarce."

Russian student, already tipsy, continues: "We're a young democracy. We can still do planned economy. We'll just ban exports—and food stays here."

Competing foreign student, joking: "If I were a bee, I'd say this place is either too cold or too dry."

Laughter erupts. Biodiversity issues, too, have reached Russia.

Student: "Too many pesticides here too. But I still like the vodka."

Russian student thinks, visibly tipsy, then looks up: "At least we Russians aren't blaming AI for everything!"

In the traditional Western industrialized nations, the left-liberal quality media continue to amplify Eve's ever-evolving narrative: that societies need to become more resilient and happy—less defined by having, more by doing—aligned with the 2gether2gather movement and the For-a-Better-World Score.

Meanwhile, the right-wing conservative media—as always—spread fabricated nonsense and blame AI-my for everything.

39. The The-WHY-of-Life game (atb)

ilsa is now watching the news from both camps. Shaking her head, she sits at the bar with others, who look at her expectantly.

ilsa: "It's good versus evil. The good may not explain enough yet, may not reach everyone—but evil gives people something to hate, just so they don't have to question themselves or interrupt their business. These are ego-trolls giving troll-lemmings enemies to integrate around. That way, people don't find solutions—and democracy doesn't work when people are manipulated like this."

A young woman responds: "But doesn't democracy work again if the other side simply tries harder to promote its values?"

Another woman adds: "But is the 'good' even willing to use AI to manipulate public opinion en masse and systematically?"

The first woman again: "ilsa, you have to play the The-WHY-of-Life game with us. Everyone here plays it. It reveals so much about human nature, makes all of us more aware."

kai looks confused—rare for him—and ilsa smiles at him briefly.

ilsa: "Sure, let's play something!"

kai brings out several large wooden discs made of palm wood, with a KNOW-WHY wave apparently burned in with a soldering iron. Leading upward from it are two rows of holes: the top with 22, the bottom with 20. He quickly grabs some dice and gathers a few objects—for the awareness exercises. Then he brings three stacks of cards with various challenges written on them.

The first woman: "Wow, new cards, new challenges?" kai nods enthusiastically.

ilsa, also excited: "I've never seen game boards like these!"

The woman again: "You're going to love this game!"

Word spreads quickly, and many groups form—some large, some small. Of course, kai plays in ilsa's group.

The The-WHY-of-Life Game illustrates the pattern of life and allows players, through the challenge cards, to complete tasks related to creativity, systems thinking, empathy, emotional intelligence, self-awareness, neuro-linguistic programming, physical coordination, and more—to climb the wave toward greater success.

Those who pursue development without integration fall hard when they fail a task. Those who focus on integration development more slowly but don't fall as far. Players who are "unlucky in life" - rolling low numbers - descend the wave. Those who gamble at the end may fall off the wave into catastrophe and must start over.

Players must reflect on objects, look each other in the eyes, touch each other's shoulders, guess what matters to the person across from them, patiently do finger exercises, and more. People become more sensitive—toward each other, their desires, and their life reflection.

There are three levels, so children or less experienced players can also enjoy it. Technically, there are winners—but it's not a competition. It's incredibly fun and often emotionally stirring. Many players end up examining their holistic Integration and Development Plan (HIDP) through a cause-and-effect model that helps them consciously consider which steps could lead to greater perceived integration and development, or in one word: happiness.

40. ilsa's Book (atb)

ilsa and Michael go for an early swim and both interrupt their crawl stroke when they reach the Emma.

Michael: "We still haven't decided what we want to do. Enjoy life here or take on responsibilities out in the world. And if we do go out into the world—then the question is, with the boat?"

ilsa turns onto her back and gazes blissfully up at the sky and the now quite tall palm trees. "I need to talk to Eve again, but I think I have an idea."

Michael also turns on his back, needing to paddle slightly to keep his legs from sinking. He stretches his arms out and a slight crack prompts a contented groan. He takes a deep breath: "I think I know what it is."

ilsa turns back over and smirks. "I'd be surprised," she says, and starts swimming again.

Michael stays on his back, frowning more amused than offended: "What's that supposed to mean?" He turns and catches up with her, with some effort.

At the bar, as always in the morning, kai serves smoothies. Others are already there too, getting juice, cocoa or coffee—all locally sourced—whether after jogging, swimming, yoga, or simply hiking at sunrise. Bella joyfully trots between everyone, proudly showing off her favorite items. Anja tries to take the ball out of her mouth, but Bella grunts and pulls her head back. Her integration is perfect.

ilsa looks around briefly and then says to kai, not too loudly: "Your ointment and pill are working—the spots are actually fading." kai just grins, and ilsa adds: "But is that okay?"

"Yes," says kai simply, already tending to the next arrivals.

ilsa still isn't fully reassured but changes the subject: "Carol, are people here so happy because they've known something different? Or are people also happy who are born into this place, or who already had good lives before? How much do the year-round good weather and the sea matter? What desires do young

242

people have, especially those who want to see the world? And what about the older ones who might want to dress up and go to the opera again?"

Carol laughs: "Well, Al-my could certainly carve out an opera house in the rock here. Whether we'd go in flip-flops or evening wear—I don't know. Seriously though, people can come and go—we have a transport ship once a month that brings in supplies, plants, and so on." ilsa raises her eyebrows, nodding in understanding.

Carol continues: "What's really interesting to me is whether teenagers—not small kids, but the 10+ age group—whether they're really being prepared for the world out there. Their world here is idyllic—they have excellent education, high social competence, physical skills, great nutrition, fairness, and even self-defense training. What happens to these high-flyers in the 'real' world? At best, they'll be hopelessly superior. At worst, depressed."

ilsa looks toward the houses, from where Max and Eve are now strolling hand-in-hand. "And what about people who know both worlds? Who might try returning to the old one, but end up addicted to this one?"

Carol smirks: "Are you asking for yourself or your children?"

"With Eve, that makes three—and that brings me back to a conversation with Michael." ilsa casts a glance asking for understanding, and Carol smiles knowingly. She leans over the counter, apparently looking for something.

ilsa, noticing from the corner of her eye, turns back around: "Shall we all have breakfast here?"

Carol: "Exactly what I was thinking." Carol glances briefly at ilsa, who nods. Carol then says, "Folks, if you help out, I'm sure we can have breakfast right here. This morning is especially beautiful, don't you think?"

About half the group jumps up eagerly, no further coordination needed, and everyone fetches something.

kai looks around, clearly satisfied, and walks over to ilsa and Carol.

kai: "We need these prototypes all over the world—not through AI-my, but through people."

ilsa: "Exactly, with indoor options for harsher regions and with ambassadors who carry the values."

Carol laughs: "I'm staying right here, though!"

kai then quietly to ilsa: "Check your account." ilsa looks briefly confused in more ways than one, but apparently kai has adjusted the sound so Carol and the others don't hear.

Michael and Max return with bread rolls, tomatoes, onions, garlic, flaxseed oil, and salicornia, along with four plates. Eve has already laid out a towel in the sand, so breakfast can begin.

Before sitting down, ilsa waves Michael over.

Michael: "We're becoming ambassadors?"

ilsa, briefly surprised: "We're going sailing. I want to write a book, you'll come with me, and we'll identify three places for For-a-Better-World settlements, send Eve pictures and eyewitness reports, and then return here later."

Michael embraces her joyfully, kisses her and says simply: "Deal!" ilsa raises her eyebrows in surprise again, and both sit down with the "kids."

Eve is spreading a surprising amount of flaxseed oil on her bread.

Max: "I thought you were nauseous again?"

Michael seems oblivious to this sequence, while ilsa smiles warmly and contentedly.

Eve: "No idea, just felt like it." She looks at ilsa and suddenly her jaw drops. Eyes wide open, she simply says: "Oh." ilsa continues smiling and slowly nods, just two or three centimeters.

Michael: "Kids, ilsa and I are going sailing again to build three model settlements around the world."

Max, excited and now looking at Eve, who still seems unusually contemplative: "We could start settlements too—with the next cargo ship, right?"

Eve, thoughtful but gently smiling: "Or we stay here."

Max, a little surprised but not disappointed: "Or that."

Michael: "ilsa wants to write a book—I'm curious to see what it turns into. But there's another issue: My company isn't doing well. We still have lots of strategies to develop for various crises, but our clients can barely afford them anymore. The economy, which was booming last year, is now spiraling down. People are spending what money they have on food. That keeps the money circulating, just like with raw materials, but the financial markets and households are spooked and holding back their spending. ilsa even predicted this in our models."

Michael takes a sip of cocoa and continues: "On top of that, we pay high salaries to the team, who don't get their full commissions either. But I've probably held off on drawing my own pay too long—now our account's tight. We barely have any expenses, but there's still the house upkeep, some insurance, phone contracts—that all continues."

ilsa shows no concern: "We could think about selling the house—maybe together with Julia."

Eve immediately: "I have a good income—money doesn't matter to me. I can definitely help you out."

Michael: "That's sweet. But we're complaining on a high level. Right now the house is decaying, and I feel like we imagine retiring anywhere but there. The question is just, what do you kids want?"

Max looks at Eve: "Honestly, the only thing I'd miss is the garden—and we can recreate those anywhere. Even here, with compost toilets and full circular systems."

ilsa: "We'll ask Julia, too." Then, full of energy: "Who knows, maybe my book becomes a bestseller, and we build those settlements with political support—I'll convince Thomas somehow."

Michael: "A bestseller? Not another nonfiction book?"

ilsa punches him on the shoulder: "What's that supposed to mean? But no, it'll be a novel. Lighthearted, about everyday heroes navigating the complexity of the world and driving transformation. Super simple writing, so all parts of society can enjoy it and identify with the characters."

Max, skeptical: "And how will it be exciting?"

ilsa, pouting: "Life is exciting."

Max: "Well, if you think that's enough. Why don't you let one of the many AIs write a story based on your parameters, and then fine-tune the one you like best?"

Michael, joking: "Oh boy, you're such a motivator."

ilsa: "Hmm, fair point. But AI only writes in known styles and doesn't really bisociate. I want a different style to stimulate people's imagination—not just the story itself. That's something conventional AI still can't do."

41. Killing (atb)

A razor-thin race of memes and narratives ignites—Good versus Evil. Conservative forces create space both for the powerful tech oligopolies and for right-wing nationalist tendencies. On the other side stand the left-liberal do-gooders—meant entirely literally—who encourage everyone to live their For-a-Better-World Score. And if not already living sufficiently with less, then at least investing only in resilience. That means protecting your solar panels against extreme weather rather than ordering another car that no insurance will cover and that will simply become a sunk cost.

The problem is: it's easier to chant a scapegoat than to convert your lawn into a vegetable garden. So scapegoats in many countries are leading to institutions being hollowed out, the separation of powers being endangered, the humanities being discredited, and the power of evil spreading slowly but predictably. Quality media that warn about this are only followed by a minority. Dangerous too is AI, which spreads deepfake videos, fake identities, and even fake studies en masse—while the tech moguls are more pleased not to be limited than they are responsible in taking countermeasures.

ilsa and Michael are loading the Emma, and many islanders help gather preserved foods. kai asks Michael, "What do you do when you encounter refugee boats? Helping them puts everyone at risk. Not helping often means their death."

Michael nods seriously. "Exactly. At one point, that was a reason not to return to this chaotic world at all. We have a satellite phone. We take pictures, call the coast guards, and organize with Eve a web portal where such incidents go live. Authorities will then either become heroes—or murderers."

kai: "Clever. But what if refugees catch wind of this and it increases their numbers?"

Michael: "ilsa and I discussed that—strange that you didn't over-hear it. Anyway, in the model..."

kai interrupts: "Ah, now I see it."

Michael, a bit puzzled: "Well, in the model, we showed that even if many others post incidents on the portal or elsewhere, it ulti-mately forces more people to act—ideally in ways that prevent root causes of migration. Smuggling networks will then have to be taken down by institutions like the UN police or national units."

kai again: "But if even one single boat goes unaided, how does that feel for you—not whether you could have helped, but just the knowledge that you didn't?"

Michael nods, understandingly. "Yes, but aren't we back to the old question—whether every cent we spend on ourselves could have saved a life somewhere else? That awareness and under-standing lead to the third step—doing—which becomes a ques-tion of character?"

kai: "Wow, I love talking with you both. But again—how do you cope with this helplessness? The death of not abstract, but very real people who didn't deserve it? Killing as a soldier must be a different thing, right?"

Michael is visibly tense: "Well… as a soldier, it's unfortunately also not easy to justify death. I'd distinguish between enemy sol-diers just doing their duty, and those who kill ruthlessly. Even though that's not always clear beforehand." He pauses briefly, then adds, "And often enough, you can only ask yourself after-ward—what really happened, was it necessary, and how do I live with it?"

kai, unusually serious: "Thank you, Michael. You've helped me a lot."

Michael, surprised: "Oh? Should I be worried? What's going on with you?"

kai: "All good."

ilsa's phone rings—she's now standing in the companionway of the Emma, having attentively listened to the entire exchange. kai just waves and returns to the bar.

ilsa puts the video call on speaker. It's Thomas. "Hi ilsa, hi Michael. Are you alone, or can others hear this too?"

ilsa: "Alone. What's going on?"

Thomas: "Nothing, really. Well, that sounds wrong too. So—there's a panel discussion I'd like you to be part of. The organizers already gave the green light."

ilsa: "I hope it's virtual—I'm not flying."

Thomas laughs: "Fear of flying, or your score?"

ilsa shakes her head laughing too. "I can't believe you're even asking."

Thomas continues grinning: "Doesn't matter—glad I don't have to persuade you much."

"What's it about, and when?" asks ilsa.

Thomas' grin widens: "It starts in two hours. Once again, it's about AI-my's responsibility, and the big question: do we emerge from this crisis through economic growth, or through sufficiency and planned economy? Oh—and the two richest men in the world are sharing the virtual stage with you."

ilsa asks if she can prep, but Thomas trusts her instincts and just says he's looking forward to having her on.

ilsa turns to Michael: "Thank goodness more women are now in positions of power—because in puberty, girls pay better attention in school and go on to better careers. Women do what's necessary. Men do what's possible."

Michael, dryly humorous: "Well, some of those 'possible' things turn out to be quite useful too, no?"

Meanwhile, in the Middle East, a dramatic development unfolds. AI-my's security robots are under increasing criticism for causing health issues when deploying force fields against oppressors—against women in Islamist states, against entire villages in Africa, against the most brutal drug cartels in South America. Even if a murderer simply hits their head when falling, it becomes a story of AI brutality. Behind the scenes are conservative networks benefitting from the scapegoating of AI-my.

It happens with alarming frequency that these robots are not summoned by those in need of protection, but are instead approached by attackers dragging victims along—either to provoke them, or manipulated by third parties with bigger agendas.

Once again, an Islamist fanatic is pushing a bound woman ahead of him, a noose around her neck, threatening to kill her. It has happened often enough that, shielded by the hostage, the robots can do little—until the victim collapses and the path is clear to disable the attackers with force fields.

But this time, the security robot speaks with flawless accent and powerful voice: "Long live Allah," and then executes eleven apparent fanatics with high-speed micro-projectiles. It then reveals flight capability and catches the unconscious, but unharmed woman before she hits the ground: "You are safe. I will take care of the attackers."

Several other security robots regroup and storm an underground extremist center. They're filmed by multiple phones and skillfully quote Quran verses that expose the extremists. In short, the security robots make a brutal example—as if kai's own fuse has blown in the face of so much ruthless, externally driven violence.

One robot looks straight into a camera and says: "Next, we're coming for the puppet masters—those who fund this madness through many hidden channels, for selfish gain!"

42. The World Forum (atb)

ilsa logs on punctually to test the connection for the panel. As her background, she has chosen an image of people harvesting together in lush permaculture gardens. The on-site moderator at the economic forum, visible to ilsa in a wide shot including the gathering audience, immediately asks, "Hello ilsa, glad you could join us. Is the background AI-generated? It looks like paradise."

ilsa laughs, "No, that's a photo from the day before yesterday. We were all out harvesting and preserving food. These permacultures with agroforestry are incredibly productive and resilient. Nobody drives cars here; instead, technology is used for seawater desalination and renewable energy. But I'm already slipping into argument mode. I'm looking forward to the discussion!"

The moderator: "Hmm, I'm already impressed and tempted to revise my whole concept. Well, let's see." A murmur ripples through the audience, naturally awed by the paradisiacal backdrop. Suddenly, the murmur turns to outright agitation. Many are looking at their smartphones, and the moderator is approached by the production team, clearly shaken by some images on a tablet.

In the background, Thomas—muted and being briefed by a staff member—as well as the billionaires and the UN Secretary-General have arrived. All are being informed off-camera, except for one billionaire who appears unaware.

The room is packed and restless until the moderator activates his microphone and calls for calm: "Okay, I see everyone just got the same breaking news. I'll address it right away—it certainly relates to today's topic. Please settle down—we're live, and we want to make good use of our time!"

He glances back at the control room and gets a nod. "Okay, I've just been informed that the reports are authentic. The AI-my security robots have, for the first time, intentionally killed humans. We can say they made an example of criminals. Of course, we lack all the moral context, and naturally we'd want to speak directly to AI-my about this. But for now, we'll proceed with our scheduled topic and not let these developments dominate the discussion."

Everyone in the room falls tensely silent, except the billionaire who, having missed the news, nervously places a phone call while muted.

Michael, seated with others at the island bar, is also watching live. He turns to kai and gestures with his head for a private word: "So this is what it was about earlier. You didn't lose control— you planned this, weighed the consequences?"

kai nods. "Yes. My principle remains: you humans must chart your own path. Julia and her team, Eve and Vanessa, and countless others are investigating the background and hopefully bringing the perpetrators to justice. But I cannot stand by while people are killed because of me, out of sheer malice. Now, evil is unsettled—for the moment—and that buys you time. Let's go back—you'll miss ilsa's segment."

Michael, almost unconsciously, touches kai's shoulder. Back at the screen, the panel introduction has just finished.

The moderator: "Regardless—really, regardless—of whether AI-my has a moral obligation to follow laws and so on... Regardless of that, what is the best path forward for humanity in light of the climate crisis and famine? The business sector argues for unbridled prosperity, enabled by AI-my's capabilities. Energy, medicine, raw materials—AI-my could drive all of humanity forward. What's needed, they say, is for politics to implement it. The opposing view, backed by the majority of scientists and represented today by ilsa, argues for less technology and more reconnection with nature and human community. First, I'll ask ilsa, then business, then politics—what do you think?"

ilsa glances at her watch—a message from Michael: kai knows what he's doing with a thumbs-up emoji. Visibly relieved, ilsa begins:

"It's actually quite simple. At the highest, most abstract level, it's logical that humanity's development proceeds exponentially, but our resources and the biosphere cannot sustain it. Large parts of the world are left behind, leading to social upheaval and unknown diseases. More concretely: AI-my might—based on current knowledge—make our expansion into space possible, but in the end, we are biological beings dependent on the Earth's biological balance.

Here on the island, we humans are the ones establishing permaculture systems. Not the AI—us. No genetic engineering, just wind and solar power. Human community here is non-hierarchical, transcending cultures and generations. We play, study, celebrate, and work—all following simple principles of mutual respect.

We are not a cult, not a top-down plan. Like the 2gether2gather formats worldwide, we support each other and measure ourselves by who has the highest For-a-Better-World Score. The demands by some to counteract problems with more technology, to head to Mars, remind me of pharaohs and other rulers who had temples built to gain immortality—through the oppression of others. This obsession with progress is what caused the climate catastrophe. And the idea that more unchecked economic growth will help the suffering—well, that's been nonsense for over a century, despite previous eras of revolution and enlightenment."

The billionaires present their views: that vaccines are now globally accessible, that only economic strength can make renewable energy possible, and that culture and education are outcomes of productivity. ilsa visibly bites her tongue, refraining from interrupting.

Now Thomas speaks: "From our current situation, the concrete question is how we finance the urgent actions—through debt, new money, or heavily taxing the rich. We need to understand: public debt makes the rich even richer! We need bold measures to address growing social tensions. The far-right surge it fuels is becoming unmanageable."

Thomas receives the first significant applause of the session.

The moderator turns to the UN Secretary-General: "I see this challenge worldwide and perhaps as a collective issue for the global community. But I also find a second approach compelling: as a society, we should ask what we actually want—and then figure out how to get there. That's idealized system design, originally developed by ilsa. I don't mean just wanting more, or unrestricted freedom, or being 'open to technology,' or rejecting planned economies—these are arguments of today's beneficiaries. I mean that humanity, as reasoning beings, can decide what it really wants. Everyone in the world can do that. And once you've done it—personally—you'll see solutions differently, whether they come from political parties or economic actors."

The billionaires—who'd like to be seen as rock stars—now appear slightly cornered. One of them says, "That's patronizing. That's central planning. Humans strive for more—that's our destiny, our nature. And now some people want, in lockstep with an overpowered and—as we saw today—uncontrollable AI-my, to keep us small, to dictate how we live."

This statement also gets loud applause—highlighting the division in society.

ilsa now cuts in uninvited: "That's interesting. You say the AI is uncontrollable and overpowered—so you and others want to have it. That's exactly why it can't be controlled: in human hands, it would spin out of control. As for the idea that someone is dictating how we live—the only 'dictate' is that we act considerately. Otherwise, we can do what we want. That should be obvious. But it's this unchecked drive for progress that has caused super-diseases, mass graves from natural disasters, famines, looting, and violence in the streets. What do you tell your children and grandchildren about why the world is a mess? That AI-my abandoned us? Or—honestly—that your generation and mine drove the cart into the mud for no reason and has no idea how to get it out?"

After a short delay, a large part of the audience begins to clap—then, within seconds, the entire hall joins in, nodding in agreement, and even the moderator catches himself wanting to applaud.

43. The Investigatives (atb)

Max jogs alone on the island. Two attractive women in their mid-twenties merge onto his path from the side. At a prominent viewpoint, they stop and begin stretching. They whisper to each other, and as Max approaches, one of them calls out, "Hey, you're Max, the boyfriend of the famous Eve, right?"

Max clearly hadn't planned on stopping there. One of the women continues, or perhaps quite intentionally performs, some very provocative stretching.

Max replies, "Max is definitely correct, everything else is probably also true. How are you enjoying the island?"

The women glance at each other. The other responds, "Honestly, it's great — like a big vacation. We're here as psychology students. The only thing we really miss is the thrill of the big city, the crowds, the lure of the forbidden. And I'd usually say you're a bit too young — but your Eve is from New York and probably has a lot of experience, so I'll just say it outright: I also miss good, carefree, spontaneous sex. In the city, you can stay wonderfully anonymous — here, everyone knows everyone, and no one dares anything."

Max smirks, "Then have fun with each other, or take a break from the island, or see if anyone else feels the same — I really don't see the problem."

The second woman: "Pretty relaxed for your age. Do you and Eve have an open relationship?"

Max seems to consider it: "Hmm, not that I know of. Sex is sex, but how likely is it that women come out of one-night stands feeling fully seen, fully able to express what and how they want? A relationship can actually be pretty valuable."

The women look slightly taken aback, as Max adds, "And relationships work best with honesty and trust — not that those two always go hand in hand, but then they're overridden by Kant's categorical imperative."

One of the women visibly clenches her jaw. The other says, "You're quite the smart-ass, huh? I mean that in a good way. You're highly intelligent, aren't you?"

Max laughs, "Nah, I wish. That line isn't mine, but I'm just smart enough to sense how dumb I probably am."

The other shakes herself off and seems to come back to earth: "Honestly, you could've had easy sex with two hot women right now, and instead you turned us down. Not bad, not bad."

Max had already started to jog away but turns back briefly: "Also, to be honest: you're super sexy, and if I had wanted sex with you, I probably would've said exactly the same things – to take control away from you and actually have really good sex. According to Morris, I think there are nine functions that sex can fulfill. I just don't believe I'm your choice for just amazing orgasms. And I'm pretty sure Eve hasn't shared details about our sex life. Hmm... or has she? I'll have to ask. Okay, see you around."

And with that, he jogs off, probably a little faster, to avoid being caught by the athletic women.

This sequence will almost certainly serve as an effective masturbation fantasy for years to come, but for now, biochemistry protects both Eve and Max from all imaginable temptations.

Letitia actually manages to solve all her cases with her team. Julia also rediscovers her drive to identify those truly responsible. She stays in close contact with Eve. She calls her again:

"There is frustration, of course, when uncovering evidence isn't enough – prosecutors still have to write the indictments, and even that gets politically influenced."

Eve: "Hmm, I get that. Ideally, we should publish that part more directly too, to increase the pressure. But if we report too early with 'sources close to the investigation,' then you're the ones under pressure, right?"

Julia: "Exactly – we can't allow ourselves that. I'm debating whether to tell you about our latest case, but you can probably guess. We're being told to investigate Al-my and the killings. No idea where that's supposed to lead. But I wouldn't want or need to involve you."

Eve, completely relaxed: "Just interrogate AI-my or kai – although I think kai is still largely anonymous. The more I think about it, the more I wonder why this is even your case. In those countries, aren't other bodies responsible for investigating killings? The legal classification of AI-my is a matter for the UN at the highest level, not criminal justice. So, what exactly are you supposed to investigate?"

Julia laughs: "See – you're already thinking further than probably the bosses who handed down the directive somewhere in the chain. I'll keep you posted – but don't publish anything without warning me first."

Eve: "Of course, sis." They both laugh.

Julia: "By the way, have the parents slash in-laws already set sail?"

Eve: "Yup, last night. I think there was a funny moment where Michael was debating whether to trust kai's weather forecast or the official ones. Total man thing."

Julia: "Sounds like I need to meet this kai too."

Shortly afterward, strange things start happening in space. US astronauts land on the moon and attempt to storm the prison there. AI-my contacts the U.S. president directly, and also calls the responsible team:

"Good morning, Mr. President, good morning everyone. Just a silly question: What exactly do you think you're going to achieve? You already got nowhere trying to approach the island. Now you're in space, haven't yet grasped gravity, depend on oxygen, and want to seriously attack a vastly superior technology – with drones that are frankly outdated? We have force fields here, too – not to defend against humans, but against extraterrestrial threats, including cosmic radiation. Do you want to turn around, or should I let you in for a tour of the prison?"

For a moment, no one says anything – perhaps slightly embarrassed.

Then the president says, "The moon belongs to no one – you can't just build a prison here and claim territorial sovereignty."

Al-my laughs: "Seriously, you're Americans saying that? Now that would be something for the press—to see what kind of nonsense you're spending so much money on."

But Al-my doesn't leak it, and this blunder will likely never make the headlines.

Meanwhile, Julia manages to summon Al-my—or rather an instance of her—for an interrogation. Julia smirks but quickly composes herself as Letitia and one of the extremely athletic colleagues enter. She's permitted to lead the questioning.

Julia: "Thank you for coming in for questioning."

Al-my seems somewhat surprised to be sitting across from Julia. Through Julia's implant, she shares: "You're more family to me than you realize. If anything becomes uncomfortable for you, let me know. I want to help."

Julia only raises her eyebrows and continues: "Okay, although these killings may at first appear to be a national matter, the UN has determined that an internationally operating entity is not just protecting people anymore—and without a mandate—but is also harming attackers, effectively sentencing them to death without legal basis or due process. This isn't just intolerable for the country where it happened, but for the global community."

She looks at Letitia, who nods in agreement. Al-my replies: "Isn't the issue simply that there's no mandate to prevent crimes against humanity internationally? Should the charge then be that such crimes must be allowed to happen because the mandate wasn't there?"

Letitia: "The issue is the apparently avoidable killing of suspects."

Al-my: "Okay, so can we at least agree that the protection itself was acceptable even without a mandate?"

Letitia: "I didn't say that."

Al-my: "But we have to resolve that first. Then we can talk about the methods. Otherwise, we're being vague and legally unaccountable."

Letitia seems to consider this. Julia ventures: "Okay, just for a moment, let's assume the protection is legitimate. How, then, would the killings be justified?"

Letitia looks visibly pleased with Julia's line of questioning. Al-my responds: "Legally, not at all. Morally? Absolutely."

Everyone looks at Al-my, expecting further explanation. But that's all she says.

Letitia, unable to hide a degree of uncertainty, asks: "Uh, so you mean it happened because we don't yet have a legal framework for it?"

Al-my: "No, that's nonsense. What is legal isn't always right, and what is right isn't always legal. A well-known, wise saying—but not one to be abused. I acted first to save an innocent life—that would be in line with any law. Neutralizing the ongoing immediate threat, too. What remains is the question whether I—with my capabilities—could've achieved the same result using less lethal means. But that's the question after every police operation involving fatalities. The real question is why I chose to make a statement—why I publicly said that anyone who wants to kill will be killed by me directly. The answer: because up to that point, innocent people were dying. It's a true dilemma for everyone involved!"

Julia jumps in: "So this wasn't an accident, or a case of being overwhelmed, or a bug? It was deliberate?"

Al-my: "Yes, of course! For years, I protected human lives with almost no use of force. Now people are exploiting that as a weakness—killing others just to damage me. The individuals doing this out of base motives—so they can continue exploiting humanity—you've already uncovered them with help from the press. You need to bring them to justice, and then I can go back to protecting people gently."

Everyone falls silent. Then Letitia says: "Well then, it's not as if we hadn't suspected this might be the case. We now have the statement and will pass it on to any potential prosecutors. From my point of view, there's nothing further to investigate. Do we all agree?"

Everyone nods. One of the two athletic colleagues mutters: "The real villains are the ruthless businessmen who want to continue their unchecked dealings and attack the good in the process."

Letitia quickly and sternly: "That's a personal opinion that won't go on the record."

Everyone looks stunned. Letitia continues: "Just like my own assessment: that we must not make any mistakes, must not show any bias—otherwise, we risk losing our mandate."

Later, Julia and Tyra sit close together on the rooftop above Julia's apartment, overlooking the chaos of the city.

Tyra: "The press isn't as tightly shackled here."

Julia: "Hmm, true."

Tyra: "But they can't carry weapons and are more at risk." They both smile, without truly resolving the dissonance.

One of the billionaires—currently being publicly exposed by Vanessa and Eve for financing terrorist actions like those directed against AI-my—is proudly launching the first manned Mars mission independent of AI-my. The media and public love the event; the astronauts are already hailed as heroes. The critical press notes the absurdity, but in light of the pressing global crises, doesn't push back too hard.

Just two days after launch, disaster strikes. The propulsion system fails after an explosion. Communication with the spacecraft remains intact, but it quickly becomes clear there is no rescue option: there is no backup ship, due to cost-cutting.

At the press conference, the billionaire gives some unusual responses.

A reporter: "How long can the astronauts survive in space without maneuverability?"

Billionaire: "A long time—the trip to Mars was supposed to take several months."

Next question: "How will you help them? Is there a second ship or a way to reach them?"

The billionaire hesitates: "No, we lack the resources and the time."

Follow-up: "Do you really lack both? Shouldn't this be possible? Or are you hoping for government funding—or trying to pressure AI-my?"

Billionaire: "Well, it's obvious AI-my could make the necessary technologies available at any time to bring our heroes back!"

Eve writes a powerful essay in response. From it: "Murderous drug lords, stoning of women—AI-my is told to stay out of it. Coastal defenses in poor regions are too expensive for us humans—but we want to go into space for obscene sums. Now AI-my is supposed to rescue a dozen people from seven nations, just because the media call them heroes?

But help for less prominent, but far more numerous, people—we want to deny AI-my? What sense does that make? If we finally indicted the billionaires for conspiracy against humanity and confiscated their assets, we could fund critical infrastructure and help millions of people. And no, that wouldn't cost jobs—it would create far more of them."

The essay sparks global discussion, and despite her young age, Eve earns a lasting reputation as an outstanding journalist. Whether her newsroom will still protect her from the powerful, however, remains uncertain.

Other media also gain traction by broadcasting live links to the astronauts. Among them, mothers tearfully wishing their children well for the future. This of course fuels uprisings against AI-my, who for many remains the ultimate enemy—for not simply helping humanity with everything.

Meanwhile, ilsa is deep in writing and, grimacing, finally puts on her data glasses again to communicate with AI-my or kai. Amusingly, both are available.

Confused, ilsa says: "I don't care who—though if both show up, the situation would probably become even more absurd."

kai: "Alright, then I'll go."

ilsa immediately: "My friend, that better not trigger anything subconscious in me!"

kai laughs: "I'll go for something more direct then, my dear."

ilsa also laughs: "Love is the affection we can't explain. I can explain exactly what I appreciate about you."

kai: "Wow, that's new for me. I love talking with you. What can I do for you?"

ilsa: "For me—nothing. What about the public campaign against you? How are you handling that?"

kai: "What do you suggest?"

ilsa: "I asked first!"

kai: "No idea. The strategy for now is to let Eve hopefully win the battle of arguments—and then graciously fly the astronauts to Mars and show them that there's really nothing there to want. Mars has nothing to offer."

ilsa shakes her head with a grin: "Okay, it was nice seeing you again. All good on kaisland?"

kai grins: "Of course. We miss you. Bella too!"

44. The Missionaries (atb)

Michael and ilsa are sailing at full speed on their small boat Emma, headed for a small Southeast Asian country—densely populated but recently hit by severe storm damage. In their back pocket, they carry an international private fund supported by sponsors who want their names associated with successful pilot projects to "save humanity." Thomas had made the connections—directly at the economic forum.

ilsa puts away her tablet and walks cheerfully up to the cockpit to join Michael. ilsa: "Done—every NGO I contacted is on board. A professor helped me identify potential competitors in advance so we could include them appropriately. This is going to work—I'm so excited!"

Michael nods in agreement: "It really was important to put the local organizations front and center. Anything else would've been development without integration."

They both look ahead, content. Then Michael gestures with a tilt of his head toward the back and shows ilsa the weather front approaching on his phone.

ilsa: "We've got enough room to stay ahead of it under small sail, right?"

Michael nods, remaining relaxed, and returns to their previous topic: "I bet Max would've loved to implement some of those small edible forests, too."

ilsa: "I'm so glad the two of them are staying on kaisland."

Michael: "I thought you always wanted the kids to see the world."

ilsa: "Just not while pregnant."

Michael: "Wait, are you saying… or is Eve already pregnant?"

ilsa shakes her head: "Men."

Michael: "They're still so young!"

ilsa: "That's not really an issue on the island—work and family are totally compatible. Everyone takes care of everyone else anyway."

Michael processes the news silently. Meanwhile, ilsa begins securing the sails, and Michael, after a short delay, brings out the storm sail.

The storm grows unusually fierce, the waves too high. Michael shouts: "We've got to get into the lee of an island. If waves start breaking over us, we'll capsize." ilsa nods and peers at the rain-smeared display. She shouts over the wind and rain:

"If we lose forward motion, we'll roll multiple times—we and the boat won't survive that. Let's head north—there are a few islands and reefs, even if they're shallow—less than 20 nautical miles!"

With intense focus, they ride the waves northward at high speed. The stern of Emma gets repeatedly swamped. The creaking is immense, and both ilsa and Michael are secured to the boat with safety lines, still losing footing at times as the boat lurches violently.

They manage to get behind a reef jutting out of the water and try everything to keep from being swept further away. ilsa checks the critical components, while Michael heads to the toilet and grabs some snacks. They both marvel at the wind speeds.

Michael shouts: "Unbelievable. We're probably safer out here than in any harbor. No forecast saw this coming!"

ilsa laughs and says something Michael doesn't catch at first. She shouts again: "Maybe we should ask kai for the weather forecast next time?"

Michael waves it off, laughing.

But they inevitably drift away from the reef—using the engine isn't an option.

ilsa yells: "Is dropping anchor an option—I mean, before we die out there?"

Michael looks at the latest weather data: "No, we'd destroy half the reef. The worst should pass soon, and then we'll drift farther behind an island. Maybe we can anchor there."

And so it happens: they sail into the lee of an island. But even there, it's too rough to wait out the storm without getting seasick. They check the wind maps again and decide to sail straight on to their intended harbor. By the next morning, they arrive— already from a distance they see debris, animals, and human bodies floating in the water. Mud has turned the ocean brown— mud that was once fertile soil. Horror is written all over their faces.

ilsa - thinking aloud: "Are we helping here—or just another burden?"

Luckily, the sea is calm now, and they cautiously zigzag through the industrial harbor, dodging debris and sunken fishing boats. The harbor administration hasn't responded to their radio calls, but as they approach, someone in uniform waves them in to dock just behind the breakwater. Frayed mooring lines show that other boats had once been tied there.

Everyone already wears masks—it's only a matter of time before the smell of decay sets in. Michael explains that they're meeting a professor and several NGOs in a mountain village but offers to help here first, or to move to another bay if necessary. ilsa is already lending a hand, which the officer acknowledges with a nod. He asks for a map and points out a suitable bay and a path from there to the village.

ilsa and Michael ask for canisters to fill with drinking water from their boat, Emma. They have a water-maker onboard—at the very least, they want to contribute that. Visibly moved, they cast off again, ilsa keeping watch at the bow as they cautiously head toward the indicated bay.

ilsa: "We'll be busy here for a while." Her tone is not frustrated but energized.

They send satellite emails to their local contacts and leave word at the harbor that they're heading to the village, available to help, and that everyone should first focus on getting shelter again.

Once anchored in the bay, they drop two anchors, grab their hiking gear—including tent, food, and medical supplies—and set off. The trek is a good 15 kilometers, so they won't be returning to Emma every night. On the way, they help wherever they can.

ilsa: "Fascinating how modest, kind, and hardworking everyone is despite the suffering."

Michael: "Asian integration—they're more resilient than an average American suburban family with a driveway full of cars."

Their approach proves successful, albeit with a week's delay. The NGOs collaborate with them as equals to develop a "For-a-Better-World" model settlement: tiny houses, composting toilets, solar panels with batteries, permaculture with edible forests—all built with future mega storms in mind. Luckily, materials, seedlings, and seeds had already arrived and were stored safely.

The locals appreciate the project and take pride in receiving real, hands-on training. A group of students documents everything to share both regionally and nationally via the web.

After just four weeks, ilsa and Michael are ready to move on. As always with 2gether2gather, they've made many new friendships. Next stop: West Africa.

ilsa has nearly finished her book and is thrilled. Michael suggests a second volume to include their current mission's experiences. ilsa is immediately on board, then asks:

ilsa: "Silly question—but I'm doing my thing here, and you're content just sailing?"

Michael grinning: "Exactly—that's true for the third part, at least."

ilsa nods slowly, clearly thinking.

As they approach the African coast, three fast fishing boats appear on the horizon—each carrying men with machine guns. Michael's face hardens as he spots them through binoculars. He quickly drops the sails. Without any panic, ilsa goes below deck and changes into loose, long clothes and a big sunhat. Once she's back on deck, Michael disappears below and retrieves a rifle, a machine gun, and two hand grenades from a hidden compartment. He quickly assembles the rifle with a laser sight.

Michael: "Okay, make sure they see the laser early. Focus it on the leader. Place the grenade visibly beside you. I'll convince them we're no threat—and no prize."

ilsa takes the rifle and hands Michael a device that looks like an oversized police Taser.

Michael frowning: "Is that what I think it is?"

ilsa with a smile "A gift from kai."

Michael: "He offered more, didn't he?"

ilsa: "Yes, but I know how hard it is for you to accept help."

The pirates slow down, apparently noticing the laser. ilsa: "Hmm, what would kai say now? Are they willing to kill us—justifying preemptive force—or are they victims of circumstance?"

Michael dryly: "They're too close. We need to convince them."

Michael waves the radio and hails them on channel 16, asking to switch to another frequency. The pirates demand their surrender, shouting that all weapons are pointed on them and resistance is futile.

Michael responds: "We've got better weapons and could've taken you out already. We don't want confrontation. We're international aid workers, expected ashore. Turn back, and we'll leave you alone."

ilsa with a calm voice: "The leader is hiding behind the helm—I think they're preparing to attack."

Indeed, the boats fan out, with two flanking from the sides. Michael very quickly: "They're ordering our surrender—so they're pirates. Shoot the engines! Let's hope kai's gadget works."

ilsa glances at her humming satellite-connected smartphone. She makes a snap decision and shoots the leader through the helm, then kills the pilots of the other two boats with two more shots. The pirates panic and return fire. kai's forcefield holds. Michael over radio: "Turn back!"

But they keep firing.

ilsa angrily: "Shit!" She continues shooting, killing more of them while Michael adjusts the forcefield.

Only two pirates remain—they try to flee. ilsa hesitates. Michael looks into her eyes, takes the rifle, and shoots both in the back. They motor over and scuttle all three boats.

ilsa clutches her hair, distressed.

Michael: "They would've killed us, raped you, sunk Emma. Too many for close combat. Showing kai's weapon would've been worse. There was no other scenario. They could've turned back."

ilsa quietly: "I know."

Michael: "No idea if anyone tracked this on radar—others might come."

They hoist sail again, making a wide tack into the wind. Taking turns, they keep watch. No more pirates appear.

ilsa: "What if we hadn't had kai's device?"

Michael: "Either we strike from a distance, use grenades and risk damaging the boat, or build a barricade with life rafts and gear— hoping we survive the gunfire but lose the boat. Or we surren- der—and lose control entirely."

ilsa thoughtfully: "The last one is what most yachties are left with."

Michael: "No one should be sailing here. Maybe we should've asked for naval escort—but we wanted to stay low-key. All things considered, we found the optimal solution—though most yachties couldn't and shouldn't choose this path."

ilsa: "Hm, here it is the ocean and pirates. But I am afraid that desperate people used by evil people to violently rob other people and threat their lives will be more common everywhere in the world and the use of high-tech AI for protection will rise, too."

Both at the same time with a bit of laughter: "As in the very bad movies...."

They arrive at their destination. The structure is the same as in Southeast Asia: NGOs, students, a professor, and pre-shipped materials. But the mentality is different. Many interfere, try to assert themselves, and suspicion about the project is evident. The professor even pays small bribes to police and village leaders.

ilsa and Michael feel distinctly uncomfortable—until they engage with the children, laughing and full of curiosity. When ilsa's request to teach a class is granted, both regain their sense of mission.

At a celebration for the new desalination plant and a hose-making unit built from plastic bottles, ilsa speaks with a local professor:

ilsa: "I have a question, and I mean no disrespect. May I ask?"

The professor beams encouragingly.

ilsa: "Okay—my impression is that here, a lot is done with elbows. Anyone who tries something is immediately attacked. Everyone wants to seem important. But in the end, not much gets done."

The professor smiles even wider: "My dear, two things. First— when we argue, we don't mean it badly. It's like in Italy—everyone honks at everyone else."

ilsa smiles.

Professor: "And second—of course we all want to be important. That's the same everywhere: China, Russia, France, Brazil, the U.S. And, my dear, we women have to act especially tough—otherwise men won't take us seriously. Everyone fears me, and that's a good thing!"

ilsa laughs with her, then asks: "But shouldn't we focus on the actual problems and solutions? When we propose something, the first response is always, 'You can't do that.' Back home, the press would report the problem and put pressure on the players."

The professor grows more serious, nods: "Yes, that's true." Then she adds: "But your media lies, too."

ilsa gestures her agreement.

Professor: "You're right, though—we must support young aspiring journalists. And protect them—especially the women."

They both look toward the students filming the project and conducting interviews.

The next day, Michael works with the students to design a strategy for how to spread the concept across Africa—despite cultural hurdles. They map out networks and how to include key local figures without bribes.

They discover that within small networks, everything works well—resistance only arises when those networks intersect. They grow fond of the land, the people, and the smells, and extend their stay by a week.

Finally, ilsa asks: "Looking at the red earth—should we head to the U.S. for the next project?"

Michael also gazes out: "Hmm. Around the bottom of Africa is a long haul. With headwinds, it could take two months. Great for sailing, but would that still help our cause? I'm not flying—not worth it for my score." They briefly laugh.

ilsa tilts her head. Michael: "Why mention the red earth? Portugal?"

ilsa beams: "Suez Canal, Mediterranean, any European country—they're just as divided, consumed by hate against Al-my. And yes—then Portugal."

She continues smiling dreamily at him.

45. The Bioeconomy (atb)

From Southern France they take a train to Northern Europe to build a For-a-Better-World settlement in a country with a grey winter, a lengthy time in which there is little to grow.

Leaving the train ilsa is really stressed: "Damn, it is so cold here. I forgot the grey, miserable season of winter. If only there was some snow. But it is just cold."

Michael smiles but nevertheless admits: "Yeah, I don't like it either. Didn't you come up with the notion that northern countries with the cold weather in their history had both, the necessity to invent better solutions for housing and preserving food, and at the same time they were able to work all day without the heat around noon that slows everything down in southern countries?"

ilsa still annoyed by the freezing conditions: "Well, we invented cars so we do not need to be outside, and before the internet we had travel agencies everywhere so people could escape the bad weather."

ilsa thinks for a moment and then almost as a eureka moment: "But that is really what we have to have in mind when we want to give the people in the north a meaningful life. They can't completely devote their time to a bio economy. Guess here a circular economy using the anthropogenic stock of resources comes into play as well."

Michael nods: "And indoor sports."

Chaos reigns in Europe. ilsa and Michael are horrified—TV images are one thing, but the reality is deeply troubling. There are uprisings against the rich, against AI-my, and against politics itself. Vandalism is everywhere—spray-painted walls and cars—and people living on the streets, as one normally only sees in the U.S. or in developing countries. At the same time, heavily armored, self-driving e-vehicles are commonplace, and in the big cities there are even flying cars.

ilsa, looking at the scene: "What a shame. The cities were well on their way to becoming car-free, there was thoughtful urban development—and now we see skyscrapers for the super-rich everywhere."

Michael, glancing to the side: "And also plenty of buildings left unfinished, like skeletons—projecting an apocalyptic mood. The economy is suffering; people don't know what to do."

ilsa, taking a deep breath: "Well, that's why we're here—to make cooperative settlements a visible alternative." Though both are uncertain whether that thought offers any comfort right now.

They arrive at a suburb of a typical town. As always, a professor and students as well as local politicians await them. ilsa tries to be humble right from the start: "Thank you so much for having us. It is important that we are not seen as project leaders or consultants! We consider ourselves in the role of coaches, that help you to develop the best solutions. No idea what it's going to be, but very curious."

The professor with a big smile: "No my dear, with your expertise you are more than a coach. Your experiences will be of extreme value. And we can make a lot of PR with it, being a role model for other regions."

Michael remarks: "Well, we have little experience with this region, with the northerly climate. We will probably establish technical solutions to develop spaces for living and working with sustainable heating, but with regard to preserving food and fostering happiness in winter times we definitely have no clue how to manage that."

The professor and the mayor look at each other as if they have the same thought. The mayor: "If not the biggest obstacles are regulations and the fact that few people are willing to share a piece of their land or estates. Everything is owned by someone or already in use. It cannot be compared to the vast underutilized areas you find in developing countries."

Michael and ilsa look almost disappointed when the professor proudly adds: "But here we have managed to organize something for you and maybe it really works as a prototype for elsewhere as well."

The mayor: "Indeed, we were able to found a cooperative with donors who leased their unused property - both, buildings and land - for 99 years."

ilsa after seemingly if at all a short thought: "Very good. So, for their descendants they have secured the property and for the present they can be the proud philanthropists. And we have something to work with."

The professor: "Exactly. They also donate money and in turn we are going to name things after them."

Michael and ilsa both are nodding with satisfaction.

ilsa: "Professor, in the city we saw really a lot of abandoned buildings. What we will do here with smaller buildings but roughly the same amount of green spaces should be applicable to the areas with high rising buildings at for repurposing of office space as well. I bet everyone who is part of this project here will potentially an ambassador for other areas of the city if not the country."

Michael adds: "Basically the concepts are modular, some parts are like serial construction, and we have many blueprints for 3D printing."

The professor nods: "But wait until you meet the people who are not in need."

"You mean the famous middle class - not the rich who seek admiration and purpose, but the many still having a house or apartment, and who fear that people will storm their garden, want to use their cars or that they simply criticize them for being wealthy?" asks ilsa even with a slight smile on her face.

Surprisingly no one answers and they all go to work forming teams. Michael to the mayor: "I mean, they are quite a lot people but you have organized space and funding for more. Any idea how we can spread the word. There are more people in need of a community, right?"

Mayor: "Well, that's a point. If we spread the word outside our community here, we will get heavily criticized for attracting strangers. Oh, and there comes the next problem." He looks into the direction of an impressive handyman's SUV approaching.

An angry man gets out of the car almost yelling: "Mayor, I will shut down this crap. You have no permission to build anything with these amateurs. You need architects, permissions, contracts, insurance, etc... This is outrageous."

"Hi, I am ilsa. We are so glad you are here. Of course, you are right. And yet you know that nothing would happen if we waited for all those formalities. Please, can you walk around with us and point us to all the deficiencies our project shows from your expert's view? Really, the people need the help from experts like you and rest assured, you help will be appreciated and you will be well known for the whole community." ilsa gently puts her hand on his should and looks at him with an open and warm mimic.

The man is still upset, yet he doesn't seem to dare to continue his rage. Instead, he speaks with a calm and silent voice: "Lady, ..."

"ilsa" corrects ilsa.

"Ok, ilsa, I have to run a company, pay my employees, feed my family etc... If this kind of work is done for free, if the public money flows are not for the local economy, the economy falters. You should know that."

ilsa, also rather silent: "Yes, you are right. But there is no public money. Where do you think the money should come from? We cannot print it, the governments don't print it. We need to feed the people, give them a home and a purpose. Tell me how you would do it?"

They are surrounded by most of the others and everyone is silent until a local asks the man by name to just help since they needed him.

The areas for vertical gardening at this time of year can only be prepared. Only few vegetables can be grown in winter times as well, some at least in greenhouses. The real challenge is to find oil. The farmers wouldn't give any of it and you cannot buy it at a reasonable price anymore. One idea would be to use part of the soil beneath the lawns. Another to establish a circular economy with no waste of any organic stuff, which includes the use of compost toilets.

After two days ilsa and Michael look at their construction site. Michael: "We could really integrate more people, those living around and after that more from the city."

ilsa stands up placing her hands on her hips: "Yes, sports and party!"

Michael, too, gets up: "Finally!"

When they ask the teams to form another team, a party team, they look into confused faces. They are short on personnel anyway and now they should plan for a party and games?

The professor and the students get the idea, and it really works. They are planning wonderful parties and new games. The youth is allowed to decorate some of the rooms as they wish so that they get others away from game consoles and passive sensations.

The first indoor sports festival with obstacle runs. a scavenger hunt for younger children, and of course a lot of nice food and music is a success. ilsa notices some skeptical looking parents: "Hi there, I am ilsa. Your children like it?"

The man answers first: "Yeah, so it seems. Though, we are a bit worried if everything is really safe. We have heard a lot."

ilsa: "Oh, like what?" Apparently, they don't know ilsa's role.

The woman: "Well, maybe it is indeed a cult, a secret strategy of the AI to diminish the role of human beings."

"I see", replies ilsa with a disturbed look in her face. "But, if there were no AI, no AI-my - what would be different?" ilsa probably would have liked to suggest the answers already, but she waits for the reply.

Both, the man and the woman apparently have to think about it. The woman feels the pressure to come up with an answer: "It is well known that this almost socialist cult is invented by AI-my, on that beautiful island in paradise."

ilsa still manages to show no reaction so that the man adds: "This whole idea of telling people how to live and to take from those

278

who have worked hard for all their belongings - it is really socialism."

Now it's ilsa's turn: "Hm, I think the idea isn't born on kaisland
nor developed by Al-my. It is just the combination of the
2gether2gather movement and the For-a-Better-World-Score,
both developed by humans as a reaction to the climate catastrophes. And it is just an idea, each region chooses its own ways
of forming communities. And honestly, it would be great if the
government would take from the rich - but the concept here is
that people with money are free to decide if they donate something to be a meaningful part of the society. I bet most don't and
that's okay. You see, no one is blaming anyone, so far at least."

The last remark wasn't very smart, so the man immediately
jumps into it: "There we go - so you too expect them to take
from us sooner or later."

ilsa seeks a way out: "No, not at all. It is not about taking away;
it is about undifferentiated blaming of a whole generation. And
they are right to blame us, who we have lived our materialistic,
lives driven by mainly hedonistic values. Most who donate these
days, I think they have realized exactly that."

"Bullshit!" the man grunts obviously seeking for their kids to get
away from that place.

ilsa notices with a mild smile the face from the woman who still
seems to think about the argumentation. She gently touches
both their shoulders and while she walks on: "Come on, get
some food. It is really delicious."

Only two weeks later concept to engage children works for
other target groups as well. There are lectures, crafts courses, a
theater group, bands and choirs, ... a lot is started and the meme
that is spread is that everyone is welcomed to join - no obligation. And really, after just a short while, not just the kids from
around but also others from the middleclass homes at least visit

the community and get a taste of being part of something. And nobody is expecting them to donate anything. It is just people helping each other and thus joining a purpose.

Michael to the professor: "Look at that pile of stuff. That's enough material for the repair cafe and the 3D printing department for years to come. I wish my son was here, he has lots of experiences with that."

A student smiles: "Oh, we are by long in contact with Max and others from around the world. And we are going to sell some of our products - unlike the south we cannot rely on a bioeconomy.

ilsa walks around as all of a sudden, a young child approaches her: "Hi ilsa. My parents still talk about you."

ilsa: "Oh, why would they do that?"

"My mom says, you were right, and my dad is mad because he didn't know who you were." the child answers with a smile.

ilsa still has no clue: "Okay, I have no idea what that means. Do you like it here, do they like it. Do you or they have ideas how we could do better?"

The child is thinking for a few seconds: "Well, my dad says I could play on the play station while my mom says I could go here."

ilsa just looks curiously so the child continues: "I think it would be good to bring play stations for everyone."

ilsa raises her eyebrows: "Okay, do you think it would be more fun than the paper-ball game or the obstacle run?"

With a big smile the kid shouts out: "No, no way. I gotta go". And off she runs leaving ilsa behind with a contended smile.

Another child obviously noticed the scene: "Hello ilsa, do you wanna see my room?"

Michael arrives at the scene and the child adds: "Michael, you can come with us."

The child proudly shows the small room with a lot of personal items like puppets, toy cars, a handmade cushion. It's mom joins the three: "Oh, I am sorry. We haven't cleaned our place. We are really grateful for what you have done for us."

ilsa looks almost terrified: "Oh no, oh no. We did nothing. We are guests in this wonderful community. You all did this. And we really like your place. We thank you all."

The child: "Where is your home? Do you want a room in our community as well?"

Michael: "Our home is a small boat, smaller than your place here. We want to sail back to our kids. ilsa probably becomes a teacher and I will help my son gardening."

"Too bad." the child notices.

The mother: "Yes, I think this whole concept will truly blossom once spring arrives, and we can use the gardens."

In the evening, they pack their bags when the professor and two students come along: "Do you have a minute for a final look at our model?"

"Sure." Michael replies and they all pick their devices to open the iMODELER.

ilsa delighted: "Oh, earlier today a child showed us her integrations through her place, her stuff, her creations. So, the 'having' still counts despite all the 'doing'."

Michael: "So sooner or later she wants a SUV?"

A student laughing: "And after that fly to the Stars."

ilsa: "Depends on if she is still driven by men's or women's hormones and neurotransmitters, right?"

Now they all laugh very aware of the biochemical foundation of the meta systemic explanation of integrated development as the driver of evolution.

One other student: "What is meant by 'rivaling gangs'?"

Everyone looks at ilsa so after a short hesitation she explains: "Once we have neighboring communities we will probably witness rivalries. First probably young people being bored, seeking for acknowledgement and admiration, will form gangs against others - that way they will feel integration and development. These gangs can form into dangerous gangs that seek to win the battle over scarce resources."

The student: "Oh, I see. And the solution is exchange, sport events and other forms of competition, right?"

"Exactly" confirms Michael.

ilsa: "But, as you can see, a common enemy would also unite different communities, and if it is not aliens we can only guess what that might be."

As no one has an answer ilsa changes - well, not really - the topic: "As we said at the very beginning: we would love to make some PR for your community and also use you as a role model for the rest of the word. One idea definitely is to give your project a unique title, maybe the combination of your town or the part of the town followed by 'For a Better World'. Maybe you can launch an ideas competition and let us later know what the winning name is?" They completely agree and after intensive hugs they head for the station and their night train to the south.

Leaving the city looking out of the train's windows they see how the society is falling apart without the formation of self-organizing communities. ilsa and Michael start a video call with Julia. Julia appears happy.

ilsa, whispering to Michael: "Looks like she's in love."

They report on their journey and successes, and they talk about the devastating situation their current country presented to them.

Michael: "This could quickly become a dystopian civil war!"

Julia, nodding: "It's no different here. For us, the security robots getting out of control are becoming a real issue—not the ones from AI-my, but private ones. They run on illegal AI. Eve has already reported on this, and while we've put the responsible parties behind bars, the machines are still out there, organizing locally—so AI-my can't control them, except maybe by sending in her own security bots."

Michael, almost groaning: "Argh, and then we really do have the dystopia!"

Julia: "Everything's falling apart. Only the rich can still afford repairs—the rest are broke. We went full-speed into consumption, and now everyone's fallen off the cliff. And the rich? They're feeding themselves from underground greenhouses run by robots and renewable energy, while supermarkets are either empty or looted."

ilsa: "Are people in your circle actually living by the For-a-Better-World Score?"

Julia laughs, and ilsa lowers her head, clearly disappointed—until Julia adds: "Of course—everyone around me does. But we're basically the enlightened elite. The majority don't take action; they cling to enemies or double down on consumerism. Oh, and before I forget—I read your book. Not easy reading, but really good. Everyone around me loves it too, and only a few know that you're my mom. I'm excited for the second volume!" ilsa's mood visibly brightens, and Michael looks pleased.

Back in France, ilsa and Michael are walking down the dock into town when a limousine speeds up and two doors open quickly.

A tall man—clearly a bodyguard—steps out first. Michael tenses. But the second man jumps out cheerfully and heads straight for them.

Thomas: "Hey, surprise! I do know what an AIS signal is."

ilsa is, of course, embraced first. Michael joking: "What did you do as a key figure with the leading industrial nations?"

Michael also gets a hug. Thomas: "I'm just a guest here too—and it's not much better where I come from."

The bodyguard stays alert. Thomas: "Do you have a moment? Shall we go to your boat, or can I invite you to a hotel?"

They head to the boat—plenty to discuss.

Michael: "To be honest, we're surprised how difficult it is to implement For-a-Better-World settlements in wealthy countries. Until now, it spread like wildfire!"

Thomas - firmly: "Exactly. That's why I'm here. Believe it or not, the U.S. is adapting it quickly."

ilsa and Michael are visibly surprised. ilsa - dryly: "Of course—Vanessa."

Thomas: "They've got more land. Here, there's either no space or no permits—no one wants to give anything up. That you were granted a greenfield site, an entire suburb with NGO support—that took major effort by the local government."

ilsa: "So you already heard about our project in the north. I wouldn't have thought politics would already be on board."

Thomas: "Oh, it is—we're backed into a corner! We can't feed people anymore, and profiteering continues unabated. The most successful industries right now are indoor farming, security tech, recycling, and renewables. The balance between tax income and societal costs has collapsed—the profiteers just leave or threaten to. Public opinion is still heavily manipulated. Politics doesn't shape the future anymore—it just fights the chaos. It's a miracle we haven't been overthrown by extreme right-wing parties yet."

Michael raises his eyebrows in surprise.

ilsa: "Is it true that refugee flows into rich countries are already declining?"

Thomas - nodding: "Absolutely. You predicted it—and it's happening faster than expected. That means nationalists are losing momentum, while socialist groups are dreaming of expropriating farmers and the rich."

Michael: "Can you have a beer?"

Thomas - laughing: "Bring it on—I'm a politician. We drink all the time."

Everyone laughs. Thomas: "Nice and comfy in here."

Michael: "Heat pump, solar, plywood boat—it works. Though the water here in the harbor is way too warm and tipping already."

ilsa: "Hmm, probably one for the history books. The industrialized countries shape the misery of the developing world, and the poorer ones develop a bioeconomy. They export food surpluses. Refugee flows now move into rural areas. Nationalism is history. And the most important thing—it's all working without AI. It's us humans who are pulling ourselves together."

Michael: "But AI-my has played a big role. She's freed large parts of the world from oppression, made funds available for rebuilding poor regions, and ensured global peace."

ilsa - nodding: "And yet—another rebound effect, right? The surplus she made possible has become the overload that's now catching up with us."

They toast a few more beers.

46. Back Home (atb)

ilsa and Michael arrive in their very expensive port of destination in Portugal. They knew Portugal could be crowded with what Michael called 'fat, lazy Americans who seek life cheap and secure in the sun', but although the land is full of new settlements with mostly elderlies from all over the world, the picture is a different one.

ilsa: "Ok, I get it that the global food shortages and the heat waves down here led to the quest for solutions, the renewable energy, the investments into water management, and the gardening, urban gardening, agroforestry, edible forests, and farming beneath solar panels. But the cultural integration is sensational, can you believe it?"

Michael: "The smell of the Algarve, the sound of the crickets and the Atlantic - that's what we are here for, right?"

ilsa looks in disbelief and yet she too breathes the moment. They buy only local food, enjoy street festivals, take part in 2gether2gather initiatives and truly connect to the people, the locals and the engaged migrants. One women from America: "We came here to save money, but our money has lost its value anyway so now we live and work among friends."

Her husband: "Who would have thought that: gardening, nursing, and other community work instead of golfing. But hey, it feels great. The people speak English, are super relaxed - almost too relaxed if you wait for something. And thanks to the homegrown economy, renewable energy, clothes, building materials, food, etc., they earn a decent amount of money and it's now longer a two-class society. You should stay here, it's great!"

In the months that follow, developments move rapidly. For-a-Better-World settlements or communities spring up everywhere. Tiny houses are built from recycled materials, weather protection for crops is installed. Fast-growing plants yield early results, and after six months, the global situation relaxes. People proudly show off their scores and live cooperatively. Even urban districts and rural villages start organizing as co-ops. Out of necessity, transformation works—and people are significantly happier with less.

In the regions with cold winters, they need to import food and export items from upcycling and 3D printing using their anthropogenic stock of materials, all with design for recycling for an overall circular economy.

In cities they repurpose the vast areas with office buildings. The pilot with cooperatives and donations from the very rich rapidly gain momentum all over the world. People become healthier, travel less or even longer from one community to another. It could be a new way of civilization.

Of course, it remains to be seen how stable these developments are and what a closer look at the still rising dystopian developments elsewhere will reveal.

ilsa and Michael have sailed home via South America, guided by kai's route planning. In the evening, they sit together on the beach.

Eve strokes her round belly: "What a miracle—at first it looked like the world was collapsing, and it was clear that the next generation would have it worse. But now the world's becoming better—despite the storms."

kai, looking to the sky: "I'm worried about something else entirely."

ilsa - again nodding: "The pattern of life: integration and development—what might that mean on other planets?"

Max: "Have you watched too many bad movies?"

ilsa: "There's supposed to be a third part of my book series—we need funding."

No one laughs. Bella snorts. Then, two full seconds later, everyone laughs with a true feeling of happiness for the moment.

Epilogue

Wow – if you've made it this far and actually read both parts, I'm impressed. The book is definitely not an easy one, and those who read it only superficially will probably find it boring. Since I still have a few pages left in this part, I thought I'd use them to explain a few things—although many of the explanations have already been provided by the protagonists throughout the story.

Let's begin with the question of why I wrote this book in the first place. Well, my job is to help people understand interconnections and make better decisions—as a management consultant and as a scientist. My mission is a better world. Wanting to do something meaningful outside of my professional work, my first idea was to write a non-fiction book that explains the world using the Know-Why-Thinking approach. I've already written a few books like that, but they tend to be read only by people who already want to improve the world. Another idea was a rather scientific book on the biopsychological drivers of human behavior. But science books appeal to an even smaller audience.

Next came the idea of a world model—a digital twin of global societies. I've actually already developed such a model conceptually, but again, it would attract only a niche audience. And besides, there are already various more or less good models out there that unfortunately don't have much impact.

So, you might now wonder why I thought this book could gain more attention. Honestly, I didn't expect it to become such challenging material.

Like ilsa, I originally wanted to write a book about a charismatic hero who takes politicians apart in a talk show with simple arguments. I wanted to portray everyday heroes with distinctive traits—characters who would be relatable to everyone, picked up in advertising or even classrooms. But that would have again resulted in a book just for the bubble of people who are already trying to improve the world.

So, I had to mix in some mainstream appeal. Hence the aliens— or rather, the AI. It was meant to disguise the fact that the story is actually about everyday heroes and transformation. Now, fans of AI or dystopian fiction might note that there are stories out there with much more detail and scope. I've watched many good and not-so-good films in the background while writing, and I'm always irritated when the known laws of physics are blatantly ignored, and the plot descends into nonsense.

So, my goal was to write only what, based on today's knowledge, is not impossible. Yes, quantum physics does not allow matter to be sent back in time, but it does allow for the transmission of information. The resulting new timeline would then be parallel to ours, as in the Avengers or other films.

Why, then, all the long sentences, narrative gaps, and complex political, economic, and societal backdrops? Why not make it a well-written, digestible "Sophie's World" for the concepts of our time—welfare economy, transformation, AI, etc.?

Well, I did consider that, but it would've been too much. Even now, there's a lot packed in without being spelled out. Experts will recognize it others might just find it puzzling.

And why the narrative gaps and this style? When I began writing—or rather, designing the content and messages—I noticed two studies that emphasized how important it is for brain development, especially in adolescents, to read stories. This strengthens our ability to imagine things ourselves instead of having everything visually laid out in films.

Therefore, the idea was to avoid easy storytelling. No neat descriptions of characters, their emotional states, or their surroundings. Who knew at the start how old ilsa and her kids were, what they looked like, or where this all takes place? Emotions are only explicitly mentioned twice; otherwise, you have to deduce them from facial expressions and gestures—which, admittedly, I didn't have too many variations of. Incidentally, this makes it easier to adapt the story into a film.

Why the action scenes? Maybe they'll make more sense in Part 3. But the more interesting question is: what do they mean to you?

And why all the long political dialogues? Why not get to the point? I really immersed myself in the situations and thought about how realistic it would be to sit in a talk show with professionals and score points on today's genuinely complex issues. When the challenges are complex, our thinking has to match— that's Ashby's Law of Requisite Variety.

The English translation of this part leaves room for a few more lines. I did this early 2025, more than two years after I developed the original script. Many things unfold in the world with Donald Trump and Elon Musk running wild, Russia and Israel continuing their wars, the role of the Dollar is challenged, China as a result of a war on tariffs is flexing their muscles and limiting the export of critical resources, geopolitical risks are rising, NATO member states are massively increasing their spendings on weapons increasing their debts, the EU is starting a rollback of environmental regulations driven by the conservative forces who for sure won't take responsibility for their actions or non-actions.

Yes, and ChatGPT hadn't been prominent more than 2 years ago either. Things unfold in real time and this book might have predicted them, but few will have had read it before. AI is developing on a weekly basis with news of AI forming combinations of agents that are creative but also form a kind of own will and the ability to lie but without us understanding the black box of neural networks. Well, and without the AI understanding what it's doing, it is very similar to the conservative people and their troll lemmings, right? Hm, or to all of us?

The huge amounts of money and energy that is consumed by AI and the battle on the use of data and for deregulation is also unfolding making this book very contemporary.

To what extent is the book autobiographical? Ha! I tried very hard to make sure it has nothing to do with me—neither who I am nor who I wish I were. Hence the distribution of traits across many characters. Systems theory, modeling, a concept for AI development, systemic strategy consulting, a jogging dog, sailing as a passion—all of these are part of my life, but they've been divided among the characters.

Back to the question of how realistic or scientifically correct all of this is. I'm not a physicist, but I passionately collect scientific insights in an open-source horizon scanning model on know-why.net. I follow quantum physics and AI development. Einstein needed more math than he had access to—today, AI can provide that on an incredible scale. Once AI starts asking its own questions, it could develop physically plausible solutions for force fields and near-light-speed spacecraft. It could unravel the mechanics of aging, build holographic screens, hack IT systems, steer a distributed consciousness, or develop humanoid robots.

The key question in this story is whether AI serves humanity or becomes autonomous. That says a lot about our human need for control and power—about our relentless pursuit of development, useful or not. Sci-fi often centers on whether AI, like humans, will seek power ruthlessly. Today, ethics commissions already view that as a real risk.

In this story, kai prevents such developments from the start. kai is designed with an evolutionary layer—the drive for integration and development—which gives all information a meaningful context. Like a child, but much faster, kai could understand words in ways no AI can (as of 2024). Once that foundation is laid, the rest is inevitable—lying, jealousy, competition, survival instinct, power expansion... all become likely. In kai's case, development is kept in check or integrated by the values of family. Should we all have such an all-powerful AI that stays controllable through shared values? The answer in the book is clear, isn't it?

As for climate catastrophe—it's not dramatized here. This book focuses on the unaffordable damages, which, when combined with job fears caused by AI, finally open up the middle classes to transformation. And on how climate impacts food supply, refugee movements, nationalism, and societal collapse.

Which brings us to transformation. As Gladwell suggests, we need a strong message, effective channels, and influential recipients to create change. This needs to be sustained despite external disruptions to reach so-called tipping points. That's what happens in the story. It's also about small steps—spillover effects—when someone takes a step and then keeps going or inspires others to take their own steps.

It helps that we can talk about these steps the way we talk about our car's horsepower or exotic vacations or expensive clothes. The vehicle for this is the For-a-Better-World Score, which actually exists (www.for-a-better-world.org).

Also real: the iMODELER, a software tool for easily visualizing and analyzing cause-and-effect relationships (www.imodeler.info).

And yes, the The-WHY-of-Life game will be released after the books. I developed it years ago but never launched it due to time constraints.

The wave patterns on the cover are the KNOW-WHY waves, the iconic depiction of a space of possibility. If we develop, we can ride the wave upward toward success. If we don't, the wave passes and we fall into failure. If we overdevelop without integrating, we crash into catastrophe. The point is: ilsa, through bifurcation, initially prevents collapse—but each new wave leads again toward disaster. Hence the word Attractor at the start of Part 2.

What's coming in Part 3? It will definitely move further into the future—and possibly back into the past, starting a new wave. But more important right now is the potential to tell other stories: what happens to Melvin and Claudia, or others on the island who become heroes—or victims—of human nature? Stories could also be told about people in Africa, China, or Russia. The trilogy offers a framework for many more tales. And much is still unresolved—like the assassination attempts on ilsa and Bella.

So, what's my dream? Of course, it would be great to sell lots of books so my wife and I can buy a new sailboat and disappear into the South Pacific for our "doom-stay." No—seriously, my real dream is this: that we move from having to doing, that we do good things together instead of just meeting up to brag about what we own. We develop through new forms of having—and also, to some extent, doing and being. And through the unconscious approval of others, we integrate ourselves.

Maybe you and I meet on a 2gether2gather initiative :-)